NOT EVERYTHING DIES

JOHN PATRICK KENNEDY

2017

Not Everything Dies © 2017 by John Patrick Kennedy
Special thanks to Kindle Press for this amazing opportunity.
Cover art by Carlos Quevedo.

Interior layout and design by Colleen Sheehan

All rights reserved
First Edition

WWW.JOHNPATRICKKENNEDY.NET/

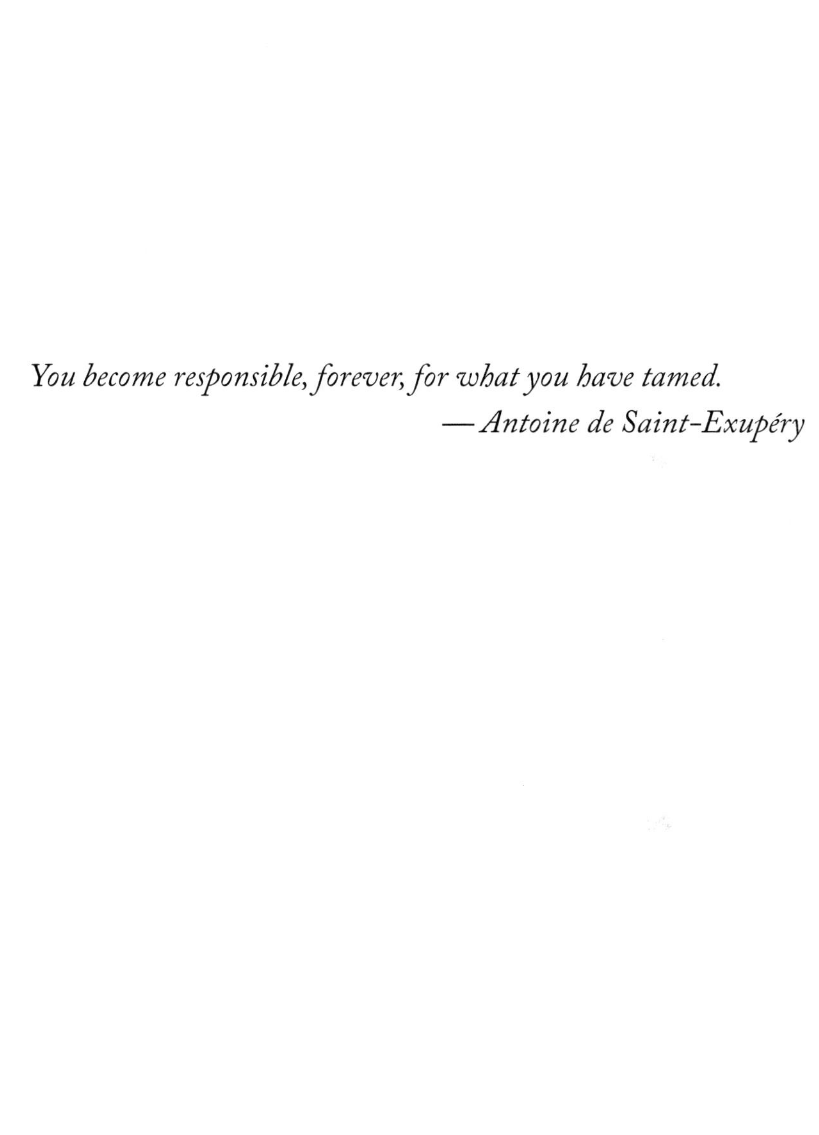

You become responsible, forever, for what you have tamed.

—Antoine de Saint-Exupéry

CHAPTER ONE

HUNGARY, 1609

The Beast woke in darkness.

For any other creature, the room would have been pitch-black. For the Beast, the stones themselves emitted light, turning the black to a deep gray that showed the length and depth of the prison cell. The room was scarcely higher than the Beast, if the Beast stood. It rarely did that these days, preferring to lope on hands and feet in a springing run that kept its nose closer to the ground—the better to sniff out prey.

The Beast had looked different, once.

Long ago it had stood on two legs all the time. Necessity had changed its body. The more it relied on scent to hunt, the more time it spent on all fours. Its arms had grown longer, its legs shorter, to compensate. Its toes grew stronger, able to flex the talons on their tips and dig them into the ground as it hunted. Its pale white skin was covered in dirt and mud, the better to be unseen in the woods. Its hair, long and red, became matted and filthy, but no longer fell into its eyes. Its neck twisted so it could easily look up when it ran. Even its breasts had changed, shrinking and clinging tighter to its body, so as not to be in the way.

The Beast paced. The room was twice as wide and four times as long as the creature. Metal bars, deeply embedded in the floor, blocked the only way out. The floor and walls were flat, cut stone, so different from the rough, natural cave wall of the hallway beyond.

It hated this place.

It didn't know how many times it had slept and woken in its prison. It didn't know how long it had been there. The Beast counted time by sunrise and sunset, and in this prison, it could see neither. It hated the unending darkness and the unchanging scent. It wanted the woods and the smells of the animals it fed on. Wanted to sniff the deer and the bears and wolves. Wanted to run thought the night, chasing down prey and drinking it dry.

It wanted out. Now.

The Beast snarled and sniffed the stale air. The musty, dank smell of wet rock permeated every surface. Beyond that, the Beast could smell the mold in its straw nest and the sharp, tangy smell of the metal bars. Beneath it all was the thin, faint scent of blood.

Not fresh, drinkable blood, but old from deaths past. The smell drove the Beast mad with hunger.

The Beast's talons scraped against the floor. It crouched low and glared at the bars. The Beast sprang forward, turning at the last moment to smash its shoulder hard against the bars. The cold metal clanged and shuddered, hurting the Beast's naked flesh, but the bars didn't give way.

The Beast hit the ground, loped back to the end of the room, and charged again. Over and over, it threw itself at the bars, heedless of the damage to its flesh. The sixth time it twisted too far and its side hit the bars.

There was a dull crack as one of its ribs broke. Agony blossomed within.

The Beast howled. It closed its eyes and waited as the ends of the ribs ground against each other and clicked back together. The pain halved, then quartered, and then faded to nothing.

The Beast smelled humans.

It scuttled to the back of the room and sank into its nest of straw. There were eight coming—six male, two female. The males' scent of musk, clean wool, and sweaty flesh was nearly hidden beneath the smell of the metal they wore. Their metal didn't smell like the bars—rust and dust and old iron. Their metal smelled of oil. From where the Beast lay, it felt the beat of their hearts and the blood rushing through their veins. The blood was a song, like the outdoors, like wildness. It called to the Beast, fixing its attention.

It had been given human blood when it first woke in this place. Human blood smelled and tasted so sweet. Sweeter and more complex than any deer or rabbit, richer than a fox's or a weasel's or even the bear the Beast had once fought. Each creature's blood had its own signature: once smelled or tasted, it was never forgotten.

Then they had switched, giving it rabbits and pigs. The Beast, starving, had drunk them all. It was used to animal blood, had fed on animal blood as long as it could remember before it came here.

The scent of humans reminded it of the sweetness of their blood, made it crave it. The Beast crouched on its haunches, hoping for a chance to drink one of them.

Two women, a light one and a dark one, stepped in front of the cell.

The light one smelled of flowers and other things the Beast couldn't name, though it thought it knew them once. The memory of those scents lingered somewhere inside, though so deep the Beast didn't bother searching for it. The dark one smelled of sweat and dirty clothing and of another woman and a man.

Both carried a faint hint of old blood on their flesh. It lingered on them, the way it did in the stones. It clung to them beneath the smells they had used on their skin: lye and ashes on the dark one, flowers and oil on the fair.

The Beast watched and waited.

The six men approached the bars and drew more metal from their sides. The Beast recognized the object and snarled. It was as sharp as the Beast's claws, and it hurt. The last time they had come, the Beast had grabbed the arm of one of the males, pulled it through the bars, and tried to bite through it. The metal on the man's body protected him, and the sharp objects the others wielded drove into the Beast's flesh over and over until the pain grew too much and it let go.

Now the Beast watched and waited as the men pointed their metal toward it.

"She isn't any better?"

The Beast heard the fair one's words but didn't make sense of them.

"Not at all," one of the men said. "We switched her to animal blood as you asked. Since then, there have been no more improvements."

"As I expected. The animal blood makes her an animal. We will switch back and see what happens."

The fair one nodded at the dark one. The dark one walked away. From somewhere nearby came the sound of wood scraping on stone, then the sound of leather striking flesh. A girl screamed, and the scent of her fear hit the Beast's nose.

It shifted in its corner, watching.

"Here." The dark one shoved the girl at the fair one. The girl began weeping, and urine ran down one of her legs. The fair one grabbed her by the hair and pulled her up to balance on her toes, then nodded to the men. All six stepped back from the bars, though their metal remained pointed at the Beast.

The dark one took a small piece of metal—old iron and rust, like the bars—out of her pocket and put it to the square in the bars. The square gave a loud click. The bars swung open with a creak and a groan. The Beast tensed and crouched. The men stepped forward, their metal pointing directly at it. It would hurt to charge them, but the Beast didn't care. If it killed the men, it could escape.

The fair woman pulled metal from her side. She slashed the naked girl's breasts with it, and the smell of fresh human blood filled the air. The Beast howled. The fair woman threw the girl into the cell and shouted, "Now!"

The dark one shoved the bars shut. The six men leaned against them. The Beast charged, ramming its shoulder against the bars.

They bounced back, but the combined weight of the men forced them shut again. The dark one struggled with the metal in the square. The Beast tried to slash at her. One of the men blocked the way. The Beast howled and drove its talons forward into the slot in the metal on the man's head.

Flesh gave way deliciously. Blood spurted from the man's face. He stumbled back, screaming. The square gave a sharp *click* and the others all jumped back. The Beast tried to grab the dark one, but she was out of reach. The men knelt to help their screaming, bleeding companion. The fair one stood still, watching.

Blood poured from the man's eyes and down his face. The smell filled the cell, shimmering with power. *Life.* The Beast howled and tried to reach through the bars to grab the man. One man shoved his metal at it. The Beast jumped back with a snarl.

The girl in the cell whimpered.

The Beast turned. The girl was bleeding from the twin cuts on her bare breasts. The Beast's lips curled up, revealing long and sharp fangs. The girl shook, her entire body vibrating with fear.

The girl's blood was different than the man's, but just as sweet. The Beast crawled forward, a string of drool oozing from one side of its mouth.

The girl sat still, weeping until the Beast sank its teeth into her neck. Sweet blood flowed into the Beast's mouth, bringing bliss. It drank until the last of the blood drained from the girl's body.

Then the world turned white and faded away.

The Beast woke in darkness.

Its stomach rumbled with hunger. It sniffed deeply. The blood no longer smelled fresh, but stale and dry. The Beast looked around.

The girl's body was gone' leaving only stains behind on the stone floor. The women and soldiers were gone.

SOLDIERS. The men in metal were called soldiers. The Beast knew that now. It also knew that it felt stronger, that its mind was clearer. Before, where there was only desire, now there was thought.

ESCAPE. It glared at the bars of the cell and snarled. *BREAK! DESTROY!*

It charged across the room and leaped at the bars. The impact hurt, and the Beast yelped in pain. The bars shook more than they ever had before. The Beast retreated, ready to jump again.

"It's awake!" someone shouted nearby. "Fetch the lady! Quick!"

A soldier ran from the hallway, sword in hand. The Beast rushed forward, and the man jabbed the its metal through the bars.

SWORD. SHARP METAL.

The Beast changed its course, bounced off the wall, and landed on all fours in a crouch. The man stepped back. The Beast smelled fresh sweat, ripe with the stink of fear, coming from his flesh.

BREAK. ESCAPE.

The Beast paced. The man's eyes and blade followed it.

KILL.

It rushed twice more. Each time the man jabbed with his blade to keep the Beast at bay. The Beast snarled. It slowly approached the bars and rose. The soldier's eyes went first to the Beast's breasts, then to the red hair above its sex. He swallowed hard and looked away.

The Beast shoved its arm through the bars, trying to catch the man's armor or helmet—*anything*—to drag him closer, but he stayed out of reach. The Beast screamed and reached with both arms.

The man stabbed the Beast in the stomach.

The Beast shrieked and jumped back. Silver blood poured from its belly. Almost at once the pain receded, and the blood slowed to a trickle. The Beast's lips turned up in a grin. It hadn't been this strong in . . .

Something tickled the back of the Beast's mind, something about how long it had been and why. The Beast shook its head and snarled. It didn't want to think.

ESCAPE!

Boots clomped in the hallway, the sound echoing through the small room. Seven soldiers, as well as two other men and the two women from before, crowded by the door. One of the men stank of the prison and had manacles on his hands and feet. The other man smelled of strange, harsh chemicals.

"Good work," the fair woman said, and this time the Beast understood the words. "What has she done?"

"Attacked the bars," the soldier said. "Then it tried to lure me closer by showing its body."

"*Her* body," the fair one corrected. "She is a woman."

"She is a mystery," said the man who smelled of chemicals. He stepped closer to the bars. "Where does she come from? Who is she under that dirt?"

"Begging pardon, sir," the guard said. "If you stand that close, she'll kill you."

"Step back, Kade," said the fair one. "Dorotyas, the door."

The dark one took out the small piece of metal and put it in the square.

KEY. LOCK.

Six soldiers formed a line and pointed their swords, ready to stab the Beast if necessary. The other two grabbed the man who smelled like the prison. The dark one clicked open the lock, and the door swung back.

The Beast charged.

It nearly made it to the door, but the two soldiers threw their prisoner into its way. The prisoner fell on his face. The Beast swerved to avoid him. The door clanged shut, and the Beast howled. There was rage, but the hunger was stronger. The Beast thrust its talons into one of the prisoner's legs and pulled him back from the bars. The man screamed, then gurgled as the Beast's teeth went into his throat.

The Beast stood on its feet and threw the man's lifeless body at the door. It hit hard, the skull cracking and an arm breaking. The soldiers flinched. The fair woman didn't.

"As soon as it is unconscious, you can go in and do it, Kade," she said.

The Beast's world started turning white again.

"Can you hear me?" The fair one's voice was sharp with excitement. "Do you understand what I'm saying?"

The Beast collapsed to the floor, and the white faded to black.

The Beast awoke to the flickering of torchlight.

HUNGRY. NEED FOOD. NEED . . .

NEED?

NEED PEOPLE. FEED.

NEED ESCAPE.

Why?

The Beast snarled and jumped away, searching for the owner of the voice. It pressed its back against the wall. Two guards, standing on the other end of the bars, jumped in surprise. One turned and ran. The other drew his sword. The Beast did not care. Its eyes darted back and forth. There was no one else near.

Why must we get away?

The voice came from inside the Beast's mind.

NO!

Space that had been empty in the Beast's mind filled with the *other.* It shoved at the Beast, trying to control it. The Beast grabbed at its skull and howled. It smashed its head against the wall.

Stop, the voice begged. *Please stop.*

OUT!

The Beast slammed its head against the wall again. Pain lanced through its skull, and the voice went silent. The Beast crouched, cradling its head as silver blood poured down its face and into its eyes.

It didn't move again until more soldiers and the two women arrived at the cell. The Beast rose and advanced to the center of the room. Its eyes were fixed on the door, its entire body tense.

"Why is it bleeding?" the fair one asked. "What happened?"

"It grabbed its head like it was in pain, my lady," the guard said, "and smashed it against the wall."

"It's insane," the dark woman said. "My lady, we need to stop trying to tame it and break it instead, like a wild animal."

"No," the fair one said. "It wouldn't work. Not with this creature."

"But it would be fun to try," the dark one said, looking at the Beast. She licked her lips. The Beast smelled her desire. The dark one wanted to dominate the Beast; to become its pack leader and to control it, The Beast snarled at her.

BREAK. KILL. EAT.

"No, Dorotyas." The fair one's tone clearly said *enough.* "Get the food."

Dorotyas disappeared down the hallway. The fair one turned back to the cage. She didn't come closer, much to the Beast's annoyance.

"Can you hear me in there?" she said. "Do you understand me?"

I do.

The response came from inside the Beast's mind, though never left its mouth.

GO AWAY, the Beast screamed within. *GO AWAY! DIE!*

The voice went silent.

The fair one waited. The dark one returned, dragging a girl. The Beast's fangs descended. It was ravenous. It watched the fair one take out her knife and slash the girl's breasts, as she had with the last one.

FEED. KILL. ESCAPE. .

No, the voice begged. *Please no, they can help me.*

The Beast screamed and ran at the wall, smashing its head against it as hard as it could. Bone cracked, and the Beast fell to the floor, howling.

When it looked up, the girl lay on the cell floor, and the door was closed.

The Beast charged the bars, screaming its rage. The men drew their swords and thrust, pricking its skin repeatedly and driving it back. Finally, the Beast slunk back to the middle of the cell and glared at the girl on the floor. The Beast knew that as soon as it drank, it would vanish again.

But the girl's blood smelled so sweet.

The Beast resisted for half an hour before jumping on the girl and tearing her throat open. Blood sprayed, and the Beast clamped its teeth down hard, drinking and drinking until the girl's life fled.

The fair one stepped forward and spoke, her voice quaking with excitement. "Do you remember me?"

The girl in the cell rose to her feet, wiping the blood from her chin. Her neck twisted and clicked and realigned. She grimaced at the pain of it. Her arms pulled in on themselves, the bones shrinking. Her thighbones stretched and lengthened.

"Countess Elizabeth Bathory," the girl said, "and with you is Dorotyas Semtesz, your servant. And my name is . . . Ruxandra."

She looked down at herself, and around at the cell, then burst into tears.

CHAPTER TWO

THE DEAD GIRL at Ruxandra's feet stared up at her with cold, empty eyes. Ruxandra frowned. "I did that. Why did I do that?"

"Because you're a vampire," Elizabeth said. "You drink blood to survive."

Ruxandra's eyes went to her blood- and dirt-stained hands. She ran them over her naked flesh, so similar to that of the dead girl's. "Only human blood?"

"We tried feeding you animal blood before," Elizabeth said. "It sustained you, but you stayed an animal. When you drink human blood, you become *more*."

"I do?"

Elizabeth smiled. "Though you've been having trouble remembering."

"I have?"

Elizabeth's laughter, short and low and melodious, filled the cell. Ruxandra's head tilted, her eyebrows rising with her confusion.

"I am sorry," said Elizabeth. "We've had this conversation five times now."

Ruxandra's eyes went to the dead girl again. "I've killed five . . ."

"Peasants," Elizabeth said. "You have killed fifteen since you have been here. Only with the last five did you start becoming sensible again."

"Fifteen…"

"They are peasants," Elizabeth said firmly. Their lot in life is to die in our service."

The words moved strangely inside her head. As if there was more to them—more meaning she didn't quite grasp.

"Our?" Ruxandra stepped closer to the bars. "You're like me?"

"No one is like you, my dear." Elizabeth moved closer. The soldiers around her tensed. Dorotyas tightened her grip on the strap in her hand. Ruxandra stepped back.

"Don't be afraid," Elizabeth took another step forward and reached out between the bars, her hand stretching toward Ruxandra.

"Why are they scared?" Ruxandra said. "I can't hurt you, can I?"

"They're scared of the Beast."

"The Beast?"

"That's what the men called it—you—when they brought you in. That was three months ago. I have watched you every time we talk. When you are this way, you are not the Beast."

Being the Beast is not a good thing.

Ruxandra frowned. "But I might become it?"

"You will become it. You have become it every time. Though with each new kill you stay yourself longer. Then you fall asleep and wake as the Beast." Elizabeth's arm was still extended through the bars, her hand reaching for Ruxandra. "Will you not take my hand, Ruxandra?"

Ruxandra reached out but stopped. She could smell the woman, feel the blood rushing through her veins, and hear her heart beat. Elizabeth was no different than the girl dead at her feet—human. Food.

Ruxandra couldn't understand it. Her hand dropped to her side.

"Why do you let me kill your own kind?" Ruxandra asked. "Why wouldn't you destroy me?"

Elizabeth withdrew her hand. "They are not *my* kind, any more than they are yours."

"You are like her. Or them," Ruxandra pointed at the soldiers. "You're all the same."

"I am *not* like them. I am a countess. These are my servants. That"—she flicked her fingers in the direction of the corpse—"is a dead peasant. None of them are like me."

Ruxandra shook her head. "I don't understand."

"I am Blood Royal." Elizabeth seemed to grow taller with the words. "I am placed here by God to rule over these people. They are all mine to do with as I wish. They live to serve me and to die for me if I require it. It is their place in the world."

"And me?" Ruxandra asked. "What am I?"

"I've told you. You are a vampire. To me, a vampire is the true embodiment of a Blood Royal." Elizabeth glowed as she said the words. Her voice swelled with passion, growing warmer and richer as she spoke. "Greater than nobility, greater than kings or even emperors. You live off the peasants, feeding on them as a wolf feeds on fawns, rather than living off the toil of their brow. If only it were so simple for the rest of us. The world would be a magnificent place."

Ruxandra shook her head again. The world was hunger, blood, and death. If there were other things—she suspected there were—she had forgotten them. She turned in a slow circle. "Why am I in here?"

"Because the Beast is not Blood Royal," Elizabeth said. "It is an animal that kills indiscriminately, without thought or purpose. It cannot be allowed to roam free."

"I don't like it in here." Ruxandra walked to the back of the cell, looked down at the nest of straw. "I can't see the sky."

"I know," Elizabeth said. "I can't risk having you anywhere else until you master the Beast within."

Ruxandra sat down in the straw, her head falling forward. *I want to leave.*

"Ruxandra," Elizabeth said. "Would you allow my men to remove the peasant's body from your cell?"

"Is there a choice?"

"Of course." Elizabeth sounded shocked. "You are a guest, and I do my best to respect my guests' wishes."

Ruxandra leaned forward. "By keeping me locked up in here?"

"My dear, it's not you we keep locked up in here. It's the Beast." She leaned against the bars. "I believe the Beast is something separate from you; something that came into existence because you drank too much animal blood. As you drink more human blood, and gain control over the Beast , you can rest assured that I will open this door and give you your freedom. But I hope . . ." Elizabeth turned away and bit her lip. For a moment she looked shy and as young as the dead girl on the floor. When she brought her eyes back to Ruxandra's, her expression was different. Desire, naked and strong, radiated from her. It made

Ruxandra's stomach flutter. "I hope you will choose to remain with me. For a little while, at least."

Ruxandra didn't know what to say. *With me,* she thought, repeating the countess's words.

Elizabeth's men opened the door and advanced in a tight group, shoulder to shoulder, their swords pointed at Ruxandra. When they reached the dead girl, one stooped, grabbed her ankles, and practically ran out of the cell, dragging the corpse with him. Ruxandra didn't move. His blood sang, but she wasn't hungry.

"I'll leave a torch for you." Elizabeth said. "The Beast did not like the torchlight. But now that you are more yourself, perhaps the light will help you further tame It. I'll be back soon. I promise."

One man put a torch into a bracket on the wall, and Elizabeth and the others left. Ruxandra listened. One man stopped at the end of the hallway as and the others continued walking. The echo of their footsteps changed, as if they were going through a larger space. Two more men stopped there. Then a door opened and shut, and the place was silent save for the soldiers' breathing.

Now what do I do? Ruxandra looked down at her hands and the dirt ingrained in her flesh. She rubbed hard at a spot on her palm. Gradually the dirt gave way, leaving a speck of pure, white flesh. Ruxandra stared at it, wondering.

I am as pale as the fair woman. Why did I become an animal?

She reached back into her mind, to see if she could rouse a memory of being anything more than an animal. All she remembered was endless forest and hunt after hunt. The smell of pine, locust, oak, of stone, water, fur, and blood. She remembered running with wolves, and challenging the alpha to become the pack leader. She remembered traveling with them through the forest, and then abandoning them when they went to places she couldn't find day-lairs. She remembered the bear she had fought and defeated, though it was five times her size.

When was I a person?

I must have been. She tried to reach farther back, but there was nothing but forest and feeding and the changing of the seasons. She could not even remember seeing humans before she had come here.

I can't have just been the Beast.

Can I?

Ruxandra sighed, and the sigh turned into a yawn. She stretched, her arms going high in the air and her back lengthening. It was a stiff movement, as if her back wasn't used to being straight anymore. As if she'd spent too long with her face near the ground.

Nose to the ground is the best way to hunt.

If I'm not an animal, what does that leave me?

A vampire, Elizabeth said.

I like that name, Elizabeth.

Another yawn took her. She blinked hard, trying to send away the tiredness. She didn't want to sleep, not if it meant waking up as the Beast. She shook her head and stared at the torch.

Her eyelids grew heavy. Her body was being pulled to the ground, every muscle and every joint now weary and tired. A strange lassitude held her, coaxing her gently to sleep.

I don't want to be the Beast was her last thought before sleep took her.

When she awoke, she was pacing the cell again.

Or, at least, her body was.

No! Stop! She thought she shouted the words, but they only echoed inside her head.

HUNGRY! Something within screamed back. *KILL!*

The Beast. Fear raced through Ruxandra.

Her body fell to all fours. Her legs grew shorter, her arms longer. Her neck twisted again. Her toes flexed against the floor, digging talons into stone. She smelled the prison and saw the flickering torch that turned the gray walls to red. She could hear the breathing of the soldier at the far end of the hallway, and other breaths, though they were too far away to know to whom or what they belonged. She could feel the stone and straw under her feet, feel her talons flexing against them.

More than anything, she could feel the hunger, gnawing at her guts like a vicious weasel. The Beast howled. It needed to break free.

ESCAPE!

No!

Her feet and hands pawed at the ground. Her eyes glared at the bars as her ears listened for the guards. Ruxandra struggled to subdue the Beast but she could not get hold. Her control of her body slipped away like water through her fingers.

No! Stop. Please stop.

ESCAPE!

The Beast charged at the bars. The force of the impact broke two of her ribs and made the bars rattle and shake. The metal around the lock bowed and stretched. The loud screech of metal made the guard in the hall shout in surprise. Ruxandra could hear him running, hear him shouting as the Beast backed her body to the far side of the cell, clutching at her aching side.

Stop. You must stop. This is my body, and I want you to stop!

HUNGRY! ESCAPE! KILL!

No!

The Beast charged forward again, slamming the other side of its body into the cage. More ribs broke, but the metal of the lock bent farther. The Beast shoved the cage with one hand. The bars moved and rattled more than before. It backed up again, ready to begin another charge.

No! Ruxandra grabbed for control. For one brief moment, she held it, making one leg bend and sending the Beast tumbling. It screamed and howled and thrashed, staring all around the cell as if expecting to find the culprit.

Let my body go! Let it go, and stay away from the door!

KILL! ESCAPE!

No!

"Hurry!"

The shout came from down the hall. The Beast charged forward. Hurt or not, damaged or not, it would break open the cage. Ruxandra tried to interfere, but the Beast blocked her attempt with a will so powerful it shoved her to the back of her own mind. She could not control her body at all, only watch as it hit the bars at a speed faster than Ruxandra thought possible.

The bars gave way.

The Beast let out a howl of joy and pain as it bounced off the far wall. One arm was broken. It staggered forward in a limping, three-footed run. Its cage was at the end of a hallway of rough-hewn natural stone. There was a door at the end of it, but it was wide open. Ahead, lit by a dozen torches, was another, larger room. In the way was a soldier, his sword drawn and pointed at her. Ruxandra could tell he was very young.

"It's escaped!" the soldier screamed. "Hurry!"

The Beast closed with the man, holding its broken arm close to its body. It was going to jump on him, Ruxandra knew, as soon as it got close enough to use both legs to spring forward.

Screams, sudden and sharp, filled the air. The soldier in the hallway backed out of the way. The Beast raced past him and into a room full of chaos.

The hallway opened into a large, high-ceilinged chamber, also made of natural stone. Ruxandra caught glimpses of strange devices all around the room. In the middle, a large brass tub sat with chains and pulleys hanging above it. There were many soldiers in the room now. Most were on the far side, their backs against a large wooden door. Others were in the large cells on either side of the room, using black whips to drive naked girls and men out of their cells.

The smell of blood hit the Beast's nose like an arrow into a bull's-eye. It froze, its head going back and forth on its shoulders like a pendulum as it saw the masses of naked, helpless human flesh around it, each thin body a frail container of glorious blood.

EAT!

The Beast launched across the room, jumping above the soldiers' heads. It hit the wall with two feet and then sprang down on one of the naked men. The man didn't have time to scream before the Beast's weight bore him down. The Beast extended its fangs and sank them deep into the man's neck.

Ruxandra could taste the smooth, rich sweetness of the man's blood. She could feel it sliding down her throat, like silk over skin. It made her dizzy.

As the Beast drank, Ruxandra felt it losing control. The blood was making her stronger. Strong enough that she drove the Beast back.

She drank deeper, sucking on the man's neck harder, draining everything she could. Each one so different. Each one with a unique life she could almost taste. Around her everything was madness. The naked men tried to fight the soldiers. The soldiers struck at them with flails and swords, leaving fresh puddles of blood across the floor and driving them back into their cells. Ruxandra didn't care. Feeding was all that mattered.

She drained the last of the blood from the man's body and felt his soul flee his dying flesh. That emotion again—she thrust it back.

When she looked up, the soldiers in the room were all pointing their swords at her. The naked men and women had all been driven back into their cells.

Ruxandra dropped the dead man and walked toward her prison. The soldier from the hallway stepped aside, keeping the sword between him and her. Ruxandra remembered how fast the Beast moved. She wondered if she'd be able to reach the man before he could raise his blade. She didn't try, though.

Instead, she stopped at the entrance to the hallway and said, "Please tell Elizabeth that I am awake."

Then she walked slowly down the hallway, back to her cell with its burst open lock. She stepped inside and swung the door closed behind her. It wouldn't lock anymore, but it would give Elizabeth and her people some security, in case she became the Beast before they arrived.

She heard one guard leave, running up the stairs. The others followed her and stood outside her cell, their swords pointed at her. She went to the pile of straw and sat, waiting. The guards remained, not speaking, until Elizabeth approached.

"Good evening," she said, stepping in front of Ruxandra's cell. "Do you remember me?"

"Yes," Ruxandra said. "I remember you, and I remember our last talk."

"Wonderful!" Elizabeth clapped her hands like a child receiving a present. "That's the first time this has happened."

She stepped forward and saw the lock. "My goodness. Did you do that?"

"The Beast did, yes," Ruxandra said. "I felt it doing it. I tried to stop it but . . . I think I need a stronger cell until it's under control."

"You felt it?"

"I could feel the Beast using my body, but I couldn't stop it. I was trapped. One of us is always stronger at any given moment. Then I drank, and it faded once more."

"You've never said this before." Elizabeth frowned. "This is the first time you've remembered so much, or stayed yourself so long."

"I see." Ruxandra stared at the filthy, stained walls and the floor. "Elizabeth?"

"Yes?"

"I . . . I don't want to live like an animal anymore." She looked down at the straw below her. "I know I can't leave but . . ."

"We will move you to a new cell," Elizabeth said without hesitation. "One with proper furniture." Elizabeth grabbed the bars with both hands. "I mean to make you whole, Ruxandra. To make you into your true self."

"You would do that for me?" Ruxandra's heart leaped up, but in the same moment, doubt wriggled in. "Why?"

Elizabeth smiled. "Because you are beautiful. Because you are the truest embodiment of Blood Royal, and because…"

Elizabeth flushed and looked at the floor. Ruxandra waited, but Elizabeth didn't say anything more.

"Thank you," Ruxandra said. "I don't want to be that *thing* anymore."

Elizabeth raised her head, meeting Ruxandra's eyes again. "In return, though, I have a request."

"Yes?"

"Promise to obey me, for as long as you are in my castle. I will help you as much as I can, but I must protect my people and myself. Will you do that?"

Ruxandra nodded. "I don't think the Beast will listen."

Elizabeth laughed. "We will worry about the Beast later. For now, we will worry about you."

Something strange stirred inside Ruxandra, a feeling she couldn't recall ever having. She must have, though, because she knew its name: Gratitude.

The muscles in Ruxandra's face felt stiff as if they had forgotten long ago their purpose. Still, she willed the corners of her mouth up until she was smiling at Elizabeth.

"Thank you."

CHAPTER THREE

THE NEXT DAY, Ruxandra moved into a new cell. It had bars for a door like the others, but Elizabeth had a narrow bed with thick, wool blankets placed in it, and a small desk with a chair. She had ordered that torches be lit at all times, so Ruxandra would have light. She'd also ordered her men to lock the door and brace the bars shut with wood posts, in case the Beast reappeared.

Unlike her last cell at the far end of the old cave, this one sat in the dungeon proper. She could see the entire room through the bars.

The dungeon's ceiling hung 20 feet above her head, though the roof in her cell was much lower. The big room was twice as wide as it was high, and was permeated with the smell of old blood, and the stink of the prisoners in the other cells. She could see the doors of the other cells from her room, though not inside. Unlike her cell, those ones had wooden doors, keeping the prisoners inside in darkness.

There were three cells on the opposite wall from her cell, two on the wall to her right. There was also the tunnel, leading to the cell they had kept her in before.

On the left was the door that led outside. She could smell the fresh air that wafted down it, sometimes. She desperately wanted to go up the stairs.

In one corner sat a large chair with short round spikes covering every surface and straps to hold whoever sat on it in place. On the second corner sat a large stool topped with a pointed, four-sided pyramid. A pair of ropes hung above it, and a large iron ball with a short shackle attached to it sat on either side. The third corner held a large wood frame with ropes in each corner and a handle to pull them tight. In the fourth corner was a post with shackles attached to it. Beside it sat a brazier filled with coals and metal instruments. Behind it, on the wall, hung twenty different straps and whips.

In the middle of the floor sat the bathtub.

It was bronze, with strange symbols that circled the outside of it. Chains and pulleys hung over it. Behind it, against the far wall, sat a cistern of water. The tub had a small bronze box beneath it and in it Ruxandra could see the remains of a fire.

It was all very strange.

Elizabeth had also given Ruxandra a long linen shift to wear. Ruxandra found the feeling of the cloth at once distracting and luxurious. The softness of it sent shivers through her. Ruxandra wasn't sure she liked it, but she knew she disliked being looked at by the guards.

She didn't know why, though.

Ruxandra spent the first day going from the chair to the floor and back again. It felt odd sitting in a chair. But people sat in chairs, so she practiced.

That evening, the man who smelled like chemicals came to her cell.

He wasn't dressed in armor like the others. He wore a long gray robe, cinched at the waist with a jeweled belt, under a blue cloak. A large silver locket hung around his neck. His beard was small and neatly trimmed. His fingers were long, delicate, and stained with chemicals. He placed a stool in front of Ruxandra's cell and bowed low to her.

"Good evening, Ruxandra," he said. "My name is Kade. May I sit with you?"

Ruxandra wasn't sure how to respond, so she said, "I suppose."

"Thank you." He sat on the stool. Ruxandra picked up the chair and moved it to the bars. She sat and waited. Kade's eyes roamed over every inch of her, studying her like a hawk studying the plains below it.

Finally, Kade straightened up and smiled. "You're very beautiful."

Ruxandra blinked. "I am?"

Kade nodded. "Or I should say, there is beauty underneath the dirt."

Ruxandra looked down at her hands and rubbed at the dirt for a moment and then saw Kade watching. She let her hands drop to her lap.

"It is nothing a bath won't cure, my dear," Kade said. "Now, how are you feeling? I imagine you must be bored, having nothing to do and no one to talk to."

"There was never anyone to talk to in the forest."

"I see. Do you remember any other places?"

Ruxandra frowned. She could see the forest in her mind, several of her favorite spots, could practically smell it and taste the clean air, but that was all. "I . . . don't know any place other than the forest. There are the mountains, of course, but they're part of the forest, like the rivers or clearings."

"Did you never see people?" Kade asked gently.

Ruxandra frowned. She shook her head. "I don't remember."

"How did you live?"

"I followed the game," Ruxandra said. "Every spring I found the new growth, and every winter I left the cold. I had lairs. I had . . ." Ruxandra shook her head again. "A pattern? That's not the word. A . . . territory? I always went to certain places, every summer and winter for . . ."

How long? Ruxandra remembered the heat of summers past and the cold of the winters, she remembered rain and times when no rain fell, when the animals could be found beside the sluggish streams, but she couldn't remember how many of these cycles she'd seen.

"It will come back to you," Kade said.

Ruxandra felt a chill pass through her that had nothing to do with the cool air of the dungeon. "What if it doesn't?"

"Then you start life over," Kade said. "Here, with us."

"Here." Ruxandra shook her head. "I don't even know where 'here' is."

"Hungary." At Ruxandra's confused expression, he continued. "It's the name of the country—one king's territory. You are in it." He clasped his hands together and leaned forward. "You will need to learn a great deal before you're ready to face society."

"Society?"

"People," Kade said. "The court and the castle, the villagers around it, maybe even the royal courts of Rudolph II."

"Who?"

Kade chuckled and covered his mouth with his hand. "I apologize. I find you fascinating."

"Which part of me?" Ruxandra asked, the sharpness in her words surprising even her. "My filthy body or my complete ignorance?"

Kade sat back on his stool, his eyes narrowing. Fear gave off a certain smell in humans, a sharper note to their sweat. Kade stank of it.

"I apologize, my lady," Kade said. "I meant no offense. I wish to help you."

"Why?"

The dungeon door opened.

"Ruxandra, how are—" Elizabeth's words ended abruptly at the sight of Kade. Anger, fast and fleeting, swept across her face and then vanished. Kade's fear heightened. "Kade, what are you doing here?"

Her words were polite yet had an undertone of danger, like the hidden claws of a mountain cat. Kade rose and bowed to Ruxandra before turning.

"I wished to see our guest," Kade said. "I was afraid she would be lonely, and thought that human company would help her with her recovery."

The words came out smooth and bland, and no offense could be taken at his tone. Even so, Ruxandra saw the skin around Elizabeth's eyes and at the corners of her mouth tighten. She found herself fixated on the color of her eyes—a glossy chestnut brown—and the shape of her mouth.

"I thank you for thinking of it," Elizabeth said. "Now that I have arrived, you may leave."

"Of course, my lady." Kade bowed, then once more to Ruxandra. "I do hope we will have the chance to speak again, Ruxandra."

"Me too," Ruxandra said. "Thank you."

Kade left the dungeon with an easy, confident stride. Elizabeth watched him go, and then turned back to Ruxandra, a charming, confiding smile upon her face. She took the stool and sat down.

"I take it he amused you?"

Ruxandra shook her head. "He confused me. Talking about society and people and King Rudolph. I didn't understand him."

"He is somewhat difficult to make sense of," Elizabeth said. "A side effect of too much reading, I suspect."

I know nothing. I can't remember anything. I can't . . . Ruxandra turned her back. Her hands clenched into fists, ready to smash something to relieve her frustration. Only she didn't want to break any of her new things. She wanted the chair. She wanted the bed. She wanted . . .

What is it I want?

"I can't imagine how frustrating this is," Elizabeth said. "To be newly awakened to your true self, trapped in here, and not able to leave—"

"I want a bath." Ruxandra held out her dirt-stained hands. "I'm dirty, and I want to be clean. People don't stay dirty, do they?"

"Peasants stay dirty," Elizabeth said. "Unless we force them to clean themselves. They're worse than animals. We of royal blood clean ourselves whenever possible."

Elizabeth put a finger to her chin. "It will take some time to make the preparations, however. Can you be patient until then?"

Ruxandra nodded. "I can."

"Good. I will return tomorrow morning."

An hour later the dark one came into the dungeon.

Dorotyas, Ruxandra remembered. *Her name is Dorotyas. The Beast wanted to kill her.*

Dorotyas looked older than Elizabeth. Pimples covered the wattles of fat on her face. Her eyes were small dark holes, buried deep beneath her oversize brow. Her dark brown hair hung limp and greasy, and her clothes strained to fit the girth of her too-large frame. There were muscles beneath her fat, and scars on her arms and face that spoke of fights.

She walked like a bear, certain of her power.

She took the keys from her belt and opened a nearby cell door. She pulled out a short, three-ended strap and entered.

A girl screamed in pain. A moment later Dorotyas stepped out, pulling out a thin blonde girl by her hair. She forced the girl down to her hands and knees and dragged her across the floor to a horizontal beam held up by two posts. Dorotyas pulled the girl over the beam so only her toes and the tips of her fingers touched the ground. The girl's backside quivered and rose high in the air.

The two guards by the door watched and grinned at one another.

Dorotyas swung the strap, cracking it across the girl's backside. The girl's flesh rippled upon impact and turned bright red. The girl screamed in pain. A moment later a welt rose, and a thin line of blood appeared on her backside. Dorotyas laid the strap to her a dozen more times, leaving her flesh crisscrossed with bright, bleeding welts. The girl wailed in pain, tears and snot running down her face. Dorotyas grabbed her hair, dragged her the rest of the way over the beam and put her back onto her hands and knees.

Ruxandra inhaled deep, pulling in the smell of the blood. It sent a shiver through her. Dorotyas dragged the girl across the floor to the far side of the dungeon, where rags hung on the wall, and a bucket lay beside a cistern full of water.

"Take the rags, peasant bitch," Dorotyas said. "Fill the bucket, clean the tub, and drain it. I want it so clean it sparkles, understand?"

She looked over to Ruxandra, lips raised in a sneer. "Our *guest* wants to wash the filth off."

Ruxandra could hear the distain in the woman's voice. It made the Beast inside her growl, and made Ruxandra want to drink the woman dry. *I mustn't.*

Dorotyas raised the strap and brought it down hard on the girl's back. "Fast!"

The girl scuttled to the cistern, filled the bucket, and took the rags back to the tub. She froze before it, her hand covering her mouth in horror. Dorotyas's strap struck out again. The girl yelped and fell to her knees. She put the water in the tub. It turned red at once.

Blood? Ruxandra leaned forward. *Is that what she was frightened of?*

The smell of blood grew stronger, and the water a darker red as the girl scrubbed.

Why was the tub filled with blood?

The girl pulled a plug out of the tub, and the bloody water swirled down and out of sight. The girl went back twice more for water. Each time, Dorotyas lashed her on the way by. The smell of her blood, fresh and warm and alive, tantalized Ruxandra.

Finally, the girl stopped and knelt before Dorotyas. "Please, mistress, it's clean."

Dorotyas peered inside the tub and ran her fingers inside it. When she straightened up, she smiled. "Fine work, peasant bitch."

Dorotyas grabbed the girl's hair and bent her over the side of the brass tub. She beat the girl across the back of her thighs, then turned her over and whipped her belly and breasts. Unlike last time, none of the hits opened her flesh. Ruxandra felt angry, but she wasn't sure why. *Elizabeth said they are merely peasants.* Dorotyas kept at her until the girl ran out of screams. Then she pulled her upright.

"Now get back to your cell," Dorotyas said. "Or I'll have the guards take a turn on you front and back."

She dropped her and watched, lip curled, as the peasant girl crawled back into her cell, pulling the door shut behind her. Dorotyas walked over to Ruxandra.

"Did you like watching that?" Dorotyas asked. "Did it excite you? Make you all wet?"

"Wet?" Ruxandra eyes focused on the woman. "What do you mean?"

Dorotyas shook her head. "Never mind. The countess will bathe you in the morning. If you hurt her, I will kill you. Do you understand?"

I'd like to see you try was on the tip of Ruxandra's tongue, but she didn't say it.

The next morning, Ruxandra smelled the hot water before she saw it. She rolled off the bed where she'd been practicing sleeping like a person and stood at the bars of her cell. The dungeon door swung open, and Elizabeth led four servants, each carrying a large bucket of steaming hot water. A fifth followed, carrying a handful of towels. Elizabeth plugged the drain, and the women poured their buckets in. The tub clanged and groaned as the hot water hit the cold metal. The servants took their buckets over to the cistern and filled them with colder water. They added bucket after bucket until the tub was filled.

Below the sound of the water pouring, Ruxandra heard every heartbeat in the room and felt the blood flowing through each person.

It made her hungry. She knew which she'd take first.

No. I don't care about that right now. I want a bath.

Elizabeth put her fingers in the tub and smiled. "Perfect. You may go."

The ones with the buckets left. The one carrying the towels stayed. She glanced at the cage, fear on her face.

"Guards, Dorotyas," Elizabeth said. The soldiers rushed forward and removed the two heavy beams propped against the door. Dorotyas unlocked the door.

"You keep control of yourself," the heavy woman whispered. "You understand?"

Dorotyas's heart beat strong and steady, not racing at all. The woman's sweat didn't smell of fear, and her expression revealed nothing. Dorotyas swung open the cell door and stepped back. Ruxandra stepped out of her cell and walked slowly to the tub.

"Guards, turn your backs," Elizabeth said. "A woman does not wish to be stared at while she bathes."

"Yes, my lady." The men turned to face the wall.

Elizabeth held out a hand. "Your shift?"

Ruxandra removed it and handed it to Elizabeth. She put one hand into the tub. It was warm—warmer than any water Ruxandra remembered. She put one leg in, then the other. The water closed around her and held her, even warmer than the blankets of her bed. She put her head under it and lay there, looking up through the water at the rippling yellow of the torchlight and the way the water distorted the world above it. She closed her eyes, reveling in the warmth.

A hand wrapped around her wrist and pulled. Ruxandra's eyes flew open, and she sat up. The cold air of the dungeon shocked her skin causing goose bumps to rise on her chest. Elizabeth was gripping her. Ruxandra felt the woman's pulse. Her mouth watered. *She would taste better than anyone.*

She swallowed, hard, before Elizabeth noticed anything.

"Are you all right?" Elizabeth asked. "You were under for so long."

"I'm fine." Something shifted inside Ruxandra. Her hunger became urgent. She pulled her arm away. "I'm fine."

Elizabeth put on a smile. "Then let's get you clean. This is soap."

Ruxandra stared at the little cake in her hand.

"It removes dirt from your skin and from your hair. May I show you?"

Elizabeth dunked the soap in the water. She rubbed it against a cloth, coating it with white, frothy bubbles. Ruxandra watched, fascinated. Elizabeth held out the cloth.

"Now, rub it against the skin on your hands first, then on your arms."

The cloth felt rough, and the soap slippery. Together they covered her hands in suds that grew darker with each rubbing.

"Dip your hands in the water," Elizabeth said. The water turned cloudy. Ruxandra's hands came out clean and white. She stared at them in amazement.

"If you stand up . . ." Elizabeth stopped and looked away. She swallowed, blinked, and when she spoke again, she didn't meet Ruxandra's eyes. "If you stand, I will help you wash."

Ruxandra wondered at the other woman's behavior but put her hands on the side of the tub and stood. Elizabeth watched her rise. Then she wet the cloth and began washing her.

Ruxandra gasped at the first touch. Elizabeth's hand and the cloth gently rubbed over the muscles of her shoulder. Elizabeth changed hands with the cloth, rubbing it up and down her back in firm strokes that caressed Ruxandra's skin and the muscles beneath. Ruxandra found herself closing her eyes again, unable to indulge in anything but the feeling of Elizabeth's hand on her body.

Elizabeth finished her back and gently turned Ruxandra around. There was a feeling about this—a memory—long, long ago—she couldn't find it. She had the idea if she did, there would be grief. So she focused on the physical, the soft strength of the hands. Ruxandra moved with them, and she felt Elizabeth's hands starting once more at her collarbones and gliding down. Ruxandra gasped again as the cloth moved over her breasts. Her nipples grew hard under the gentle rubbing.

"Your scars." Elizabeth traced four thick, pebbled lines of flesh across Ruxandra's left breast and down across her stomach with the cloth. "Where did you get them?"

"A bear," Ruxandra said. "We crossed paths one winter."

"It must have hurt terribly."

"Yes." Memories of the bear's claws ripping into her flesh made Ruxandra shudder. She turned her mind away from it and focused on Elizabeth's cloth moving across her body. It crossed Ruxandra's stomach, bringing such profound comfort that she wanted to cry, and then swept around her hips to her backside. The touch made Ruxandra shudder again but in a different way, reminding her of a time when she once loved the sun. Elizabeth's hands went down, covering Ruxandra's legs with the suds and leaving them tingling with the memory of her touch.

"You look so young," Elizabeth said. "Like a girl, fresh into womanhood. How old are you, my dear?"

Ruxandra shook her head. "I have no idea."

Elizabeth stepped back and looked her over. "Your body looks no more than eighteen. Now sit. Rinse your body, and we'll start on your hair."

Ruxandra sat. Elizabeth dunked the cloth and rubbed it over Ruxandra, getting the soap off the half of her torso above water. Ruxandra kept her eyes closed. Elizabeth's scent—roses, lavender, and sweat—rose above the sweet smell of the soapsuds floating in the water.

It shouldn't smell like that.

Ruxandra sat up. "The soap."

Elizabeth stopped rubbing at her flesh. "Yes?"

"It's wrong." Ruxandra opened her eyes, looking down at the gray water and the slick of oil and bubbles. "It smells wrong."

Elizabeth sat back from the tub. "Wrong how?"

Ruxandra shook her head. "It should smell like . . ." She struggled. "Lilacs?"

A boy. A pond. Music. Soap. Soft clothes. Hunting rabbit. Hunting deer. Feeding but growing hungrier.

"Elizabeth . . ." Ruxandra said. Elizabeth's scent filled her nose. The beat of her heart rang in Ruxandra's ears: she saw its color, rose-red. "Something's wrong."

Elizabeth leaned closer. "What?"

"I don't know. I'm . . ." Music. Singing. A cabin in a clearing. A boy with a strong back and white teeth. Lips touching lips. Hands touching her flesh, touching her breasts. *Oh.* Hunger and hunger and hunger. *Love will flee, will die. Why is that?* "Run."

"What?" Elizabeth rose to her feet and stepped back.

"Run!" *Had flown. Was gone.* Something chasing her. Some *wrong* thing. It wanted to kill her, to drink her. She was too weak. She needed to stop it before it killed her. She needed to be stronger. She needed to be—

"Run!" Ruxandra screamed. Then the Beast roared and leaped out of the tub, talons extended, aiming for Elizabeth's flesh.

KILL!

CHAPTER FOUR

Ruxandra tried to seize control of her body. It stumbled but didn't stop moving. Dorotyas lashed out with her strap, snapping it on her face, causing one eye to rupture in a burst of fluid. Pain ripped through Ruxandra, tearing away her control. The Beast screamed in agony and scrabbled at its dripping eye socket. Dorotyas whipped the strap again, ripping open the flesh and muscle on the Beast's arm.

Dorotyas swung again, aiming for the Beast's good eye. The Beast ducked, and the strap snapped above its head. Then it sprang.

Dorotyas's punch met the Beast halfway. It tried to knock the fist aside, but the missing eye had ruined its depth perception. Dorotyas's punch crashed into the Beast's nose, breaking it. It wasn't enough to stop the Beast's momentum. The Beast smashed into Dorotyas with all its weight, sending her sprawling. The Beast snarled and jumped again, talons aiming for Dorotyas's stomach.

Stop! Ruxandra wrenched control from the Beast long enough to pull her arms apart. They hit the ground on either side of

Dorotyas, the talons scraping on the stone. Dorotyas grabbed the Beast's head and rolled it over. She sat astride its chest, letting her full weight rest on the Beast's rib cage. She raised the strap again and brought it down hard toward the Beast's face.

The Beast bucked its hips, and Dorotyas flew across the room. She hit the far wall with a crunch and yelled in pain. The Beast flipped over, ready to spring again.

I said stop! Ruxandra tried to control the Beast's legs to keep it from springing. The Beast's mind, savage and wild, pounded down on Ruxandra's.

Two swords sank into the Beast's back. Pain, sharp and sudden, tore Ruxandra's control away. The Beast spun away from the soldiers' blades, tearing its flesh open to free itself.

It howled again, the noise reverberating through the dungeon.

"Get back, countess!" Dorotyas shouted.

The Beast turned. Elizabeth ran toward it. The Beast snarled and crouched low. *KILL!*

No, I won't let you! Ruxandra tried to stop. It felt as if Ruxandra's own muscles had turned against her, refusing to do her will. The Beast tried to shove her into a dark space in her head where she had no strength or control. The Beast wanted to gauge how far it had to jump to reach Elizabeth. With its eye missing, it couldn't be sure, and hesitated.

Run! Ruxandra screamed in her mind.

Elizabeth grabbed the girl who had carried the towels.

She was crouched on the floor by the tub, forgotten by the Beast. Her eyes were wide with fear, and her fist was crammed in her mouth to keep her from screaming. Elizabeth grabbed her hair and hauled her to her feet. In one swift motion, Elizabeth pulled a knife from inside her dress and cut the girl across the chest. The girl screamed and Elizabeth shoved her toward the Beast.

The smell of the girl's blood filled the Beast's nose, driving out any other thought except *HUNGRY.*

The Beast jumped and sank its teeth into the girl's neck, cutting off her screams. Blood, warm and rich and so delicious, filled its mouth. The Beast pulled hard at the girl's throat, draining her as fast as it could. The fresh blood flowed over the Beast's tongue: food, bliss, relief.

Out of the corner of her eye, Ruxandra spotted Dorotyas climbing to her feet. She cradled one arm against her body. Her face was pale with pain, which made Ruxandra feel at once ashamed and satisfied with herself. Elizabeth stood behind her soldiers, her eyes wide. Ruxandra could smell the fear on them all. She continued drinking, taking the last of the life from the girl before letting her drop.

She stood, swaying and dizzy, but in control of her body once again.

The girl's blood ran down Ruxandra's breasts and dripped toward her legs and sex. Ruxandra looked down. She stumbled over to the bathtub, grabbed the cloth, and slowly, meticulously, washed all the blood off her body. When she finished, she picked up her dirty shift, put it on, walked back into her cell, and closed the door behind her.

Dorotyas ran forward, shoved the key in the lock, and turned it. The guards rushed to brace the two beams against the door. Ruxandra sank to the floor and put her head in her hands. *Elizabeth will never trust me now.*

She thought of the dead girl—then made herself stop. Not yet. She couldn't think about it. She needed to not be the Beast anymore.

The wounds on her back started to heal. Pain and relief blended into one as the flesh and muscles stitched back together. Stranger, still, she could feel her eye reforming, swelling to fill the space in its socket.

When her eye had rebuilt itself, Ruxandra lifted her head and looked around. The dungeon was empty, save for the two guards in front of her cell. Both had their weapons out, and both looked ready to kill her. Ruxandra put her head back down into her hands and wept.

The guards changed six times, but none came near. One prisoner was brought into the dungeon—a teenage girl with bruises on her face and a torn skirt. Later, two guards dragged a man from the cells, kicking and pleading for his life. Ruxandra watched it all with dull, bored eyes. There was nothing to do save sit on her chair or lie on her bed or pace the cell for hours. No company, no Elizabeth . . . How quickly she had gotten used to speaking like a person.

She was getting hungry again.

How often do I eat?

I still don't know how much time is passing. I don't know if its daytime or night.

Am I going to be stuck in here forever like this? Just stuck here, only thinking about my next meal?

The faint smell of chemicals caught her attention.

Kade.

She went to the bars and looked, but the man was nowhere in sight. She frowned and sniffed again. It was definitely he. Then she heard footsteps, coming down the dungeon stairs. The door opened, and Kade stepped inside.

Once more, Kade placed the stool in front of Ruxandra's cell, far enough away that she couldn't reach him. Ruxandra picked up her chair and moved it away from the bars. She didn't want to lose control and attack him.

"Is Dorotyas all right?" Ruxandra asked as he sat. "She hit the wall rather hard."

"She had a dislocated shoulder," Kade said. "The surgeon put it back. She's still in a fair bit of pain."

Ruxandra's head dropped. *Elizabeth will be angry.* "I'm sorry."

"So is she," Kade said. "You are not to blame. It was the Beast."

"I am the Beast."

"I don't think so." His voice was warm with interest.

Hope, small and fragile, blossomed in Ruxandra's chest. Her head rose. "Why?"

"Remember what Elizabeth said to you before. The Beast came into being because you were feeding on animal blood." Kade scratched his beard as he put his words together. "I believe that the Beast is your will to survive. When everything about you that had been human faded, from drinking the animal blood, the Beast took over."

"Human?" Ruxandra frowned. "Was I human once?"

"According to all the stories I've read about vampires, yes. In every one, the vampire was human before he—or she—changed."

"Do they ever change back?"

Kade shook his head. "I'm sorry, no."

"Oh." His voice was admiring, she noted. *He wouldn't find it so fascinating if it had happened to him.*

"Ruxandra," Kade asked gently, "what happened down here?"

Ruxandra stared at her hands again. She couldn't bring herself to look at him. He didn't move or speak, just sat there, waiting.

Finally, she mumbled, "I got hungry."

"Hungry?" Instead of sounding dismayed or upset, Kade seemed excited.

Ruxandra felt tears coming again. "I knew I was hungry, and I knew I needed to eat, but I wanted the bath more. I thought I could control my hunger. Then I smelled the soap and suddenly the Beast was there and I couldn't stop it!"

She dropped her face into her hands and turned away so he wouldn't see her cry. Her back shook as the sobs racked her body.

"I didn't want to kill Elizabeth!" she howled between sobs. "I just wanted a bath! I was so dirty!"

"Ruxandra," Kade said softly, but she didn't stop crying. He raised his voice. "Ruxandra! Stop! It wasn't your fault!"

Ruxandra shook her head and didn't look up.

"Ruxandra, no one knows how vampires work!" Kade's words penetrated through the fog of her weeping. "No one knows how often they must feed, or what happens to one who's been living off animal blood. No one blames you—in fact, you are quite remarkable: vampire, woman, Beast. You are amazing, a . . . *treasure.* Elizabeth is unhurt, and you've discovered something vitally important!"

Ruxandra raised her head. She snuffled back her tears. "I did?"

"Yes!" Kade's face glowed with excitement. "You recognized the feeling of hunger. Before, you'd fall asleep, and the Beast would take you. This time, you felt the Beast advancing! You *saved* Elizabeth because you were able to warn her. Do you know what that means?"

Ruxandra shook her head. She didn't understand anything, and she didn't dare say more for fear she'd start crying again.

"It means you have control! This is a huge improvement!"

"I still put people at risk. My control is . . . limited."

"Everyone's control is limited. If we are frightened or starving . . . any being will react to protect itself, to live. You are no different. You merely have different instincts."

It was disconcerting to look at herself from this perspective. As if she were a creature like any other, one that God had made to live on this earth. But she wasn't.

How do I know that?

Kade rose to his feet. "I'm going to tell Elizabeth. She'll be thrilled. I will be back soon, I promise."

Ruxandra reached for him. "No, wait! Stop!"

She shouted loud enough that the guards on the other side of the room winced. Kade hunched over a moment from the force of it.

He straightened up. "What's the matter?"

"I'm hungry again," Ruxandra said. "I don't want Elizabeth coming down when I'm hungry."

"Of course." Kade sat back down, not moving the stool away but seeming to hold himself back. "Is the Beast emerging?"

"I don't think so." Ruxandra reached inside her mind, searching for the Beast. It was there but not trying to take over. "I'm not that hungry yet."

"We could feed you now. But it might be better to discover what your limits are. Why don't we wait until you start to feel the Beast emerge? Then we'll get you something to eat."

"Someone, you mean." Ruxandra couldn't see the other cells, but she could hear the prisoners talking in low voices or trying to sleep or weeping to themselves.

"Some*thing*," Kade repeated. "Peasants aren't human. They're animals bred for labor."

Ruxandra looked away. She knew that wasn't right. She also knew she was not ready to think about it yet.

"Now," said Kade. "Shall I teach you about the world while we wait?"

Ruxandra's eyes lit up. "Yes, please!"

"Then I'll begin by telling you it is the year of our lord, 1609…

Kade talked for hours. He described the marvelous inventions and discoveries of the last fifty years: magnifying lenses that allowed one to see the world eight or nine times bigger than it was; spyglasses that allowed one to see at a distance; thermometers that could measure heat and cold in units. He talked about the discovery of a place called America, full of curious savages and even more curious animals, and the burning at the stake of a famous philosopher and alchemist, Giordano Bruno.

He told her about the Hungarian Empire, about King Rudolph, and about the ranks of its nobility. Ruxandra learned that the Bathory Family was one of the preeminent noble families in the kingdom, and that Elizabeth had four children, one married, the rest living with her family in other parts of Hungary.

He talked of Vienna, where the king lived, and Ruxandra's eyes went wide at the idea of a place so large and so filled with people.

Ruxandra grew hungrier with each passing hour, but the Beast wasn't yet stirring.

Kade talked about the castle. Elizabeth's late husband had given it to her upon their marriage. He told her that Elizabeth had established a *gymnaesium*—a school for young women—to help educate the daughters of the nobility in their duties and responsibilities.

In the midst of it, the Beast awoke.

It didn't feel separate from Ruxandra. Rather, it felt as though part of her mind was trying to tear itself away from her control and take her body with it. Her legs began trembling, and her hands shaking.

"Kade." The panic in her voice stopped him midsentence. "It's happening."

"Guards!" he shouted, rising to his feet. "The man in the third cell. Bring him!"

The guards ran.

Ruxandra stayed in her chair. The Beast wanted to rise and throw itself against the bars, to grab Kade and rip his throat open. It wanted to eat, and it didn't care whom. Ruxandra refused to move. She wouldn't let it take over. Not this time. Not even a little.

"What do you want? Stop!" a man shouted. Then steel-wrapped fists slammed repeatedly into flesh. The man cried in pain. Ruxandra smelled blood, fresh and flowing.

KILL!

"NO!" Ruxandra grabbed the chair with both hands. "Kade, hurry! It's nearly free!"

"They're coming," he said. "Just keep fighting it!"

"I can't!"

KILL EAT HUNGRY!

The soldiers dragged the man to the bars. Kade pulled out the cell key and shoved it in, then kicked away the two beams from the door.

KILL KILL KILL!

"Shut up!" Ruxandra screamed. "Kade! Hurry!"

Kade swung the door wide, and the soldiers hurled the man in. He fell at Ruxandra's feet. He jumped up at once, but Kade and the soldiers had already pushed the door closed. Kade turned the key and jumped back. The man swore and rattled the cell door. Then he spun and faced Ruxandra. He was a rough, wiry man of about thirty, with rusty hair and narrow, angry eyes. Thin-faced, with bad teeth, a dirty neck. His hands clenched into fists, and he crouched.

The Beast leaped forward. *KILL!*

Moments later, there was only Ruxandra, looking down at the body before her.

"You held off the beast."

"Barely," Ruxandra said, and not when I finally had prey."

"Barely controlled is still controlled," Kade said. "Control is the difference between an animal and a person. You recognized when you were hungry and you managed to hold off the Beast until you had. You've never done that before and that is a great deal of progress."

"I suppose." She looked at the body. "Who was he?"

"A criminal," Kade said. "A peasant who attacked women as they walked in the woods. His sentence was castration and impalement through the hole. You gave him a cleaner death."

"I see." That helped.

Kade opened the cell door. "The guards will take the body away."

Neither of the guards looked happy about the idea. Both grabbed their swords. Ruxandra reached down and clasped the arm of the limp corpse. With ease, she dragged it to the front of the cell and tossed it out. The body flew fifteen feet and fetched up against the tub.

"Impressive." Kade closed the door and locked it. "I'll return with Elizabeth. Hopefully, she will let you out of this cell soon."

Soon, Ruxandra thought. *How long is soon?*

Elizabeth came down after two more changes of the guards. She wore a blue velvet dress and cloak, wrapped tight around her body. She walked across the dungeon and stopped in front of Ruxandra's door. Her beautiful face was expressionless as she watched Ruxandra. Then she took out a key and unlocked the cell door.

"It's time for you to leave this place, Ruxandra."

CHAPTER FIVE

Ruxandra stared at Elizabeth, unable to believe what the woman had said. Elizabeth turned her back and walked to the dungeon door. She opened it and looked at Ruxandra over her shoulder. Regal, trusting, so feminine. Ruxandra felt butterflies in her stomach again.

"Come, my dear."

Ruxandra didn't move. Fresh, cool air flowed down the steps and through the dungeon door, bringing scents so different from the blood and mold and filth filling the dungeon.

Suddenly, Ruxandra was terrified.

Elizabeth smiled, the serene expression a stark contrast to the two fear-filled faces of the guards on either side of the door.

"It's all right, Ruxandra. Come."

"Why now?" The words escaped Ruxandra's lips before she could stop them. "Why let me out now?"

"Because Kade told me what you did." Elizabeth smiled. "You felt the hunger and controlled it. You kept the beast from escaping and you came back to yourself immediately after you drank."

"I don't know if I can do it again."

"You will." Elizabeth sounded so confident that Ruxandra believed her. "Now, come."

Ruxandra had to prepare herself to take the first step out of her cell. It felt wrong. Forbidden. Something she would be strapped for . . . like . . .

Like who? Whose strap? Not Dorotyas's . . .

The feeling faded, and Ruxandra couldn't bring it back.

Ruxandra took another step forward. Part of her wanted to run, now that she was out of the cell, to be free and away from this dank place. She wanted to sprint out of the dungeon and up into the open air, feeling the strength of her limbs and the fullness of her power. She didn't want to scare Elizabeth, though. Or panic the guards. She walked with a deliberate, even pace to the doorway.

"Well done, Ruxandra." Elizabeth cupped Ruxandra's cheek for a moment. "Now follow me."

She went up the stairs, with Ruxandra dogging her heels. With every step, the stench of the dungeon faded, and the smells from outside grew stronger. Before they reached the top, Ruxandra counted ten separate human scents, and a dozen animals. She smelled burning wood and hot metal, meat cooking and bread baking. Wool, silk, perfume. It was a tapestry of scent, and she paused to appreciate it.

Then Ruxandra followed Elizabeth out of the dungeon and into the night.

It was cold, and snow lay in patches on the ground, but Ruxandra didn't care. She passed Elizabeth and stood in the courtyard of the castle. The thick, gray stone of the castle walls rose high around them. Guards on the walls looked out to the world beyond. Above, a thin sliver of a moon hung on the purple and deep blue blanket of the night sky, surrounded by stars.

Ruxandra stared at the sky in wonder. The distance was like mercy.

The smell of hot metal filled her nose. Ruxandra ran around the little building beside the dungeon door and found an open-fronted space with a large pit of glowing coals in the middle of it.

"The smithy." Elizabeth stood beside her. "They make horseshoes."

Ruxandra nodded but didn't stay to look more. She could smell animals. She ran to the middle of the courtyard, sniffed, and then ran to another building. She moved so fast that Elizabeth gasped behind her.

"What's this place?" Ruxandra asked.

"It's a stable," Elizabeth called. "We keep horses in there."

Ruxandra heard the horses nickering and neighing sleepily to one another in the stable, and the sound of men snoring in the loft above it. She closed her eyes and listened. She heard the tread of the guards' feet as they walked the castle walls, each a little different from his fellows. Somewhere in the castle, someone sang a lullaby to a crying girl. Somewhere else a man and a woman gasped together, their breaths coming short and fast, and the woman crying out softly.

"Ruxandra!" Elizabeth called. "There will be plenty of time to explore later. For now, you need to come with me, please."

"Yes." Ruxandra ran to her. "I'm sorry, Elizabeth—I mean, my lady. Kade said I should call you 'my lady.'"

"He's right." Elizabeth tucked Ruxandra's arm in her own. "Whenever we are with other people, you must call me that. But when it's only us, you may call me Elizabeth."

"Yes, Eli—" Ruxandra caught herself. "Yes, my lady." *I like calling her Elizabeth.*

"Now come."

She led Ruxandra across into the main hall. The few candles burning in their sconces flickered and danced. Tapestries covered the walls. Deeply etched carvings circled the stone pillars leading to the ceiling. The tiles created black-and-white patterns beneath her feet. At the far end of the hall, a dais held a pair of lavishly carved wooden chairs. Ruxandra stopped by them.

"One was my husband's," Elizabeth said without slowing her pace. "He was an adulterer and a lecher, but he was a good ruler, so I keep his chair there, to remind the peasants whose wife I am."

She took Ruxandra out the door and through a dimly lit back hall. They went up three flights of stairs and down a short hallway to a heavy wooden door. Elizabeth took out a key, put it in the keyhole, and turned it. The lock clicked, and the door swung the slightest bit away from her. Ruxandra put her hand against it and pushed. It swung open, and Ruxandra's eyes went wide at what was on the other side.

The room was round, with shuttered, curtained windows on two sides. Tapestries hung on the whitewashed walls to ward off the winter chill. A tiny fire blazed in a small fireplace in the wall. A large bed with a chest at the foot of it took up most of the rest of the room. The tall bedposts held up a dark blue canopy above and curtains that closed around it to keep the sleeper warm.

Beside the fireplace, a girl rose to her feet and curtsied. "Welcome, my lady."

She was short, yet too old to be called a child. Ruxandra guessed she was thirteen or so. She had mouse-brown hair and dark brown eyes. Her face was pretty and freckled. Small breasts sat high on her chest under a faded brown dress, belted with a rope above newly widening hips.

She stank of fear.

Elizabeth stepped into the room, ignoring the girl, as Ruxandra remained at the threshold. "Do you like it?"

"It?" Ruxandra repeated, unable to take her eyes off the terrified girl. The girl stared back, her lower lip trembling.

"The room," Elizabeth said. "It's yours."

"What about—"

"Yours," Elizabeth interrupted. "For as long as you stay here, which I hope will be a long time."

Ruxandra swallowed hard. "What if I get hungry?"

Elizabeth pulled out a second key and handed it to Ruxandra. "This key opens your cell downstairs. From now on, it's your larder. Whenever you are hungry, you may go to the dungeon. There will be a prisoner in the cell for you to eat."

"Oh."

Elizabeth leaned close and whispered in Ruxandra's ear, "Of course, if it is too much, you can always feed on the girl."

Ruxandra looked to the girl, smelled the fear on her. *Does she know what I am? Did Elizabeth tell her?*

"You are now properly my guest," Elizabeth said. "You may come and go from the castle whenever you wish."

Ruxandra's hand rose to her mouth of its own accord. She felt tears welling up the corners of her eyes. "Oh my, Elizabeth."

"Come in, silly." Elizabeth took Ruxandra's hand and pulled her in. She held on as Ruxandra looked around, taking it all in with wondering eyes.

What mattered was that it was beautiful. *Hers.*

"I don't know what to say." Ruxandra swallowed the lump in her throat. "It's so . . ."

"Don't say anything." Elizabeth put her free hand on Ruxandra's cheek again. Then she leaned close and kissed her on the forehead. The warmth of her lips sent a shiver through Ruxandra, setting off a storm of emotion. Elizabeth squeezed Ruxandra's hand and stepped away.

"I must go," Elizabeth said. "I'll see you tomorrow evening if that's all right."

"Of course." Ruxandra's eyes roamed the room and fell once more on the girl. "My lady, who is she?"

"The peasant?" Elizabeth's lips twisted up into a smile. "She's your servant. She will help you bathe and dress, and take care of your clothes and your room."

The girl bobbed down into a deep curtsy.

"Kill her if you like," Elizabeth said. "She's easily replaceable. Do beat her tonight before anything else. Otherwise she'll not know her place." Her eyes sparkled. Ruxandra watched the play of light on her face, letting the words flow past.

Elizabeth patted Ruxandra's shoulder and left the room. Ruxandra watched her go a moment and then closed the door. She opened it again, to be sure she could. She squeezed the keys in her hand.

It's mine! I can leave anytime I want and lock it when I don't want anyone else coming in! She turned a slow circle again, and her eyes fell once more upon the girl.

Tears streamed down the girl's face.

"Please . . ." The girl's entire body shook. She tried to curtsy, but her knees gave way, and she collapsed. Ruxandra reached out to help her, but the girl crawled forward and wrapped thin arms around Ruxandra's legs. She pressed her wet face against Ruxandra's dirty bare feet.

"Please," the girl whispered between sobs. "Please don't kill me. I beg you. Please."

Ruxandra's mouth fell open.

"I'm a good servant!" The girl's words tumbled out, fast and terrified. "I'll take care of your clothes and help you dress and fix your hair. I'll air out the bed every day, I'll sweep the room, and I'll fetch you whatever you ask. I swear I will. Please!"

"All right!" Ruxandra pulled her feet away. "Please let go of me."

The girl scrambled away on her hands and knees until she hit the clothes chest.

"I'm sorry!" Her voice was high with panic. "I'm so sorry, my lady. I didn't mean to touch you without permission. Please don't kill me. Please!"

"I wasn't going to—"

"Beat me instead. Please! Just don't kill me. Here."

The girl spun about and opened the chest. She fished inside and pulled out a thick leather belt. She ran to Ruxandra and pressed it into her hand. The girl ran back to the clothes chest and dragged it in front of Ruxandra. She grabbed the bottom hem of her dress and pulled it over her head. Then she bent over the rounded top of the chest.

"Please, my lady," the girl said, her voice now a whisper. "Please beat me. Don't kill me."

Ruxandra looked at the belt in her hand. Then she looked at the bare skin of the young girl. Three angry red scars crossed her back. Two more marked her pale backside, the lines running diagonally across the skin. Another two crossed her legs.

Ruxandra reached out and touched the lowest mark on the girl's leg. The girl flinched and cried out as though she'd been hit. Ruxandra left her hand there until the girl's muscles relaxed. She traced her fingers over the scar. The girl looked over her shoulder. Ruxandra moved her hand upward to the scars on the girl's back and traced over them.

"Did it hurt?" Ruxandra asked.

The girl's chin quivered. She swallowed hard.

Ruxandra stepped back and pulled her shift off over her head.

"Stand up," she said.

The girl rose from the chest, one thin arm crossing over her small breasts, the other dropping to cover her sex. Three scars crossed her belly as well. She was still shaking and didn't look up. Ruxandra waited. Slowly the girl's head lifted.

"Oh!" The girl's eyes went wide at the sight of thick white scars that covered Ruxandra's body. Her hand went to her mouth. "Oh, my lady, what did they do to you?"

Ruxandra looked down at the scars. They had faded even more since the bath. The angry red had turned white, as if she'd had them for many, many years. She ran a hand over the ones that cut through her breast. She remembered the fight, like she remembered all her time in the woods. She only wished she could remember the times before.

"I got in a fight," Ruxandra said. "With a bear."

"What?" She sounded so shocked it made Ruxandra laugh. The girl blushed and looked at the floor again.

"It really, really hurt." Ruxandra reached out and touched the scars on the girl's belly. "Did it hurt?"

The girl nodded, and fresh tears made her eyes shimmer in the light of the fire.

"What's your name?"

"Jana, my lady."

Ruxandra stepped past Jana to the clothes chest. She opened it and looked in. Dresses, shirts, shifts, and scarves lay in neatly folded rows beside stockings and shoes. All of it felt alien to Ruxandra.

As alien as the idea of beating someone.

"I don't hurt people for fun." It was a realization, more than a statement. "And I won't hurt you. Ever." She felt a rush of relief, knowing who she was. What she would not do. "I promise."

Jana snuffled and wiped her tears. She then raised her eyes and smiled shyly at Ruxandra.

Ruxandra smiled back.

"I don't know how to wear any of these," Ruxandra said. "Can you show me?"

"Of course, my lady!" Jana practically jumped. She stopped, clamping her arms over her chest and blushing bright red. "My lady, may I get dressed first?"

It was past midnight when Ruxandra stole out of her room.

She had tried on every piece of clothing in the chest. Jana patiently explained how to wear each one. She showed Ruxandra the clothes she could put on by herself, and the ones that required help. Toward the end Jana was yawning so wide Ruxandra could see down her throat. Now, the girl was sound asleep on the bed, curled up amid the pile of dresses and stockings.

Ruxandra wore a blue dress that reached to her ankles over a pretty shift whose beaded collar showed through the neckline of the dress. She'd put a gray cloak over it. Jana assured her that it looked wonderful before she fell asleep.

The outer clothing felt odd, but not as odd as the underwear. The shift she understood, but there were drawers that went under it, and stockings. It felt very peculiar—*confining*—having all that cloth against her skin. It felt stranger still having shoes on. She couldn't sense the ground beneath her feet properly.

Still, she was dressed as a person, now.

Ruxandra explored the dark, silent hallways of the castle, peeking into all the unlocked rooms. She found Elizabeth's chambers and listened at the door to Elizabeth's deep, even breathing. With a smile on her lips, she found a room with a loom, a spindle, and piles of wool. She found another with chairs set around a big table. She peeked in on the kitchen, with its large fireplace, big tables, and sides of pork and beef hanging from the ceiling. She went out into the courtyard, then up onto the wall. The guards there watched her, but none came near.

The castle stood atop a high hill, a road leading from its gates to the sleeping town below. A pale, thin layer of snow lay over everything, making it sparkle under the stars. Beyond that, the forest spread out, covering the hills and valleys beyond.

It was beautiful.

Ruxandra breathed in the cold air. She could smell all the scents of the castle, and the wood smoke from the town, and the crisp, cold snow. She could even smell the trees of the forest, each one, like people, like animals, a touch different from the others.

She stayed there until the sky began to brighten and the first discomfort moved under her skin. Then she stole back through the castle to her room. She put her cloak over Jana to keep her warm and then slipped out of her clothing. Jana had shown her how to pull the curtains on the bed. Ruxandra shut them tight and slipped into the bed and beneath the covers. The soft warmth embraced her, and she was asleep in moments.

She woke to a rapping on the door.

"Welcome, my lady," Jana said after opening the door.

Ruxandra peeked through the bed curtains. The room was clean, with a fresh fire in the fireplace. Elizabeth stood in the doorway, Jana kneeling in front of her.

"Dress your mistress and have her come down to the grand hall, please." Elizabeth saw Ruxandra peeping through the curtain and smiled. "It's time to begin her proper education."

CHAPTER SIX

JANA DRESSED RUXANDRA, her small hands deft at tugging and smoothing until the clothing fell right. She brushed her hair very gently, getting out the tiniest knots, and then brushed more to make it shine. After what seemed like too long to Ruxandra—though the girl's ministrations were very pleasant—she declared her ready to go. Ruxandra thanked her and headed down. The sun was below the horizon, leaving the last traces of day to fade slowly to darkness.

Elizabeth stood in front of the door to the great hall. She smiled at Ruxandra. "Welcome, my dear. You look quite lovely. A perfect young lady."

"Thank you. Jana helped me dress."

"Don't learn their names, dear. It only makes it harder when the time comes." Elizabeth reached forward, cupping Ruxandra's cheek. Ruxandra leaned into it, enjoying the warmth of the woman's flesh and the gentleness of her touch. She pushed Elizabeth's words away. She would explain how she felt later.

"You will be joining society soon," Elizabeth said. "You must treat the peasants as peasants and learn how to act when among your equals, which is why we are here tonight."

She leaned in and kissed Ruxandra's cheek. Ruxandra smiled. It didn't matter whether she agreed with Elizabeth about everything. She was her friend. Elizabeth took Ruxandra's hand.

"None of the girls of my gymnaesium know what you are," she said as they stepped into the hall. "As far as they are concerned, you are another pupil."

Fourteen girls stood silent, their breath making small clouds of frost in the cold hall. Dorotyas stood before them, her hands on her hips and her strap tucked into her belt. Some of the girls were nearly adults. Others looked no older than Jana. All wore gray dresses, their hair pulled back and tied with gray ribbons. They wore no jewelry; there was nothing of value on them. Several had gaunt, underfed faces, with sharp cheekbones. They stood in three straight lines with hands clasped in front and heads bowed.

All smelled of fear.

If they don't know what I am, why are they afraid?

"We are here," Elizabeth said.

"Ladies!" Dorotyas's voice cracked through the hall. "Curtsy!"

All fourteen dropped into low curtsies and stayed there. One of the younger ones wobbled slightly but managed to catch her balance. Elizabeth smiled. She left Ruxandra by the door and walked slowly up and down the rows of the girls, her eyes going from one girl to the next.

"Marsca, your bow needs straightening." She touched the girl's hair ribbon and kept going. "Csilia, your collar is askew. Agota, you have a stain on your skirt. Hanja, your nails are dirty. This is the third time for you, I believe."

Hanja began trembling from head to foot. Tears started to well up in her eyes. Elizabeth didn't look at her. She nodded to Dorotyas.

"Rise!" Dorotyas called.

The girls straightened. Several winced from being so long in the curtsy, but no one made a sound. All of them kept looking at the ground.

"Where are Nusi and Sasa, Dorotyas?" Elizabeth asked.

"Sasa is sick," Dorotyas said. "The women are looking after her. Nusi is still in contemplation, reflecting on her behavior yesterday."

"Very good." Elizabeth stepped up on the dais beside the chairs. "We have a guest joining us in the evenings from now on. She is of royal blood, and you will treat her with the same respect you treat me. Understood?"

"Yes, my lady," the fourteen girls said in unison.

Elizabeth nodded her satisfaction and then held out a hand to Ruxandra.

Ruxandra's feet froze in place. It wasn't fear, not exactly. It was something different. The thought of seeing so many new people sent butterflies dancing in her stomach. She felt a sudden, desperate need to flee.

"Now don't be shy," Elizabeth called. "Come in and let me introduce you."

Ruxandra swallowed the urge to bare her claws and fangs and roar at the girls, to show them she was powerful and not afraid. *They're just people.*

That was the problem. Ruxandra was not accustomed to people. To be in a room with so many others made her nervous.

They cannot hurt me.

Maybe some of them will like me.

Ruxandra wasn't sure why that mattered.

She walked out and took Elizabeth's hand. The warmth of her skin and the strong pulse beneath it calmed Ruxandra's nerves. Elizabeth squeezed her fingers and turned back to the girls.

"Ladies," Elizabeth said. "This is Lady Ruxandra. Welcome her."

"Welcome, my lady!" the girls chorused as they dropped into a short curtsy.

The butterflies in Ruxandra's stomach beat faster. She looked at the ground, unable to meet the numerous eyes studying her.

"These are my students," Elizabeth said. "The younger daughters of many fine nobles and princes of the Hungarian empire. They're here to learn the proper skills of a lady: deportment, dancing, entertaining, and the day-to-day running of a household. I thought this would be an excellent place for you to learn."

She raised her voice. "Ruxandra was in an accident. She has lost all memory of her family and how a lady should behave. So I ask you to work with her to help her relearn."

"Yes, my lady," the girls chorused again.

"Tonight, we shall begin with the curtsy," Elizabeth said. "Ruxandra, please stand with the other girls, in the second row, perhaps. Ersok, Ferike, make room for her, please."

The girls stepped apart, leaving room for Ruxandra between them. Ruxandra took her place and smiled at each of them. They didn't look back at her. From this close range, the sharp smell of their fear filled Ruxandra's nostrils. It was almost painful.

What is so frightening?

"Now, eyes up, please," Elizabeth said. "Each of you shall demonstrate the three curtsies. Ruxandra, you watch and try to imitate."

"Yes, Eliz—" *There are other people here.* "Yes, my lady."

Ersok shot Ruxandra a look of terror, mixed with sympathy.

"Begin," Elizabeth said.

For the next hour, Ruxandra watched the girls and imitated. Elizabeth corrected her posture, foot placement, and hand placement with calm, gentle words and directions. By the end of the lesson, Ruxandra could perform all three curtsies—formal, informal, and royal—correctly. She learned the correct address for the girls ("miss," followed by their names), for other nobles (my lord/my lady), for princes (Your Highness), and the king (Your Majesty).

"Very good," Elizabeth said at last. She clapped three times. "Girls, you are dismissed. Ruxandra, you too. Marsca, Csilia, and Agota shall remain with Dorotyas to be reminded of the proper way to dress. Hanja, come to my study and we will…discuss… your mistakes. Good night, ladies."

"Good night, my lady!" the girls said. They gave deep, respectful curtsies. Then ten fled the room, leaving three to go to Dorotyas and Hanja, biting her lip and barely holding back tears, to follow Elizabeth.

The next night, they danced.

Hanja was not in class, though Nusi and Sasa rejoined the class. Sasa's skin was pale, and she sweated as she moved. She didn't utter a word of complaint, though, and she moved as gracefully as any of the others. Nusi did not move gracefully. She walked bowlegged and limping. Several times she bit her lip and blinked back tears. She didn't say anything either.

Dorotyas clapped the beat, slow and steady, and the girls danced in groups and pairs, taking the lead by turns. Elizabeth stood beside Ruxandra, guiding her through the steps of each of the dances. None of the girls spoke.

Ruxandra found it strange. She had hoped to talk to the girls, to learn about them, but not one said a single word the entire lesson.

After, Ruxandra followed them out into the courtyard. The girls stayed together, their eyes down. Two held Nusi's elbows, helping her walk. The group moved quickly and fearfully, like deer passing through a grove wherein wolves lurked. They stopped against the outer wall of a long, low building.

As one, they turned back to watch Ruxandra following them.

Ruxandra did not know what to say or what to do. She stopped ten feet away.

One of the taller girls stepped forward. "May we help you, Lady Ruxandra?" The girl's eyes did not meet hers, nor avoid them—instead they stared slightly to the left of where their gazes would lock.

"I thought we might talk."

The girl shivered under her thin dress, but she made no move to go inside the building. The others stayed as well. Nusi was in agony, from the expression on her face. Sasa leaned against another girl, the sweat on her pale skin starting to freeze.

"What do you want to talk about?" asked the older girl in a polite monotone.

Ruxandra searched for something to say. "I don't . . . know."

"I see."

With those two words the girl built a wall between them. Ruxandra didn't understand why. She didn't think she'd done anything to make them upset. Sasa's legs gave out, and the girl she was leaning on grabbed her to keep her from falling. Another girl moved to help.

"She needs to go inside," Ruxandra said.

"Yes," said the first girl. "She does."

Still, no one moved.

They're like wolves defending their territory. They won't let a stranger in, and they won't back down.

Why are they so frightened?

"I'm sorry." Ruxandra stepped back and then dropped into the formal curtsy. "I'll go. Please take your friends inside."

She turned and walked away, listening as she went. None of the girls moved until she was well across the courtyard. Then they helped their friends inside and shut the doors. If they spoke inside the building, she couldn't hear them, though she tried.

The next night, Ruxandra woke up hungry.

She lay in the darkness, not moving. The Beast prowled inside her, moving in her mind like an animal pacing a too-small cage. Her body was as taut as a bowstring. Her fangs poked out through her lips, and her talons were ready to shred her blankets.

Beyond the curtains of the bed, she heard the fire crackling, warming the room. Jana was laying out her dress and shoes on the chest.

She smelled delicious.

She's so close.

Ruxandra felt the muscles in her arm move without her volition. She saw her hand reaching for the bed curtain. Ruxandra grabbed at it with her mind, trying to capture control of her hand. It froze but didn't pull back. The Beast growled with hunger, the low sound making the bed vibrate.

"My lady?" Jana's voice was bright and cheerful. "Are you awake?"

Jana walked toward the bed. To Ruxandra, Jana's light footsteps sounded like a hammer striking an anvil. Ruxandra kept her body still, despite the Beast's struggle to break free.

"My lady?" Jana said. "Would you like some—"

The Beast growled again, frustration and hunger mingling and making the bed vibrate.

"My . . . my lady?" The cheer vanished from Jana's voice. "Are you all right?"

Ruxandra fought for control.

The bed curtain began to move.

"Don't!" The word rasped out of her mouth, like jagged steel dragging across stone. "Don't open it!"

"My lady?" Concern and fear filled Jana's voice.

"Get out," Ruxandra said. "Go to the kitchens. Wait there for me."

"My lady—"

"GET OUT!" Ruxandra's voice echoed off the walls.

Jana squeaked. She ran, her feet moving fast and light. Ruxandra heard her wrestle the door open, heard it bounce off the wall as the girl dashed down the tower stairs. She felt the cool air from the staircase invade the room, even through the thick curtains.

In her head, she could feel the Beast rushing forward to take over.

It came at her like a river in flood, rushing at her, slamming into her, and driving her back. She clawed against it, holding her place, holding onto control. It wasn't at full strength yet, and so, like a dam against a raging flood, she stopped it. She made her talons retreat into her fingers, pulled her fangs back into her gums.

When she had control, when the Beast was locked in an iron grip, she reached out and opened the curtain.

The only light came from the flickering yellow flames. They danced and jumped in the breeze from the hallway, setting all the shadows in motion.

Ruxandra rose from the bed, picked the keys off her side table, and wrapped them tight in her fist. The keys were good. They would remind her of her humanity and the privileges it brought. Then, with slow, deliberate steps, she walked out of the door and down the stairs.

I'll be fine as long as I don't see anyone. I'll be fine as long as no one talks to me.

The smells of the castle filled her nose, stronger than ever. She could smell every person in the rooms she passed. One had three men sleeping in it. Another had four women. A third had a man and woman, panting heavily and smelling of sweat and sex. The pull to that door was ferocious: such rich blood, flavored with pleasure, tasting like wine. *If I could taste them while they still coupled.* She fought with all her might to keep the Beast from rending their flesh, ending their passion with its hunger.

I won't. If I do, I will be sent back to the cage, and I cannot go back there. Will not go back there.

Finally, she crossed the great hall and stepped outside. A strong wind pushed at her and filled her nostrils with the sharp, cold smell of snow to come. She breathed deep, letting it clear her head. Then she walked across the courtyard, pulled open the dungeon door, and walked down the stairs. The glow of the stones, visible only to her, lit her way.

She pulled open the dungeon door, and the smell of blood hit her hard. The Beast emerged wild and fast, taking control of her mouth and howling with glee before Ruxandra suppressed it again. In the darkness beyond, the prisoners cried out in fear. Whispers came next, voices asking each other what had happened, or if they could see anything.

The tub in the middle of the dungeon was stained with day-old human blood.

Blood puddled on the floor, too, dripping from the chains that swung over the tub. Ruxandra remembered the girl who Dorotyas forced to clean the tub, and how the water swirled red down the drain.

Why does Elizabeth have this?

Why keep blood in a tub?

Her mind was muzzy with hunger. All she could think of was storing blood, which made no sense. Elizabeth didn't drink blood.

The Beast growled, loud and angry. It wanted control. Ruxandra held it tight. She forgot the tub and approached her old cell. A woman sat in the corner in a pile of straw. Her eyes were wide, trying to pierce the darkness. Ruxandra put the key into the lock and clicked it open.

"Who's there?" The woman rose to her feet. "Who is it?"

Then the Beast took control.

Shortly after, Ruxandra slipped into the kitchen.

Jana sat on a stool in the corner of the fireplace, her back against the mantle, her face lit up red by the glowing coals of the fire. She was sound asleep, her head on her chest. Ruxandra looked at her for a moment, feeling a sorrow she couldn't name, then touched her shoulder. The girl started and sat up, her eyes wide.

"Shh," Ruxandra said. "It's all right."

"My lady!" Fear filled the whispered words. "Where were you?"

"It's all right," Ruxandra repeated. "Everything is better."

"But . . ."

"Don't worry. You don't have to be scared."

"But . . ." Jana swallowed hard. "There's blood on your shift. And your face."

Ruxandra put her hand to her mouth. It came away sticky. Jana reached out and touched the blood spatter on Ruxandra's shift.

"I'm sorry," Ruxandra said. "I thought I'd gotten it all off."

Jana put on a shaky smile and nodded. "Yes, my lady."

The next evening, Ruxandra met Elizabeth outside of the great hall.

"We missed you last night," Elizabeth said.

"I'm sorry," Ruxandra said. "The Beast came out."

"I see. I thought the girls might have offended you."

"Not at all." The words tumbled fast out of Ruxandra's mouth, though she wasn't sure why she so desperately wanted to defend them. "They were very nice."

"Good. I take it you need a new servant?"

"No," Ruxandra said. "I managed to get down to the dungeon and open the cell before the Beast could escape, as you instructed me."

Elizabeth cupped both of Ruxandra's cheeks. "That's wonderful! You're getting stronger every day! How long did you stay the Beast?"

"Only as long as I fed," Ruxandra said. "Then I was myself once more."

"I am so proud of you." Elizabeth leaned forward and kissed Ruxandra on the mouth.

The touch of her was warm and soft and made Ruxandra gasp.

Elizabeth leaned back and looked into Ruxandra's wide eyes. She smiled.

She kissed Ruxandra again, longer, slower, and gentler. The heat spread from Ruxandra's face to her breasts and her belly and between her legs. Ruxandra kissed her back and leaned in. Her arms went around Elizabeth, gently pulling their bodies together.

Elizabeth pulled away first and put a finger to Ruxandra's lips. "Our secret."

Ruxandra didn't understand why—wasn't Elizabeth the mistress? Everyone did her bidding. She saw how serious Elizabeth looked and nodded.

"Good." Elizabeth stepped back and smiled again. "Now I need you to attend classes and learn as much as you can, because King Rudolph has summoned me to Vienna, and I want you to come along."

CHAPTER SEVEN

RUXANDRA COULDN'T FATHOM it. "Me? Travel to Vienna?"

"To King Rudolph's court, yes." Elizabeth sighed. "I had hoped he would leave alone matters concerning my estate until spring, but he insists that I come at once. Fortunately, the snow is not deep."

Ruxandra suddenly felt afraid. She had just arrived at the castle, just learned to control the Beast. To go to Vienna . . . She was not afraid of any one person, but many . . .

"It is a week's journey, with coach and escort."

"I'm not sure I'm ready to leave the castle."

Elizabeth's lips tightened. She looked at the floor a moment before raising her eyes to meet Ruxandra's. Her face was so full of loneliness it made Ruxandra's heart ache. "I have enemies in the king's court, Ruxandra. Enemies who would take my home from me if they could."

"How? You're a Blood Royal. Doesn't that protect you?"

"Not from others of the blood," Elizabeth said. "Not all of us are considered equal, Ruxandra. Some have less and want to take from those who have more. Some have more but are never satisfied. Now they're coming to take what is mine."

Ruxandra frowned. "That's wrong."

"If my husband were alive, they would never dare. They have the ear of the king, and I am but a lone woman. So I must go to him and plead my case." Elizabeth reached out and took Ruxandra's hands. "Please. Come with me. Help me protect my lands."

Ruxandra shook her head. "How can I help? I know nothing."

Elizabeth raised Ruxandra's hands to her mouth and kissed each. "You know how to kill."

Ruxandra pulled her hands back to her chest. "Who would I need to kill?"

"The ones who are threatening me. The ones who would take *my home* from me. This is my place, Ruxandra. I won't lose it."

"They're not peasants. You said I could kill peasants. Not royalty."

Elizabeth stepped forward, halving the distance between them. "Do you think I want this? I, who believe so strongly in the importance of bloodlines? Sometimes, it is necessary. One cannot close one's eyes to the injustice. They must be stopped before they destroy the kingdom with their greed."

"I don't understand."

"I know," Elizabeth said tenderly. "I do. I know my enemies. I wish this were not happening now—poor innocent Ruxandra—but it is. Will you help me?"

"I . . ." *Why don't I want to do this? I kill to survive.*

"Please," Elizabeth said. "Please help me."

"I . . ." *They'll hurt Elizabeth if I don't stop them.*

"Ruxandra?" A note of desperation underlay Elizabeth's tone.

I must help her. "I will do my best."

"Thank you!" Elizabeth wrapped her arms around Ruxandra, holding tight. She put her face against Ruxandra's neck. Her breath was warm and tickled Ruxandra's neck. Ruxandra hugged her back, feeling the strength beneath Elizabeth's skin, her rose-red heart, and the blood she did not want to take, only smell—like a perfume . . .

Elizabeth kissed Ruxandra's neck.

Ruxandra swallowed, hard.

Elizabeth kissed her neck again, then again, each kiss sending a tremor through Ruxandra's body. Slowly, Elizabeth worked up to Ruxandra's ear. Her breath felt hot against Ruxandra's skin. She kissed her ear, then turned her head and kissed her mouth. Elizabeth's tongue pushed gently against Ruxandra's lips. Ruxandra opened her mouth, and Elizabeth's tongue slipped inside. Intoxicating as blood but even sweeter.

Ruxandra gasped, her knees trembling. Her entire body felt hot. She felt as swollen as the tongue that was enormous, blotting out thought. Petal soft. That made her dizzy. Had she thought of it as enormous? No, it was delicate and nimble. She opened her mouth wide, letting Elizabeth's tongue play inside it.

Elizabeth pushed Ruxandra against the wall. Her lips pushed, hard and urgent, against Ruxandra's mouth. Her hands left Ruxandra's back and ran up and down her arms. Ruxandra felt hotter than ever before, and between her thighs, there was a warm dampness she hadn't felt since . . .

When?

"No!" Elizabeth practically shouted the word. Ruxandra started in surprise, her reverie broken. Elizabeth pushed her back. Her hands came up to cover her face, and she fell to her knees.

"I'm sorry," Elizabeth said between her fingers. "I'm sorry. I'm sorry. I'm so sorry."

"Why?" Ruxandra reached for her, but Elizabeth pulled away.

"Because I took advantage of you!" Elizabeth's shoulders began shaking. Her eyes closed tight, and when she opened them, they glistened with tears. Sobs punctuated her words. "You're so innocent, so beautiful, and I'm lonely, and I wanted . . ."

She stopped speaking and took several deep breaths until the last of her sobs vanished. She stood up, straightened her back, and faced Ruxandra. Then she dropped into a deep, formal curtsy.

"Please," she said, her voice tinged with regret, "accept my apology."

"Of course." *But I liked it.*

"And please, if you care for me . . ." She took another deep breath. Her deep brown eyes pierced Ruxandra's soul. "Even if it's only a little bit, if you care, please come with me to Vienna."

"Of course I will."

"Thank you." Elizabeth took another deep breath. "These feelings I have for you . . . we shall keep them secret. Others mustn't know, or they will use them against us. Do you understand?"

Ruxandra nodded. "Yes."

Elizabeth took her hand, squeezed it, and then let it go. "Let us begin class."

The following two weeks went by in a whirlwind of activity. Jana spent most of it dashing back and forth, securing travel trunks, proper clothes, boots, and bedding for the trip. Every evening Jana explained what she'd accomplished, to Ruxandra's amusement and delight. Then Ruxandra went for her lessons.

She learned very quickly, she discovered. Sometimes the lessons felt almost familiar. But every time Ruxandra searched her memory for why, she found nothing.

The other girls were far ahead of her, and Ruxandra strived to be like them. They recited their lessons in clear tones, hardly ever forgetting their posture or their manners. The few who did were sent to Dorotyas, or occasionally Elizabeth's study, at the end of class.

The girls looked thinner and more tired with each passing day. Some days they winced or limped when they walked, while on others a girl or two would miss class entirely. Those days, Ruxandra realized, coincided after a visit to Elizabeth's study.

She must set them lessons to learn or words to meditate on.

This didn't sound quite right, but she found she didn't want to think about it.

At the end of the evening's class, the girls would leave together, huddled in a clump as they walked back to their dormitory. None of the girls spoke to Ruxandra, except as required in class.

She still did not know why.

Every fourth night she woke hungry, and the Beast woke with her. Jana had learned Ruxandra's patterns and knew better to be in the room on the fourth evening. Ruxandra fought to keep the Beast from breaking free long enough for her to reach the dungeon and the prisoner waiting in the cell.

Then the Beast would emerge and drain the prisoner dry.

She tried to maintain power and feed herself, but the Beast was too strong and always took her kill.

On the twelfth night, Ruxandra woke with the Beast stirring. Ruxandra's clothes lay on the chest, and a fire crackled in the fireplace. Ruxandra slipped out of bed. She kept better control now, though she still did not want to risk Jana's life on it. So she made her slow, silent way to the dungeon, avoiding other people.

When she opened the dungeon door, the smell of fresh human blood filled her nose. The Beast roared, causing Ruxandra to stagger and fall against the wall as she fought for control. The Beast raged and tore at her mind.

BLOOD! The Beast screamed in her head. *BLOOD! FEED! KILL!*

No! Ruxandra clamped down on it hard. She held still against the wall until she forced the Beast back down. When she had control, she began down the steps again.

With every step down, the smell grew stronger. The Beast slathered and hissed and yowled, fighting to charge forward and find the source. Halfway down the stairs, Ruxandra heard pleading screams suddenly muffled and then sharply cut off.

The Beast nearly took over, then. Ruxandra stumbled and fell backward, her hands clenched in her hair, using the pain of it to distract the Beast and drive it back. When she regained control, she walked down the final steps.

The Beast's roar nearly drove Ruxandra insane.

Torches lit the dungeon. The cell doors and the small windows in each were closed. There were no guards, no prisoners in sight save a man in Ruxandra's cell.

The man was staring, his eyes and mouth wide, his entire body trembling. Tears rolled down his face, and he uttered a low, dull continuous moan. Ruxandra turned, her eyes following the man's gaze to the center of her room.

In the middle of the room, two teenage girls hung naked from the chains over the tub. Their bodies bore the marks of a fresh beating, their skin faded purple and red, and the flesh open in a dozen places each, though no blood came from them. Their arms were bound tight behind them. Their ankles were in shackles, hooked on to the chains that held them suspended in the air. Each girl had a gag on her mouth, long, thin piece of wood protruding from her urethra, and another, much thicker piece, from her anus. Dorotyas stood between them, holding their hair back in tight fists. Their mouths and eyes were wide open, their faces frozen in terrified screams.

A wide red gash stretched across each girl's throat from ear to ear.

The first girl's had stopped bleeding.

The second girl's blood still spurted from her neck.

Below them, her naked body half-submerged in the blood-filled tub, sat Elizabeth.

Her eyes were closed and her face turned up to let the blood spatter down on it. She wore a beatific smile, and stretched languidly under the hot red flow.

Ruxandra convulsed. The Beast wanted to claw at the bleeding girl to drink the last of the blood before the girl's life went with it. Ruxandra's knees buckled, and she fell. She forced her talons out, forced them to dig into the floor and turn away from the bloody girls.

Inside, the Beast screamed *BLOOD! EAT! FOOD! FOOD!*

The Beast wanted to turn around. Ruxandra didn't let it. She crawled, inch by inch, to the cell. The man inside didn't see her.

His eyes were still fixed on the girls. He'd voided his bladder. The sharp stench of his urine mixed with the coppery smell of the blood in the air.

Ruxandra reached the cage. She grabbed the bars and pulled herself to standing. The man didn't move, didn't take his eyes off the tub. Not when she put the key in the door, or when she pulled it open. He didn't even move when she stepped close enough to touch him.

The Beast roared and tried to charge forward.

With a supreme act of will, Ruxandra drove it back to submission and made it watch as she grabbed the man's neck and sank her teeth deep into it. The large artery ruptured, and she drank and drank from it until the man collapsed in a heap on the ground.

The Beast faded away, and Ruxandra wiped her mouth.

I win.

She turned around to face Elizabeth.

Thick, dark red blood coated the woman from head to foot. It covered her long, dark hair, the skin on her face and neck. It ran in thick rivulets over her breasts and belly. Elizabeth smiled at Ruxandra and sank into the tub until she disappeared beneath the surface.

Still feeling the contentment of her meal and pleasure at her victory over the Beast, Ruxandra walked to the tub. Slowly, she became aware of her bewilderment. What was Elizabeth up to? She watched the ripples on the surface grow smaller and smaller until it became a single, smooth mirror of near-black red.

Ruxandra waited.

Slowly, smoothly, Elizabeth broke the surface, rising like a Venus from a deep red sea. She stood, letting the blood drip down her hair and her body until the red gave way to streaks of white flesh. The blood still filled her hair, both on her head and between her thighs. It still dripped from the hard tips of her breasts and the end of her fingers. She raised her head and opened her eyes. The whites stood stark against the red of the flesh around them and made the dark brown of the eyes even darker.

"Dorotyas," she said. "Now."

Dorotyas let go of the girls and picked up a large bucket of water from the side of the tub. She raised it high and poured it over Elizabeth's head. Elizabeth shuddered, and her skin broke out in gooseflesh. The blood sloughed away from her face and ran out of her hair.

Dorotyas poured a second bucket, then a third, and went to refill them from the cistern. Elizabeth smiled at Ruxandra. "How was your feed?"

"I controlled the Beast," Ruxandra said. "I didn't let it come out the entire time."

"Very good!" Elizabeth clapped her hands, sending droplets of blood flying through the air. A few landed on Ruxandra's dress. "That's wonderful!"

Ruxandra looked at the swirling red mess in the tub, then at the two girls hanging from the chains. They were so young, and they'd been so frightened. "Why do you do this?"

Elizabeth followed her gaze. "The gags and the plugs keep other fluids from flowing out."

"Not those." Ruxandra looked down at the tub. "Why do you bathe in their blood?"

Elizabeth smiled. "Power."

"Power?" Ruxandra shook her head. "I don't understand."

"A woman's power comes from her beauty. With beauty, a woman controls the men around her. She bends them to her will."

Elizabeth stepped delicately out of the tub. "Without beauty, a woman has nothing in this world. No husband, no power, no control. I have learned how to preserve mine."

She walked to the cistern, leaving a trail of bloody puddles behind her. Dorotyas was waiting and poured bucket after bucket of water over Elizabeth's head. The water splashed and foamed on the floor before disappearing into the drains in the floor.

"I learned of it years ago," Elizabeth said. "A peasant girl seduced my husband. She dallied with him in the hayfields. I caught her while he was away at war and brought her down here. I racked her for three days. Then I suspended her by her elbows and whipped her. Back, legs, face, belly, breasts, and cunt. Her blood spattered me. When I washed it off, I realized my flesh was firmer and stronger. So I cut her throat and rubbed the blood over my body."

Elizabeth spread her arms wide and turned in a circle. The flesh on her body was taut and the muscles beneath it strong. There were few wrinkles in her flesh and little sag in her breasts.

"I am *forty-nine* years old, Ruxandra!" She grabbed her breasts and squeezed them. "I suckled four children and saw them grow to adulthood, yet my breasts do not sag. I have the body and face of a woman of thirty-five. When I bathe in blood, I absorb strength and youth. It fills me with vitality!"

Elizabeth's eyes were bright and wild. Her lips pulled back wide in a grin that made her teeth flash in the firelight. "I cannot grow old, Ruxandra. Not while I need to protect my family and my lands. So these girls must be sacrificed, like the ones we sacrifice to your appetite. Do you understand?"

Ruxandra nodded, though her mind was a swirl of confusion. *Elizabeth kills girls and bathes in their blood to look young.* The revulsion was sharp and immediate, but it did not seem to affect her attraction to the woman. *Maybe I'm being hypocritical.*

"Oh, but if I were like you," Elizabeth reached for her but stopped. Her smile became rueful, and she shook the cold water from her hand. "If I were like you, I wouldn't need to bathe in blood any more. I wouldn't need to do anything to keep my youth and beauty and strength."

She stepped closer. Her cold, wet hands closed over Ruxandra's arms.

"Ruxandra." Her grip was tight and her expression deadly serious. Her face was only inches from Ruxandra's. "Could you make me like you?

CHAPTER EIGHT

"I . . . I DON'T KNOW how," Ruxandra said. "I don't even know if I can."

"You can," Elizabeth said. "In every story, vampires have a way to turn humans into vampires. Someone did it to you once."

"I don't remember . . ." Ruxandra felt a terrible wave of fear rising in her, threatening to drown her. She looked at Elizabeth with wide, frightened eyes. "I'm scared."

Elizabeth leaned in close. "Why are you scared?"

"I don't know."

Visions filled her head. Jumbled images of a cave and men and something far stronger than her. Then blood in her throat and something with the stench of death chasing her, killing everything in its path.

Ruxandra clutched her head and fell to her knees, crying out. Elizabeth knelt beside her, pulling her into her strong, warm arms.

"I remembered," Ruxandra whispered. "I remember something…"

"What?" Elizabeth asked. "What do you remember?"

Ruxandra tried to reach deeper, but nothing else came.

"Shh," Elizabeth said. "It will be all right."

"I'm sorry," Ruxandra said through her tears. "I'm so sorry. I don't know. I don't understand . . ."

"Shh," Elizabeth said gently, like a mother soothing a tired, crying child. "No more for today. I promise."

Ruxandra nodded and pressed her face into Elizabeth's breasts, clinging to her cold, wet flesh and taking comfort from the steady pulse of Elizabeth's heart.

"We will speak again of this," Elizabeth said, "after we go to Vienna and face our enemies."

The night before they left, Jana was teaching Ruxandra how to play Flor, a game with three cards and much betting. Ruxandra had no idea about either. She was finally beginning to grasp the concepts when there was a knock at the door.

Jana answered and curtsied deeply to Kade. "Good evening, sir."

Kade ignored her and smiled at Ruxandra. "Good evening, Ruxandra. May I come in?"

"Of course." Ruxandra stood and curtsied. "Please, join us."

Kade raised an eyebrow at Jana, who flushed red. "It is not seemly to play cards with the servants."

"I did not know." Ruxandra looked at the deck on the small table. "I have no one else to play with."

"Then I will join you." Kade took Jana's chair, picked up the deck, and began shuffling the cards. Jana stood behind Ruxandra. "What game was it?"

"Flor. I do not fully understand it yet."

"It is deceptive in its simplicity." Kade dealt a card to each of them. "Are you ready for your trip?"

"I think so." Ruxandra's eyes went to the three chests in the corner. "Everything is packed, aside from what we're wearing tomorrow."

"Very good. Have any memories returned?"

"Flashes, nothing more." Ruxandra shuddered. "A cave and several men and something frightening. Then I remembered being chased in the woods. I have no idea by what, but it terrified me. It was… dead but it still chased me."

She shook her head, trying to clear the images. "Why can't I remember anything else? What's wrong with me?"

"I don't know," Kade said. "I do know that the more you drink, the you experience, the more you become yourself. You will find you memories, I am sure. It will just take time."

Ruxandra nodded miserably.

Kade put down the cards and looked at Jana. "Get some tea."

"Yes, sir." Jana curtsied. "My lady?"

"None for me, thank you."

Jana left, closing the door behind her. Kade waited a moment, listening to her retreating footsteps.

"Another vampire . . ." Kade said. "Is that what was chasing you?"

Ruxandra shook her head. "No. It wasn't like me. It was dead."

Kade frowned. "How can something dead chase you?"

"I don't know."

Kade leaned forward and took Ruxandra's hand in his own. It was as warm as Elizabeth's, but with a roughness that Ruxandra found both strange and intriguing. He leaned close to her.

"My lady." His voice was quiet and gentle. "I'm worried for you."

"Why?"

"You haven't even been to the village yet." He squeezed her hand gently. "Vienna is a city with more people than you have ever seen. Thousands of them. If those people discover your true nature, they will hunt you down and kill you."

No! Not when I have people to care about again . . . She stopped, her thoughts confused. *I had people to care about before? Yes, I must have.*

"You must protect yourself, remain above suspicion, and appear to be a proper young lady at all times."

Ruxandra thought about the other girls, and how much more polished they were. "I will do my best. And I'm sure Elizabeth will help me."

"Of course she will," Kade said. "But she is only one woman. She cannot defeat the strength of the court, and certainly not the king." He looked away, his face flushing slightly. "I have a gift for you."

He reached into his pocket and pulled out a necklace. As he held it out to her, the close-linked pewter rings of the chain gleamed dully in the firelight. A small pendant with a single red gem hung from it.

"It's beautiful!" Ruxandra exclaimed.

"A good luck charm to wear on your trip," Kade said. "May I put it on you?"

"Of course!"

Kade undid the clasp and stepped behind her. Ruxandra gathered her long red hair into her hands. Kade laid the necklace against her neck and slid his hands back to fasten the clasp. The metal was cool on her skin, a sharp contrast to the heat of

Kade's hands. He released the necklace and rested his hands on her shoulders.

"There," he said. "May it keep you safe in all your travels."

His hands stayed on her shoulders a moment longer. Then he let go, walked to the door, and bowed deeply.

"Travel well, my lady."

"Thank you, Kade."

With that, he was gone, leaving Ruxandra to hold the pendant and relive the memory of his warm hands on her shoulders.

They left Castle Csejte at dawn. Ruxandra dashed from the hall to the carriage, wearing the heaviest hooded cloak Jana could find to keep her skin safe from the sun. She sat in the middle of the seat, with the curtains pulled closed.

It was still horrible.

The bumpy road jolted the carriage with every turn of the wheels. The sun beat down on the carriage roof, like an angry creature ready to break into the carriage and rip her to shreds. Ruxandra didn't let it touch her but she still wanted to see where they were going. So she looked out the window on the side away from the sun. Even there, the sun was too bright. It made her squint and gave her a headache. She could last only a few moments before huddling back into the stifling darkness behind the curtains.

But what she saw was wonderful.

A line of carriages and carts stretched out around them. On the curving mountain roads, Ruxandra could see them all. There were four carriages—Elizabeth's, Ruxandra's, and two for the ladies and servants of Elizabeth's court. There were another four carts carrying everything the household needed for an extended stay. Six knights rode ahead of them, and eight more behind, all in gleaming armor.

After the first morning, Ruxandra sent Jana to sit with the driver. There was no reason for the girl to sit in the dark with her. That evening, Jana reported to her everything she had seen. The driver was an older man who wrapped the girl in the big fur blanket he wore and treated her well. He told her where they were going, and the names of the little towns they passed, and the animals they saw. Jana passed it all on to Ruxandra.

They stayed at an inn the first night. Elizabeth had her men clear the building first, and no one other than their party stayed with them. Then she took Ruxandra to her room.

"It is important you stay in your room," she said, "even if you are hungry. You cannot be seen walking the streets. It will lead to talk."

Ruxandra spent the night in her room playing cards with Jana until the girl fell asleep, then looking out the window at the village. The houses were all dark, their windows shuttered tight against the cold. She still wanted to wander through them. To see what they were like up close and maybe talk to some of the people who lived there.

The next morning, she woke up hungry.

It was a small, niggling hunger. Not enough to stir the Beast, and certainly not enough to make Ruxandra lose control. Even by evening it wasn't enough to cause worry, but she knew she did not have much time before the Beast stirred again.

At the end of that day's journey, Ruxandra found Elizabeth sitting in the common room of the second inn, sipping a glass of red wine. Dorotyas stood behind her, glaring at Ruxandra like something to be wiped off her shoe. Ruxandra ignored her and told Elizabeth everything.

"Fortunate, then, that you have the girl." Elizabeth took a sip of her wine.

"I don't want to feed off her."

"It's why I gave her to you." Elizabeth put her glass on the table. "Feed off her. Anyone else will draw attention."

"And feeding off Jana won't?" Ruxandra asked.

"We can say the girl was sickly and died in the night. Then we can take her body when we leave and dump it in a ravine. By spring, the wolves will have taken her."

"That's—"

"What she's here for." Elizabeth stood and put a hand on Ruxandra's shoulder. "I brought several extra girls with me to act as your servants, once you are done with her."

Please, no. I like Jana. I don't want to kill her.

Elizabeth put down the wine and rose from her seat by the fire. "No hunting, Ruxandra. I won't stand for it. Do you understand?"

"Yes, my lady."

She walked back to her room, remembering what Kade had said: if people learned her true nature, they would hunt her down and kill her. Elizabeth was trying to protect her. *I'm not ready to die.*

The next night, they stayed in a castle.

It was larger than Csejte, and the count and his wife greeted Elizabeth with a cold deference. They housed her knights in their grand hall and gave Elizabeth and Ruxandra each their own room. Ruxandra, at Elizabeth's insistence, claimed weariness from the trip and retreated to her room with Jana as quickly as possible.

Ruxandra began pacing the moment she closed the door. Jana sat in the corner, watching her with wide-open eyes. Inside Ruxandra, the Beast growled and whined, its voice becoming louder and louder in her head.

"My lady?"

Ruxandra spun, her talons and teeth nearly descending at the fear in Jana's voice. The girl's smell filled her nose. Her heartbeat, fast and hard, like a bird desperate to take flight, pounded in Ruxandra's ears. Jana's hands went over her mouth, blocking any sound. Tears rolled down her cheeks.

Ruxandra spun away. She stood at the window, breathing the cool night air that flowed through the gaps in the shutters. It smelled of the oncoming winter. It also carried the smell of the castle. Of men and women and children. It made her dizzy with hunger.

"My lady?" Jana's voice was small. "What will happen if you don't eat?"

Ruxandra swallowed hard. She didn't turn around—wouldn't turn around for fear of attacking the girl as soon as seeing her.

"I know what you are," Jana said. "I know what you do, and I know this is the fourth day. But . . . I don't know what happens when you don't eat."

"I change," Ruxandra said. "My mind gives way, and I become a mindless animal. The Beast kills whoever is closest, and I feed until I regain control."

Ruxandra heard the girl's breath begin to shake, heard her muffled sobs. When Jana spoke again, her voice quivered with fear.

"Does it hurt?"

The Beast growled, long and low, like a cat about to pounce.

Ruxandra walked to the door.

"You can't!" Jana cried. "The countess said you must stay here!"

Ruxandra opened the door and stepped into the empty hallway.

"She'll hurt you," Jana whispered.

"I'll be back before morning." Ruxandra closed the door without turning around. Inside, the Beast's growls had become a whine of displeasure.

Shut up. We're getting food. We just can't get it here.

She listened hard, tracking the sound of every person inside the keep. Most were asleep. Some were fornicating. A few poor souls were working. Jana was crying. Dorotyas was snoring. Elizabeth was breathing deep and easy.

Three guards were coming down the hallway toward her.

No, no, no, no, no!

She stopped.

I wish they couldn't see me. I wish they wouldn't notice me at all. She said it over and over, as if by willing it to happen, she could keep from being seen.

The guards rounded the corner and walked straight toward her. *I am a lady. I could not sleep, and I am going to the kitchens. That's what I'll tell them.*

They continued walking, three abreast, talking in low voices about the day. Not one of them spoke to her. Ruxandra watched them, watched them stare right through her.

She stepped aside and pressed her body flat against the wall. The three marched past without the slightest turn of their heads.

What happened?

I was right there. They could not have missed me. It's not possible! Is it?

There were guards on duty, standing outside the door of the great hall. Ruxandra could hear their breathing through the door. She stopped in front of it.

There is one way to find out.

She willed them not to notice her and gently pulled open the door. Both guards turned and stared as it swung open.

Neither stared at her.

"You said it was closed tight, idiot," said the first guard.

"It was," groused the other. "I swear it."

"You swore wrong," said the first, reaching inside to grab the ring on the door.

Ruxandra twisted out of his way and jumped out of the grand hall into the courtyard. Neither guard took any notice of her. Even when they went back to their positions, neither looked at her.

Curious, Ruxandra stepped in front of one. His eyes went to the side, refusing to look in her direction. Ruxandra walked back and forth in front of them. Each time she appeared in one's line of sight, his eyes went elsewhere.

They don't see me.

Ruxandra slipped across the courtyard. The front gate was shut, the portcullis down. She had hoped to slip out the front, but it wasn't possible. Someone would surely notice if she opened everything. She couldn't get out the front gate and had no idea whether there was another. There was no way out unless she could fly.

She stared up at the fifteen-foot wall and remembered how the Beast had moved in the dungeon.

I'm fast and strong. Maybe . . .

Ruxandra bent her knees, stopped, gathered up her skirt, and then bent them again.

I hope this works . . .

CHAPTER NINE

Ruxandra cleared the wall with five feet to spare. She was so surprised that she looked back. The movement sent her off balance, and she hit the ground hard, landing in a heap. It hurt, but nothing felt broken or even badly damaged. A moment later the pain faded.

Ruxandra sat up slowly and looked down at her body. She didn't have a single bruise. She looked back up at the wall and started laughing. Then she clamped her hands over her mouth, fearful someone had heard her.

The night was still quiet, save the steps of the guards atop the wall.

Now what?

Ruxandra stood, brushed off her clothes, and walked through the village. She heard the breathing of the people in each house as she passed. The Beast rumbled inside, wanting to feed.

I can't hunt in the village. Elizabeth will know.

I shouldn't go too far, though.

She sniffed the air, looking for scents of people outside of the village. A hint of wood smoke rode on the wind, coming from not too far away. Ruxandra walked toward it. The Beast growled, wanting her to speed up. Ruxandra didn't want to, for fear of ruining the dress.

CLOTHES STUPID.

Shut up.

HUNGRY.

Stupid Beast. Shut up.

Except the Beast wasn't as stupid as it had been. It was still separate from Ruxandra, still an animal, but filled with cunning. It knew what it wanted, could communicate so. The fact that it spoke to her . . .

Is it really part of me? Or is it something different?

HUNGRY.

Shut up.

She stopped at the edge of the woods. Most of the animals had gone to ground for winter, or fled the oncoming cold. The trees had long since lost their leaves, and spiked branches stuck out like skeleton fingers waiting to grasp and tear at passersby.

The woods called to her like a siren's song.

How long has it been since I've run free?

Elizabeth will know if I ruin this dress.

DRESS STUPID. NO DRESS.

Tempting. Though what if someone sees?

They can't see me. Not if I don't want them to.

Ruxandra willed herself to be unnoticed and stripped off her clothes. She hung them on the branches and put the shoes in the crook of a tree. The ground beneath her bare feet felt cold and solid and *alive* in a way that shoes could never match. The cold breeze brought her skin to gooseflesh and made her nipples so hard they nearly hurt.

Ruxandra breathed deep, taking in all the smells of the night and pinpointing the direction of the wood smoke. She started running, and the world rushed past is a blur.

When did I become so fast?

The Beast had always been quick. Ruxandra had chased down game many times, either for herself or the wolf pack. She was much faster now. She sprinted through the trees, faster than any deer. She jumped over fallen logs and hollows in the earth, and across a stream without slowing once. She ran off all her confusion about Elizabeth, her fear of Vienna, and her concern for Jana.

Deep in the woods, she found prey.

The old hut looked abandoned at first glance. The roof was sagging, the shingles on it old and worn. There were holes between the planks of the walls, and the clothes that hung over the windows were ragged and torn. Only the thin stream of smoke coming from the chimney suggested that someone might still live within. Ruxandra slowed and sniffed the air. Beyond the smell of wood and decay was the scent of an old, unwashed body.

She heard a grunt. Then another.

Ruxandra sank deeper into the bushes, her hunter's instincts coming to the fore, even as she remembered she couldn't be seen. The hut door opened, and an old, frail woman emerged. The woman groaned and tottered out of the hut. She had both hands wrapped around the grip of a long stick and leaned on it as she staggered out into the night. On each step, she gritted her teeth, and a low moan of pain escaped.

What's wrong with her?

Suddenly, Ruxandra *saw* the woman's pain.

It looked like red flags wrapped around her aching joints. Her knees hurt the worst, her hands and wrists only slightly better. Every step she took caused her pain.

Ruxandra was so stunned that she couldn't move.

Why can I sense all this?

The moment she started wondering, the sense disappeared. Ruxandra frowned. She inspected the old woman more closely, but nothing came.

Before, I was wondering what she was feeling.

She focused on the woman's feelings, and the images in her mind returned.

The woman was weary. Not tired, but weary of living, weary of struggling against the pain. Lonely and missing those she loved who had died. She wanted desperately to not hurt anymore—to leave this world for whatever might come after.

It works as long as I concentrate.

The woman leveraged her backside over a log and pulled her dress out of the way. She hissed in pain and let loose a few spurts of urine. Ruxandra watched the red flaring in the old woman's belly as she urinated, felt the despair in her mind as she struggled to stand back up afterward.

She remembered when she ran with the wolves. How they separated the old and weak from a herd of deer and cut them down. She started moving, her steps silent on the cold ground.

HUNGRY.

I know.

Ruxandra caught the old woman at the door of her hut. The pain the old woman felt as Ruxandra sank her teeth into her neck flared bright in Ruxandra's mind, then faded to darkness as she drank her dry.

Ruxandra slipped back into her room just before dawn. Jana was asleep on the floor in front of the fireplace. She had Ruxandra's cloak wrapped tightly in her arms, her face nearly buried in the folds. She looked like an infant finding comfort in her mother's scent. Ruxandra put a gentle hand on the girl's shoulder and shook her awake.

Jana blinked, her eyes red from tears and lack of sleep. She realized who it was and jumped back in fear. Ruxandra caught her shoulder.

"It's all right," Ruxandra said. "I'm fine. It's all right now."

Jana looked uncertain. "Then . . . you . . ."

"Yes." Ruxandra pulled the girl close and hugged her. "I promised I'd never hurt you, and I won't."

Jana squeezed her, hard, and snuffled against her bare skin. Then she pulled back, her eyes wide.

"My lady, where are your clothes?"

"Right here," Ruxandra handed her the pile. "Now help me get into them before Elizabeth comes to see us."

An hour after dawn, Dorotyas banged once on the door and flung it open. Elizabeth strode forward and froze in the doorway. The four women behind her barely managed to keep from knocking her over.

"Good morning," Ruxandra said brightly. "Are we ready to leave, then?"

Elizabeth looked from Ruxandra, sitting in the room's only chair, to Jana, pouring two cups of tea from a small kettle on the fireplace. Jana paused her pouring and sank into a deep curtsy.

"We are." Elizabeth glared at Jana. Then she put on a false smile for Ruxandra. "It will be a long, dull day, so I suggest Jana stay in the carriage with you, so that she may . . . entertain you."

She turned away. The four women behind her nearly fell over themselves to get out of her way as she strode back down the hall. Dorotyas stayed in the doorway, looking the two of them over.

"Is there something else?" Ruxandra asked.

Dorotyas glared at them both and walked out, practically slamming the door behind her. Ruxandra looked at Jana. They both began giggling.

Four nights later, Ruxandra killed an old man who lived alone in the forest, draining him and leaving his body for the scavengers. In the morning, Elizabeth glared at both her and Jana but said nothing.

The next night they reached Vienna, and Ruxandra nearly burned herself to a crisp trying to see it.

She peeked out at first. Then she stared, eyes wide and mouth open. Forest gave way to fields and orchards. Farms dotted the landscape. As they drew nearer to the city, the houses grew closer together. Most were wood and stucco, their white walls gleaming below wooden shingles or thatch roofs. Others were stone, with tile roofs. Beyond them rose the thick, wide walls of the city, so different from the tall walls that surrounded Castle Csejte. . They rode closer until the buildings rose up on either side, putting the carriage in shadows.

There were so many people in the streets riding horses and pulling handcarts. They were everywhere, and the clamor of their speech nearly overwhelmed Ruxandra. She had to pull her head back into the carriage and close her eyes.

By the time her ears adjusted to all the noise, they were in the empty area and then crossing the Danube. She risked looking out again. The reflection of the sun from the river nearly blinded her. She squinted and tried to see anyway.

"There's Saint Stephen's, missy," the driver said to Jana. "Biggest cathedral in the city. Maybe in the whole empire."

Ruxandra risked another glance. On the far side of the city walls, she spotted Saint Stephen's steeple rising from the middle of the city. Then they were across the river and through the gates to the city itself.

So many people.

If the outer city was noisy, inside was cacophonic. It smelled, too, of humanity, of animals and sewage and the blood of the butchers and the bakers cooking and a hundred other scents. It was rank and ripe and so, so alive. Ruxandra sat back again, trying to adjust. She wondered what it felt like, living with so many people.

Curiosity got the better of her, and she reached out for their emotions.

Suddenly she felt them—all of them. Every emotion, every pain, every pleasure, coming from thousands of people at once. Ruxandra barely got her hands to her mouth in time to muffle her cry of surprise and fear.

Stop! It's too much!

The feelings vanished at her command. Ruxandra gasped in relief and fell back against her seat. She stayed there as the carriages rumbled toward the center of the city.

"There," the driver said. "The Hofburg."

"My lady," called Jana. "Look! The Hofburg!"

Ruxandra pulled the curtain back and risked another peek outside.

The Hofburg was the royal palace of Vienna, Jana had explained, and all the streets around it were its property. At the center sat a large, square castle of pale stone that loomed over the streets. It was old and solid, unlike the beautiful newer palace to the north of it.

"Jana!" she called up. "What is that place?"

Jana asked the driver and called back, "It's the Amalienburg! It's where the Emperor stays when he comes to Vienna! We're staying in the Stallburg!" Jana sounded excited enough to dance. "On the other side of the castle! It's where Emperor Maximillius used to have his residence!"

Ruxandra watched the palaces and the immaculate grounds for as long as she could before the light drove her, head aching and flesh hot, back into the darkness of the carriage. She laughed in delight at everything she saw.

I want to visit the entire city! I want to see everything!

The carriages went through the gates and into the massive, square block of the Stallburg. They stopped in the courtyard—in the shade, to Ruxandra's relief. All around them were arched balconies, going up three stories and leading to the rooms of the residence. Ruxandra stepped out and stretched. Her skin felt hot. Her eyes hurt from squinting, and her head throbbed. Still, she joined the line of waiting courtiers for Elizabeth to step down from her carriage.

As they gathered into a line, a contingent of footmen stepped out of the Stallburg to take their luggage. A pair of guards and a tall, thickly bearded man followed. He was walking with a proud, upright bearing.

One of the footmen opened Elizabeth's door and held out a hand. Elizabeth took it and stepped down. That morning she had dressed in style for her arrival. She wore a fine red dress, with a sumptuous blue cloak over it, and a shining white wimple.

She smiled as she descended. "Gyorgy! How good to see you, my lord."

"And you, my lady," said the big man. He bent over her hands, kissing them both. "You look radiant, and I swear, younger than the last time I saw you."

Ruxandra wondered if anyone knew what Elizabeth did to keep her youth, and what they would think if they did. *Would they also see them as peasants, to be disposed of at Elizabeth's whim?*

"You flatter me," Elizabeth declared. "It's so generous of you to meet us."

"How could I resist? In fact, there are many in the city who would be pleased to visit with you, if you will see them."

"I would very much like to," said Elizabeth. "I want the girls at my gymnaesium to have more company. The more they have, the better they learn before coming to court and meeting suitors."

"I have heard a great deal about your gymnaesium," said Gyorgy. Something in his tone made Ruxandra pay more notice, headache or not. "I'm *very* interested to learn more about it."

"Of course," Elizabeth said. "Speaking of that, Ruxandra, come here."

Ruxandra went to stand beside Elizabeth. "Yes, my lady."

"Ruxandra, this is Gyorgy Thurzo, Palatine of Hungary and a longtime friend of my deceased husband. It was into his care we were delivered after my dear Ferenc passed. Gyorgy, this is Ruxandra, one of my newest pupils."

Ruxandra dropped low into the formal curtsy, as she had been taught for meeting with nobility. "My lord."

"A pleasure to meet you, young lady." Gyorgy looked her up and down. "Are you happy at Elizabeth's gymnaesium?"

"Yes, my lord."

"Excellent."

"Now come, Gyorgy," Elizabeth said. "Tell me all that has happened at court this year." Elizabeth and Gyorgy walked into the Stallburg. The waiting line broke apart. A handsome young footman led Ruxandra and Jana to a large room with an impressive bed, ornate chairs and a table, and a good-size fireplace. To Ruxandra's relief, the large windows faced away from the sunlight.

She grabbed a chair, pulled it to the darkest part of the room, and sat down on it. She closed her eyes and breathed a soft sigh of relief.

"Are you all right, my lady?" Jana asked.

Ruxandra didn't open her eyes. "My head hurts from all the sunlight."

"Lie down, my lady," Jana said. "I'll take care of our things."

She helped Ruxandra to stand, though Ruxandra didn't need it, and gently unfastened her clothing, taking off each piece carefully. Her touch was soothing and kind, and Ruxandra felt calmer when she climbed into the bed. Jana undid the curtains and let them fall, creating a warm, dark box for Ruxandra to lie in.

Ruxandra sighed in relief and snuggled down in the bed. She closed her eyes and listened to Jana bustling about the room. The sheets were soft linen, and the weight of the wool blankets pressed softly on her body.

I have been awake too long, today . . .

"My lady," called Jana. "My Lady Ruxandra. It is evening, and Lady Bathory wishes to see you. Your dress is ready, and I will brush your hair."

Ruxandra blinked awake, stretched, and smiled. The headache had faded, and she felt delightful. "Are we to go out?"

"To a concert!" Jana was nearly bouncing, even though she wouldn't get to go. "Lady Elizabeth said to be ready in an hour."

An hour later, cleaned, brushed, and wearing her prettiest dress—dark green with white stitching along the sleeves and collar, worn under a cape of deeper green—Ruxandra stepped out of the Stallburg. An open-topped carriage pulled by four horses stood before the foyer, with an escort of two knights before and behind, all carrying torches. Elizabeth was seated inside. She wore a beautiful blue dress, stitched with gold brocade across the bodice, and black fur cape over it. The rich coils of her hair spread out against the fur. Even sitting in the carriage, she looked stunning. *Regal*, Ruxandra thought, not for the first time.

She smiled as Ruxandra stepped inside. "How are you, my dear?"

"Very good," Ruxandra said. "I had a headache earlier, but it's gone now."

"I see." Elizabeth sat back in her seat and signaled the driver. He whistled once, and the knights and carriage started moving. "How is your servant girl?"

"Quite well." The carriage rolled out of the Stallburg into the streets. Even now, in the dark, people moved about, carrying torches or small lanterns. In the distance, a bright yellow glow lit up the streets and the sky.

"Is that so?" Elizabeth smiled at Ruxandra. "Because I told you to feed on her. Which invites the question: why didn't you?"

CHAPTER TEN

ELIZABETH'S TONE WAS flat and angry. "I told you to stay inside and not hunt."

Ruxandra winced. "I *like* her. She's nice, and she takes good care of me."

"So you risked exposure?"

"No one saw me."

"They *could have.*" Elizabeth leaned forward in her chair. One hand came down on Ruxandra's leg, gripping it hard. "Do you know the danger you will put me in if they see you? Do you know the danger *you* will be in?" She leaned closer, her next words desperate with desire. "Do you know what would happen to me if I can't have you near me? I *need* you, Ruxandra."

The sudden change from anger to need sent Ruxandra's mind reeling. Heat grew in her belly and spread down.

"I need you by my side." Elizabeth's eyes bore into hers. "Especially right now. Especially at a time like this."

Ruxandra grabbed onto the words, used them as a wall between her body and Elizabeth's desire. "A time like what?"

Elizabeth fussed with the collar of her cape as though straightening it could make everything better.

"Like what, Elizabeth?"

"Rumors have been spreading. Stories about me and about the girls of my gymnaesium."

"What sort of stories?"

"Vile ones of how I abuse the girls in my gymnaesium. Worse, stories of how I treat my peasants, as if that is any concern of these self-serving sycophants."

Ruxandra frowned, remembering the fear that radiated from the girls. She had not seen Elizabeth abuse them, but they were all terrified of her. As for the peasants…

Ruxandra had a vision of the girls hanging above the tub and looked away.

"Now the worst of the rumormongers has invited us to a concert on the very night we arrive." Elizabeth let go of her collar and threw her hands in the air in disgust. "Lady Czobor is a favorite of King Rudolph. She commands respect and fear in his court, and she *insisted* that we attend this concert. She is very curious about you, Ruxandra."

Ruxandra looked at the pretty dress and thought about how Jana had made sure her hands and fingernails were clean, her hair perfectly combed. She'd been looking forward to the concert, but there was no need to take risks. "Maybe I shouldn't go. I have yet to learn how to behave properly."

"You must come. She heard a young lady from my gymnaesium was with me and insisted you attend," Elizabeth said. "We shall say that you are my ward. Your parents are dead, and you were sent to me. They were very provincial and raised you poorly.

You will tell Lady Czobor what wonderful things you've learned, though you have only attended two weeks."

"I will."

"You'll need a last name as well," Elizabeth said. "Rozgonyi. One of my more distant relatives. Say it."

"Rozgonyi."

"Very good. Stay by me at all times."

"I will."

The carriage rolled around a corner, in front of a grand building. A hundred torches lit up the square in front of it. People—far more people than Ruxandra ever thought could be in one place—moved slowly up the wide steps to enter the hall. At the top of the stairs, an older woman in a deep red cloak stood, greeting each person as they arrived.

"There she is," Elizabeth said through gritted teeth. "Of course she will have us wait in line to pay court to her."

They dismounted the carriage and stood with the others in line. Many people, Ruxandra noticed, went around the line, directed away by men in red livery. Twenty people stood ahead of them, and the line moved slowly as the woman at the top greeted each. Ruxandra spent the time looking at the lovely clothes and listening to the many conversations around her. It had never occurred to her there could be so many ways to dress or do hair, or so many people to talk about.

Finally, they reached the top.

The woman looked older than Elizabeth, with a long, narrow face and faded eyes, but stood straight and tall and looked at them both as if her very presence was a gift to them. Her gray hair was swept up in an elaborate coiffure set with pearls, and around her neck she wore a thick gold chain. A coterie of seven women, each nearly as elegantly dressed, stood behind her.

"My dear Countess Bathory." The woman spoke the words without the slightest enthusiasm. "So good of you to join us on such short notice."

"How could I refuse such an invitation?" Elizabeth said sweetly.

"I am pleased you did not," Lady Czobor said. "I would have been most upset. And who is this young creature?"

"My young cousin and ward, Ruxandra Rozgonyi. Ruxandra, this is Lady Czobor."

Ruxandra dipped into a deep, formal curtsy. "I'm honored to meet you, my lady."

"Rozgonyi?" Lady Czobor looked Ruxandra up and down. "You are very fair, I must say. Tall, but that is your parents' fault. How long have you been with Lady Bathory?"

"Since two weeks before we left to come to Vienna," Elizabeth said.

Lady Czobor did not acknowledge Elizabeth. "Are you enjoying your stay with Countess Bathory?"

"Yes, my lady."

"Is that so?" Lady Czobor turned to Elizabeth, giving her a cold stare. "We hear how . . . *strict* you are with your servants. We should hate to think you are as strict with girls under your care."

"Servants need correction as you know," said Elizabeth calmly. "But Ruxandra can tell you how well I care for her and the other girls."

"I'm sure she can," said Lady Czobor. "And I'm sure she will, given the chance. Tonight, however, we are here for a concert, are we not? Shall we, ladies?"

Lady Czobor walked past the women and into the hall. The other ladies turned and followed. Lady Elizabeth caught Ruxandra's arm.

"None of the others greeted me, though I outrank all of them." Elizabeth's grip on Ruxandra's arm was like iron. "It was a deliberate snub, and it was at Lady Czobor's instructions."

Elizabeth fixed a smile on her face and tucked Ruxandra's arm into her own. "Now, act impressed, my dear, and *don't* let that woman get you alone."

It turned out Ruxandra didn't need to act impressed. The concert hall held five hundred people, and every seat, from the boxes in the sides to the farthest seats in the back was taken. The audience were dressed in their finest clothes, silks and satins and fine wool, embroidered and beribboned, jewels in the women's hair and around their necks, sparkling like stars. A thousand candles burned in candelabras above their heads. The people talked continuously, and the clamor and color together nearly overwhelmed Ruxandra.

She held tight to Elizabeth's arm, making her wince. Ruxandra loosened her grip but didn't let go. When they found their seats and sat, Ruxandra still clung to Elizabeth like a child at a circus.

"Lady Czobor provided these tickets for us," Elizabeth whispered in Ruxandra's ear. "Notice where she is."

Ruxandra looked around and spotted Lady Czobor and her ladies. "The boxes, near the stage. The other ladies are with her."

"In the seats reserved for the upper nobility, which I am." Acid dripped from Elizabeth's words. "She gave us seats here that they may all look down upon us."

"You're not in the pack."

Elizabeth pulled her eyes from the crowd and turned to look at Ruxandra. "What?"

"Like wolves. If a stranger comes, the leader makes the pack keep their distance, to show the intruder he is not a member."

"You know this how?"

"I ran with a wolf pack."

Elizabeth's eyebrows went up. She looked back up at Lady Czobor. The woman saw and waved down, a smile on her face.

"Not in the pack," Elizabeth said. "Yes. Exactly like that."

Fifteen musicians took the stage. Fourteen carried their instruments. The fifteenth sat on a bench before a large, curved box. Ruxandra whispered to Elizabeth, who smiled.

"The box is the pianoforte. The other ones are"—Elizabeth pointed at each—"violin, violin, viola, viola, cello, and a bass. Also, two flutes, two trumpets, two horns, and two oboes."

Then the music began and Ruxandra forgot everything.

The music from each instrument wove in and out of the others, the sounds building on one another into a harmony that made Ruxandra's mind quake with joy. The trumpets and violins soared together. The bass and cello glided with the horns and oboes. The pianoforte brought them all together. It was like the conversation of angels, where each voice added—and sometimes argued—but never in any way unbeautiful. The melody rose up and down the scale, dancing in and out of Ruxandra's mind, leading down to her depths and up to the wide, bright world.

Her hearing, so much better than anyone's, caught every single note, every vibration of string and reed and brass. It felt as if her brain itself were being played, rearranged into exquisite patterns. The music entranced her in a way that made everything else fall away.

When it was over, Ruxandra remained entranced, even as Elizabeth led her back to the carriage. She hummed the tune as she walked, and practically danced the rhythm. Elizabeth watched her the entire ride to the Stallburg, then led her back to Elizabeth's drawing room.

"You certainly enjoyed yourself," Elizabeth said.

"It was marvelous!" Ruxandra gushed. "I've never heard anything like it. I've never even thought there could be music like that!"

Elizabeth looked at the servants. "Leave us."

The anger in Elizabeth's voice made Ruxandra self-conscious. She stopped talking and looked at the floor. The servants left without a word.

"She snubbed us a third time," Elizabeth said. "She left without speaking to us or asking that we meet again. It was a grievous insult, one meant to demean me in the eyes of Rudolph's court."

"Oh." Ruxandra felt her pleasure at the evening diminish.

"Worse, no one had the courage to challenge her by speaking to us! *No one!*" She stomped across the room, her hands clenching and unclenching. "Not one person dared come near because of that greedy little bitch!"

"Greedy?"

Elizabeth rounded on her. "Do you think Rudolph is targeting me on his own? No! It's her, and it's people *like* her who are making him pursue my land."

"I'm sorry."

"You?" Elizabeth snapped. "What do you have to be sorry for?"

"I . . . I don't . . ." Ruxandra felt her eyes growing wet.

"Oh, my dear," Elizabeth's tone changed in an instant, and the desire in it made Ruxandra's knees tremble. "Don't be sorry for enjoying this evening. Your passion was wonderful to watch." Elizabeth cupped Ruxandra's face in both hands. "You are a beautiful creature, Ruxandra."

They kissed, long and deep. Elizabeth's tongue slipped between Ruxandra's lips, and the feel and taste of it was immediately, madly intoxicating. Her hands wrapped around her waist, and Ruxandra felt new melodies arise—similar to the music from the concert. Where she was touched, her body sang. Their mouths pressed hard, and their bodies pushed close. Elizabeth's hands roamed Ruxandra's back, from the nape of her neck to the cleft of her buttocks. Everywhere they went they left trails of heat and song.

Ruxandra let her own hands wander down Elizabeth's back, and she was rewarded with a gasp. Elizabeth pushed her mouth harder against Ruxandra. One hand left Ruxandra's back and slipped up to cup one of her breasts. The touch made Ruxandra's flesh burn with pleasure.

She reached up and took one of Elizabeth's breasts in her hand. They were soft beneath the cloth of her dress, so much softer than Neculai's chest.

Who?

"Stop," Elizabeth gasped, pulling Ruxandra away from the memory. "Oh please, please stop."

Ruxandra did so, and Elizabeth stepped back. Her face was flushed red, and she was panting with desire. She smiled at Ruxandra, and Ruxandra knew that if Elizabeth were to devour her on the spot, she would not have minded in the slightest.

"We must stop"—Elizabeth's eyes were gleaming, her body trembling—"because I want so much to continue."

Ruxandra shook her head. "That doesn't make sense."

"I will not take you here." The wave of Elizabeth's hand took in the entire drawing room. "I will not have our first lovemaking be rough and tumble on the floor of this room."

"Our first . . ."

"Oh, my sweet, sweet girl." Elizabeth took a deep breath and stepped farther away. "I promise to teach you all about love, but not tonight. Tonight, I must sleep, so that I may face Rudolph in the morning and protect my lands."

She stepped forward again, caught Ruxandra's hand, and kissed it hard. "Will you forgive me?"

"Oh yes." Ruxandra moaned the words as Elizabeth's lips caressed her skin. "Always."

"I'm so glad." Elizabeth dropped Ruxandra's hand. "Good night, Ruxandra. I will see you tomorrow."

Elizabeth retreated into her bedroom. Ruxandra stared after her, the feeling of Elizabeth's hands and mouth still reverberating through her body.

Is that love? Why does it seem familiar, yet not familiar at all? There is no one like Elizabeth.

The picture in her mind was of her friend in her beautiful gown and cloak, hair dark as night, jewels not as bright as her eyes, her face sweet and rosy with desire. She knew it wasn't the whole story, but it was the one that mattered—that drew her like a flame.

She turned to go to her room and realized she was in no way tired. So she wished herself unseen and slipped out of the Stallburg and into the night.

The air was cold against her skin but not enough to make it unpleasant. The night was darker now. Few people wandered the streets, and few torches burned anywhere. Ruxandra didn't mind. She could see clearly, and she wanted to see everything. She walked in ever-widening circles around the Stallburg, learning the streets the way she had learned the forest.

Every building was a revelation. The way the stones were cut, the way glass hung in so many windows. The way the buildings crowded one on another. Everything was new and exciting, and the rhythms of the concert seemed to dance through the darkened city.

She was so enthralled that she forgot to stay unnoticed.

"Pardon me, miss," a man's deep voice asked behind her. "Spare some change for a poor beggar?"

Ruxandra turned. The man was squat and wide and well fed. His right hand was behind his back, his hat in his left, pressed over his heart. He bowed deeply.

"I'm sorry," Ruxandra said. "I don't have any money."

"That's too bad." The man looked up, a gleam in his eye. "I'll have your dress, then."

He threw the hat at her to divert her attention and charged. His hand came out from his back, the knife in it slashing toward her face.

Only Ruxandra wasn't there anymore.

He spun, saw her, and launched at her. Ruxandra moved.

When was the last time I ate?

The Beast was sluggish, but the first feelings of hunger danced in her stomach.

The man leaped at her again, and Ruxandra dodged again. The man swore and spun.

Memories of the wolf pack, of challenging the leader, of other wolves seeking to supplant her filled her mind.

Ruxandra *growled.*

The sound came from deep in her chest. It was an animal noise, not a human one. It made the man freeze. Then he grinned and launched himself at her once more.

The man was bulky and slow compared to Ruxandra. His movements were predictable. Even so, he was strong, and several times he nearly caught her before she grabbed his right hand in her own.

He kicked at her and smashed at her hand. She pulled him to keep him off balance and leaped onto his back. She sank her teeth into his throat, and he shouted in surprise. She latched on hard to keep the blood from spurting out and staining her beautiful dress. The man struggled desperately, slamming her against the wall and reaching over his shoulder to gouge at her eyes. She drove her talons into his body to pin him to her.

His struggling stopped, his knees collapsed, and he fell to the ground. Ruxandra released him and caught her balance. She swallowed the last of his blood and felt a tremor go through her. Then she realized what she'd done.

A quick look showed her the street was empty, but it didn't change the fact that a man's body sprawled at her feet with two holes in his throat.

Elizabeth will be furious . . .

CHAPTER ELEVEN

N*ow what do I do?*

Ruxandra stared down at the man's body. His face was frozen in a scream. His eyes stared wide in surprise and fear. Worst of all, he was lying where everyone could see him.

Ruxandra's eyes darted around looking for someplace—anyplace—to get rid of the body.

If this were the forest it would be easy, but here?

The moat was her first thought, but even if no one saw her dump the body in, surely they would notice his corpse floating on the surface. There was the river itself, but she needed to cross most of the city and get over the wall to get there.

If I cut his throat and dump him in the moat, everyone will likely assume he died and bled out there.

She picked up the man's knife. It was heavy, and the blade looked keen and sharp. Strangely, the idea of cutting into his flesh left her feeling squeamish.

Yet I tore his throat open and drank all his blood. What's the difference now?

It took her a moment to build enough nerve to kneel on him and press the blade to his throat. It took more to start sawing. After three strokes the blade bit in, opening the flesh. She saw the muscle and the small bones floating in his throat. She saw the openings where breath and food passed down into the body. It was fascinating and repulsive.

She stood, grabbed the bloodless corpse by its belt, and tossed it over her shoulder. It was easy. She wished herself unseen and ran across the city, the body bouncing and flopping as she went. The corpse's bladder released, then its bowels, leaving a stench that made Ruxandra's nose wrinkle. Both messes stayed in the dead man's breeches, though they would soon start to leak through. She sped up.

The city wall was tall and thick. She found a set of stairs and climbed to the top easily enough. She dodged three guards and slid down the rough, sloped front of the wall, and set the body gently into the moat. It slipped beneath the surface and out of sight.

Ruxandra stood, her back against the wall, and she stared up at the sky. The moon was out of sight, and the stars shone like the eyes of old pagan gods—eyes that approved of her daring and her skill. She was practically gasping with exhilaration, at one with the wild night.

I killed him and I hid him and I got away with it.

It was different, fighting someone. It was thrilling and challenging. Not like killing the poor helpless girls in the cell or the old lady and the old man. It was like running with the wolves, or fighting the bear.

But better.

Ruxandra had been a hunter in the woods. She had liked it. The chase and the fight roused her in the same way the hunger roused the Beast. That sort of hunt was more than just feeding.

It is what I was meant to do. Made to do.

She grinned at the sky, her fangs bared. She wanted to howl like she had with the wolves. Instead, she extended her talons, climbed the wall, and slipped through the night back to her rooms, without waking a soul.

"I need you here," Elizabeth told her the next morning. "For the next two days I will be in discussions with many of the nobles. If they wish to see what I have been doing with the ladies of my gymnaesium, I need to be able to present you at a moment's notice. Do you understand?"

"For the next two days," Ruxandra said. "Yes, my lady."

Elizabeth patted her cheek. "Good girl. I shall see you again as soon as these meetings are finished."

Ruxandra spent the following two mornings asleep and the afternoons playing cards. Since she had promised not to go out, she spent the evenings experimenting with her ability to feel others' emotions.

The first time, she opened her mind wide. Suddenly, she could feel everyone's emotions at once, for miles in every direction. She cried out in pain, shocking Jana awake, and held her head until the feeling of being overwhelmed went away.

The second time, she looked at Jana, asleep on Ruxandra's bed. Contentment and happiness radiated from her, with a hint of fear at the very center. Ruxandra expanded her reach, taking in the building. She could feel fifty people she didn't know, mostly asleep, some awake in passion, one awake in misery. She found Dorotyas and felt her anger and jealousy. She lingered for a moment, wondering if there was anything else, but found nothing interesting at all. She found Elizabeth's servants and felt their fear and pain, their persistent weak prayer.

By the end of the second night, she could control how far she reached and whose minds she looked into.

On the third night, she was growing hungry again.

Elizabeth said two days. This is the third.

She slipped out the window wearing only her shift. Her feet were bare to better feel the ground. She made herself unnoticed and stalked the streets, listening for the sound of people and following them to a tavern where poor men drank together.

It was a dangerous place if the smell of fear from the serving girls was anything to go by. Ruxandra stepped inside, still unnoticed, and opened her mind to the people's emotions. Anger, happiness, sadness, and grief radiated from the men and women there. Some more complex, nuanced feelings that she didn't have time to explore. She felt the pain of their injuries as well. The stump at the end of one man's arm throbbed with memory of the hand that had once been there. Another man's back burned with the flogging his master had given him.

One man burned brighter with rage and hatred than any of the others.

Still unnoticed, Ruxandra slipped through the crowd. People stepped out of their way to avoid her without wondering why. She found the man sitting in the corner watching the serving girls, with bloodshot eyes and a heart seething with hatred. Ruxandra stayed against the wall, unnoticed and patient, like a cat waiting on a rat.

The woman who served his table, a young blonde thing with a low-cut blouse and wide eyes, was terrified. She kept out of hand's reach of him, didn't answer his questions, and avoided his eyes. The man's eyes never left her, and when she told the barman she needed to step out, the man finished his drink in a single swing and followed her.

Ruxandra slipped out behind him.

The girl squatted in the alley, her skirts hoisted. Urine spattered on the cobblestones between her feet. The man watched her, and Ruxandra felt rage and lust and pure hatred coming off him in waves. He slipped up behind the girl and raised his boot to kick her over.

It was as far as he got.

An hour later, Ruxandra slipped through the dark streets toward the cathedral. She had glimpsed the steeple on the way in and was curious to see it up close. Jana had told her the other servants called it one of the greatest cathedrals ever built. As the night was still young and the cathedral was only a short walk from the Stallburg, there was no reason not to see it.

Soon, she stood at the front door of Saint Stephen's Cathedral, gawking.

The steeple was taller than anything she had seen. The building was as long as the blocks surrounding it. The door was twenty feet high and mounted by an animal bone that was as long as she was tall. The towers flanking the doors were at least sixty feet high, and each was only half as high as the great steeple.

I must get inside. I must see it.

The doors were shut and locked, the windows all closed. She didn't want to break anything to get inside, but she was desperately curious. She looked closely over the building, searching for an entry point. High up, near the top of the steeple, was a balcony. Two men stood there, looking out over the city.

It would not be too difficult to climb, she thought. *They wouldn't see me at all.*

She tied up her shift, grinned, and jumped.

Upon her return, Ruxandra told Jana where she'd gone. Her descriptions of the cathedral made the girl nearly squirm out of her chair with excitement.

"It sounds wonderful!" Jana said as she helped Ruxandra get ready for bed. "I wish I could see it."

"Then go," Ruxandra said. "I don't need you during the day. You can go see it and come back after."

Jana shook her head. "Dorotyas will strap me if I go anywhere without my mistress."

"That's not fair." Ruxandra put her hand on her chin and thought about it. "If I go out after sunset tonight, we should be able to see some of the city before it gets too dark. Would you like that?"

"Oh yes!"

That evening, as the sun went down, Ruxandra led Jana out of the Stallburg and into the streets. Ruxandra wore a plain dress and cloak at Jana's suggestion, and the two of them walked arm in arm through the streets.

The evening light felt too bright and made Ruxandra squint. It was worth it, though, to see the delight on Jana's face. The girl leaped around like a wolf cub, exploring one place after the next. Together they found an open-air market and browsed through the stands. Most were already closed, but they saw chickens and fresh bread, winter apples and jewelry.

The woman selling jewelry worked very hard to sell it to Ruxandra, but they had no money. *Which is too bad, because I would have liked to buy one of those.*

They were leaving the market when the smell of lilacs caught Ruxandra's attention. She turned, half expecting to see Neculai, holding the bar of soap he'd given her.

Neculai?

The image faded nearly as quickly as it came, leaving Ruxandra dazed. She sniffed the air, found the scent, and followed it to a small shop. Jana trailed after her, mystified. The door to the shop was closed. Ruxandra knocked at it without thinking. A woman opened it and looked Ruxandra up and down. "Yes, m'lady?"

"That smell. What is it?"

The woman frowned. "One of my perfumes, I suppose."

"May I see it?" Ruxandra asked.

"We are closed for the day, m'lady—"

"Please!" Ruxandra desperately wanted the perfume, wanted to put her nose in it and breathe the lilacs. "I've never smelled anything so good. *Please, may I come in?*"

The change in her own voice startled Ruxandra so much she nearly fell over. Her words throbbed with power. She felt it floating in the air like the scent of the perfume, felt it twisting the woman's will.

The woman's face went slack. She stepped back. "Come in."

Ruxandra hesitated, still struck by what she had done. The woman stared at her, waiting. Ruxandra stepped inside, Jana trailing her.

The shop smelled even better inside. Fifty different scents competed for Ruxandra's attention. She walked through the small, cluttered shop with its embroidered hangings and deep-shelved cabinets, watching the candle flames reflected in the mirrors and sniffing bottle after bottle. Then she picked up a small glass vial, and the scent of lilacs filled her nose.

The water in the pond was ice cold and turning gray as she used the soap to scrub away the accumulated dirt of months. She hurried. He said he wasn't coming back, but she didn't want him seeing her like this.

"An excellent choice," the woman said. "I extract the lilac scent and wear it myself. It is very expensive. Ten soldi."

Ruxandra's insides twisted as she looked at the little bottle. "We have no money."

Jana shook her head. "No, my lady, we don't."

The woman frowned again. "I cannot give it away for free."

"*Can we pay for it tomorrow?*" Ruxandra tried to keep the desperation from her voice. "*And take it now?*"

For the second time, Ruxandra's words filled with power—with conviction and certainty and a strength that said *obey me.* The woman's face went slack again. She nodded.

"Very well, my lady," she said. "I will look for your servant tomorrow."

Ruxandra cradled the perfume in her hands like it was a baby bird as they left the little shop. Her mind was spinning.

I made her do something. I made her do it just by asking. Can I control people?

She looked around the market square. A large man stood in front of baskets of wilted turnips and cabbages. He tipped his hat to everyone who went by and kept up a stream of patter. Ruxandra walked to him, listening as he extolled the virtues of his turnips and cabbages—the last from the fall harvest, you know.

"Good evening, my lady," he said. "Turnips for the household?"

"No thank you."

"Then some cabbages perhaps?"

"No." She didn't want to humiliate the man, but she needed him to do something a man wouldn't normally do. "Do you ever balance turnips on your head?"

The big man laughed. "Now why would I do such a thing?"

Ruxandra put all her energy into the next words, concentrating on *knowing* he would do it. *"Balance a turnip on your hat and keep it there until I leave the square."*

"Of course, my lady."

He turned to his basket of turnips, went through several, and put them aside as unsuitable. Then he picked up a small round one and weighed it in his hand.

"Perfect, I'd say," he announced. With that, he put it on his head and crushed it into his hat so it stayed in place. "How is that my lady?"

"Wonderful," Ruxandra said. She bit her lip, turned around, grabbed Jana's hand, and led her from the square. When she reached the edge, she looked back. The man waved at her, took the turnip off his head, and put it back in the basket. Ruxandra managed to get around a corner before collapsing into a fit of giggles.

"My lady?" Jana said. "Are you all right?"

Ruxandra nodded. *I can command people to do things! I could tell people to take me places and show me things. I could show Jana things. We could visit the city together.*

"Jana," Ruxandra said. "Do you want to see the Hofburg?"

Jana's eyes went wide. "Can we?"

Five hours and an exhaustive tour of the Hofburg later, Ruxandra carried the sleeping Jana to their room. The guards at the Hofburg, at her command, had led her to a butler who declared himself more than happy to show them around once she commanded him. The building had been filled with art, with religious relics, arms and armor, and magnificent staterooms. They even got a glimpse at Maxmillius's bedroom.

It was wonderful. Ruxandra pushed open the door to her room and laid the girl on her small pallet bed in the corner.

"Where have you been?" Elizabeth demanded.

Ruxandra spun. Elizabeth sat in the chair, glaring furiously. Ruxandra had been so distracted by the evening she hadn't noticed Elizabeth's presence. She looked for words, but none came.

"I told you to stay here," Elizabeth snapped. "I told you to stay where I could find you."

"For two days," Ruxandra protested. "You said two days."

"That is no excuse!" Elizabeth rose and strode to the door. "Come with me."

Ruxandra slipped the bottle of perfume into Jana's hand and followed Elizabeth to her rooms. All her maids stood outside the drawing room. They looked terrified and exhausted. Dorotyas stood beside the door, a three-pronged strap in her belt.

Elizabeth shoved the door open, snapping, "Close it behind you!"

Ruxandra stepped inside and froze.

"I said close it!"

Dorotyas shoved Ruxandra from behind, sending her stumbling forward. She heard the door slam shut. Still, she didn't turn around.

"Why?" The fury was gone from Elizabeth's voice. In its place was a terrible sadness. "Why did you leave me?"

Ruxandra could only stare.

A wide, low-backed chair stood in the middle of the room. One of Elizabeth's maids was tied facedown over the back of it. She was naked, save for the thick strip of cloth holding a ball of rags in her wide-open mouth. Her clothes lay beneath the chair, spattered with blood. The skin on the woman's back, buttocks, and thighs had been torn open in a hundred places.

It was hideous.

"What . . ." Ruxandra's voice came slowly alive. "What happened?"

"I wanted to see you, Ruxandra." Elizabeth's voice was small. "I've been sitting in Rudolph's court for four days now, waiting on his pleasure. Not once has he seen me. Not once has *anyone* spoken to me. The servants ignore me except to tell me to continue waiting or to leave. The courtiers don't come near. They move away when I talk to them. They say things—cruel, heartless things—where they know I can hear them. I tried very hard not to burden you with this, Ruxandra. I tried to keep you out of it. Tonight I desperately needed to talk to you."

That isn't my fault. There is no excuse for this. Ruxandra wanted to say the words, but they stuck in her throat.

"But you weren't there." The anger came back, a fury that burned into Ruxandra's ears. "I wanted to see you. I wanted you to comfort me, and *you weren't there!*"

She shouted the last words, and they echoed off the walls. The sound of her voice somehow nullified the sight of the maid. She became small, not quite real, almost a doll. Only Elizabeth mattered.

"I'm sorry!" Ruxandra cried. "I did not know you needed me."

"You risk everything by doing that! And now look what you've done!" She pointed at the bloody corpse.

"The one day I needed you! The one day I was so full of anger and so upset that I had to tell someone, and *you weren't there!*" Elizabeth kicked the leg of the chair. "I need to talk to someone of the Blood Royal, and all I have are these stupid peasant *bitches* who don't even know how to properly clean a room!"

"So you beat her to death," Ruxandra said quietly. "You didn't have to—"

"She was mine to beat!" Elizabeth drove the toe of her boot into the thigh of the corpse. "She was mine to do as I please with because *she* was a useless peasant bitch, and what I needed was *you*!"

Tears still wet the dead woman's face. She'd made her wrists raw and bloody with her struggles against the ropes. Ruxandra tried to reconcile the Elizabeth she liked she knew with the woman who did this. The dead woman was a peasant, but even so the punishment had far outweighed any mistake she had committed.

"Now I have this." Elizabeth's voice went quiet again as she turned away. "How do I explain this, Ruxandra? There are already rumors about me. When the courtiers learn about this, the rumors will grow worse. That bitch Czobor will alert Rudolph, and he will take my lands, and my children will inherit *nothing*."

She turned a tear-stained face to Ruxandra. "All you had to do was stay in your room, Ruxandra. Why couldn't you do that?"

"I . . ." *I was bored. I wanted to see the city.* None of them seemed like good enough reasons, looking at the corpse of the girl.

"What do we do now, Ruxandra?" Elizabeth's voice was frail and tired. "Tell me. What do we do?"

CHAPTER TWELVE

RUXANDRA TOUCHED THE dead woman's shoulder. *If I'd been here, would she have done this?*

Somehow it was easier to think she wouldn't have—that Ruxandra had had the power to prevent this.

"I'll say she fell sick," Elizabeth shook her head. "The other servants will say nothing. Dorotyas will see to that. I think I can find a doctor to verify my story. It will cost money, but I—"

"I can hide her." The words rushed past Ruxandra's lips, practically of their own accord. "I can put her in the river if I hurry."

Elizabeth shook her head. "You can't. You'll be seen."

"I won't."

"Ruxandra . . ."

"No." Ruxandra willed herself unnoticed. "I won't."

"Ruxandra?" Elizabeth's voice rose an octave. Her eyes went wide, and her mouth fell open. "Ruxandra!"

"I'm here." Ruxandra let go of her will.

Elizabeth gasped and stumbled away. One hand clutched at her chest while the other clung to the wall for support.

"How?" Elizabeth demanded. "How did you do that? When did you learn?"

"When I first went hunting," Ruxandra said. "That night in the castle."

"Why didn't you tell me?" Elizabeth's voice grew loud. "How could you keep this from me?"

"Because you wouldn't let me hunt!" Ruxandra's hands clenched into fists. "I *like* hunting! And I didn't want to kill Jana."

"Well"—Elizabeth shook her head—"I didn't know you could do *that*!"

"Neither did *I*."

"How . . ." Elizabeth's eyes lit up. "It's the blood. You're finally drinking human blood and look what power it is giving you."

Ruxandra nodded.

"I only want what's best for you, Ruxandra." Elizabeth spoke slowly, as if to a difficult child. "You know that. If I'd known you could hunt without being seen, I wouldn't have worried."

Ruxandra bit her lip. "Truly?"

"Truly." Elizabeth stepped forward. "I love you, Ruxandra."

Ruxandra's mouth fell open. "You love me?"

"Yes." Elizabeth took both of Ruxandra's hands and kissed them. "I love you. You are the most magnificent creature I have ever seen, and I loved you from the moment I saw you. I would never do anything to hurt you. I swear."

She loves me.

Elizabeth kissed Ruxandra on one cheek, then the other. Then she planted her mouth hard against Ruxandra's. She stepped back, her breaths coming in heavy bursts, lust written clear in the red of her cheeks. "How . . . will you get rid of her?"

"I'll carry her." Ruxandra started undoing the ties on her bodice. "No one will see if I'm carrying her. Help me get these off, so I don't ruin the dress."

"All right." Elizabeth helped her with the ties and the belt, and when the dress fell to the floor, she helped pull the shift over Ruxandra's head. Ruxandra kicked off her boots and started on her stockings.

"My word," Elizabeth said. "You are beautiful."

Butterflies danced in Ruxandra's stomach.

"After this," Elizabeth said, her voice filled with passion, "you can have anything you want."

Ruxandra's eyes went wide. "Anything at all?"

"Anything I can give."

"Then I . . ." Ruxandra fell silent.

"Then you what?" Elizabeth stepped closer. "What do you want, Ruxandra?"

Ruxandra felt embarrassed, though Elizabeth said she could ask for anything. "May Jana and I go out and explore the city? And may I have some money as well to buy things when we're out?"

Elizabeth's lips rose up on one side in the smallest of smiles. "Of course."

She turned, drew the knife from her bodice, and cut the ropes on the dead girl.

"Thank you so much," Ruxandra said.

Elizabeth nodded but didn't stop cutting. Ruxandra stripped the last of her clothes away and waited.

Elizabeth cut the last cord and stepped back. "Ruxandra?"

Ruxandra picked up the body. "Yes?"

"Can you do anything else?"

Ruxandra stopped with the body half over her shoulder. Suddenly she wanted to keep quiet about her ability to sense emotions and to command people. *But it's Elizabeth. She's helped me all this time. She loves me.*

"Yes." *Why don't I want to tell her?* "We don't have time to talk about it now if I'm going to get her to the river."

"Of course," Elizabeth said. "After, then. If you would."

Ruxandra opened the window. Night was fading, the sky slowly changing from black to deep blue. She climbed into the frame. "I'll be back soon, I promise."

With that, she willed herself unseen and jumped.

Ruxandra returned and found Dorotyas waiting.

"My lady is asleep," Dorotyas said as soon as Ruxandra appeared in the window. She pointed at the closed bed curtains. "She is exhausted from the ordeal you put her through."

"Oh." Ruxandra climbed down. "Where are my clothes?"

"In your room." Dorotyas walked to the door. "Where you were supposed to be."

"I already apologized to Elizabeth." Ruxandra realized she sounded like a sulky child and resisted the impulse to growl. "I'll go to bed then."

"Bed?" Dorotyas shook her head. "You'll not parade through the halls naked. You can wait here until Elizabeth wakes."

"Can't you fetch my clothes for me?"

"No." Pleasure laced the word, and a hard smile grew on Dorotyas's face. "You can wait."

"Did Elizabeth say so?"

"No. *I* said so."

Ruxandra's hands curled into fists. She wanted to stomp her foot in frustration but knew she would look stupid doing it. She wanted to growl, but she wouldn't give Dorotyas the satisfaction of seeing her as an animal again. Instead, she walked toward the door.

"No, you don't." Dorotyas stepped in front of her. "You'll do as I say and wait here."

"You don't get to give me orders," Ruxandra said. "Move."

"No."

Ruxandra wished herself unseen.

Dorotyas stared wildly around the room. "Where did you . . ."

Ruxandra walked past her, opened the door, and stepped out.

There was a purse waiting for Ruxandra when she awoke. Jana opened it, whistled, and poured the contents on the bed.

Her eyes went wide. "Gold florins. The small ones are four florins each. The large ones are eight. There's ten of each."

"Is that a lot of money?" Ruxandra asked.

"More than I've ever seen!"

"Is it enough to pay for the perfume?"

"One of the four-florin coins would pay for twenty bottles of that perfume." Jana shook her head and started putting the coins back in the bag. "We can't carry all this around with us."

"How much should we take?"

Jana picked up three of the smaller coins. "That's more than enough for anything we want, I think."

"Good." Ruxandra smiled wide. "Let's go exploring!"

For the next three nights, that's what they did.

They returned to the perfume shop and paid the shopkeeper for the lilac perfume. The woman didn't seem surprised to see them—apparently she'd had no doubts they'd return. Then Ruxandra and Jana strolled through the city, looking at the fountains and statues. They went to concerts and taverns. Ruxandra discovered she liked the taste of wine, though it did nothing to fill her or make her intoxicated. She also discovered that the boys and young men in the taverns found both Jana and her worthy of attention.

Jana made Ruxandra promise never to go off alone with them because Lady Elizabeth wouldn't approve. The men did their best, but Ruxandra remained firmly by Jana's side. So the men took them around the city. Ruxandra learned new dances. Several of the young men suggested more, but Ruxandra managed to fend them off.

Jana, on the other hand, ended up kissing one of the boys on the second night. Ruxandra caught them at it and laughed herself silly. Jana spent the trip home bright red and blushing.

On the second night, after carrying Jana home to sleep, Ruxandra stripped to her shift and went hunting. The young men they met had told her which areas of the town were dangerous for a young woman to walk alone at night. It was there Ruxandra went.

The young bravo she found swaggering down the street smelled of sex and blood and radiated self-satisfaction. Ruxandra made sure he saw her and followed her into an alley.

"Hey there," she said when he grinned and came toward her. "Want to fight?"

It was almost like hunting with the wolves.

The next afternoon, Ruxandra woke to a knock at the door. Jana opened it. "Yes?"

"Tell your mistress she cannot go out tonight," Dorotyas said. "Lady Czobor is having a party, and Lady Elizabeth wants Ruxandra to join her."

There was acid in the woman's words. Ruxandra knew Dorotyas's thoughts about her without even reaching for her emotions. As far as Dorotyas was concerned, Ruxandra was not in the slightest worthy to join Elizabeth anywhere.

Neither are you, Ruxandra thought.

"She'd better look her best, or you'll get my strap, you hear me?"

The threat in Dorotyas's voice brought Ruxandra upright in bed. She opened the curtain, ready to tell Dorotyas to leave, but the woman was already gone. Jana closed the door, took a deep breath, and turned to Ruxandra. She put on a bright smile that did nothing to hide the trembling in her voice.

"A party, my lady," Jana said. "Isn't it exciting! You'll need your best dress. We should braid your hair, so that everyone can see how pretty your face is."

Ruxandra slipped out of the bed and wrapped her arms around the girl.

"I'm fine, my lady." Jana's voice was muffled in Ruxandra's breasts.

"She won't hurt you," Ruxandra said. "I won't let her."

Jana nodded. "Yes, my lady. You should wear your perfume, so you smell as pretty as you look."

“Of course.” Ruxandra let Jana go. The girl stood straight and tall, refusing to show her fear. Ruxandra ruffled her hair. “Please make some tea, and then we’ll decide what I’m going to wear.”

It took two hours before Jana declared Ruxandra properly attired. Instead of boots, she wore soft-soled shoes for dancing. She’d put on her best blue dress and her cleanest shirt and shift. Jana combed and braided her hair, so the braids became a crown, framing her face, while the rest of her hair hung free down her back. She stood back, looked over her handiwork, and declared Ruxandra done.

“I’ll try to stay up until you get back,” Jana said.

“Even if you don’t,” Ruxandra said, “I promise to tell you all about it.”

She gave Jana a hug, holding the girl’s small body close. Jana hugged back, and for a moment Ruxandra could pretend they truly were sisters.

Jana let go first. She stepped back and curtsied. “Have a good night, my lady.”

Ruxandra curtsied back. “Good night to you, Adela.”

As soon as she said the name, memories came flooding back.

Ruxandra was smaller, younger, and running with two other girls through the yard of the abbey. She worked in the kitchens and was terrible at weaving. She snuck into Adela and Valeria’s rooms to hug and hold them. They all comforted each other after facing Sister Sofia’s strap. And one night . . .

Ruxandra stumbled back and sat heavily on the bed.

“My lady?”

“I had a friend,” Ruxandra whispered. “Her name was Adela, and when she was young she looked like you.”

Tears, unbidden and unreasonable, welled in Ruxandra's eyes. "She and Valeria. They were my best friends. How could I forget my best friends?"

"My lady . . ." Jana looked helplessly at the door. Ruxandra knew she must go, knew that Dorotyas would blame Jana if she were late. But she didn't want to move. She wanted to remember more. She wanted to see them again and ask how they were and what had happened to them.

They must be grown now. They probably have their own children.

Oh God, how long has it been?

More tears rolled down her cheeks and spotted her dress. Jana dashed forward and dabbed at her eyes with a handkerchief. "Please, my lady. You mustn't cry."

Ruxandra sniffled and took the handkerchief. The memories sank back in her mind, but they didn't fade away.

Maybe I'll remember more soon. Maybe I'll know who I am.

Or who I was once, before I became this . . .

She snuffled back the last of her tears, wiped her face again, and gave Jana her handkerchief.

Jana kissed her hand. "You'll be all right, my lady. I'm sure you will."

"I will," Ruxandra agreed. "Thank you, my friend."

Jana's eyes lifted. "Friend?"

Ruxandra nodded. "Always."

She straightened her shoulders, took a deep breath, and headed for Elizabeth and the party that awaited them.

Elizabeth spent the ride giving instructions, but Ruxandra hardly listened as she replayed the memories again and again. It wasn't until Elizabeth grabbed her arm and shook it that she returned to the present.

"Ruxandra," Elizabeth glared at her. "Why aren't you listening?"

"I'm sorry." Ruxandra meant it. Even so, she couldn't concentrate. "I remembered some things about when I was young."

"That is important," Elizabeth said, "but not as important as what I am trying to tell you." Elizabeth let go of her arm. "Then, for the *second* time, Lady Czobor holds her parties to extend her influence and the influence of the king, to promote her daughters for marriage, and to subject those she wishes to under her thumb. Which one of those do you think this is?"

"The . . . the last?"

"Precisely. She invited *you* to this party, and me as your guardian. She wants you under her control, so she can turn you against me. Do you understand?"

Ruxandra nodded.

"Instead, you will show yourself to be a model young lady, a credit to me and my gymnaesium. You will talk very little about yourself. Only dance those dances I taught you, and never with the same man twice. Otherwise, it may be construed as showing favor. Further, you will not, under any circumstances, show yourself to be other than what you appear. This woman wants to humiliate me and she *will* use you to do it. Do not show your strength, do not show your abilities, and in the name of God do not show your fangs. Otherwise, she will use you as proof that *I'm* the monster, and she will destroy us both."

"I understand," Ruxandra said.

"This is my last chance to negotiate with the courtiers," Elizabeth said. "It is my last chance to keep things as they are without resorting to other . . . methods. Do you understand?"

"Yes, my lady."

Elizabeth gripped both her hands. "If you love me as I love you, do not show your true self tonight. No matter what. *Promise.*"

"I promise," Ruxandra repeated. "I won't. No matter what."

"Good. Because we are here."

The carriage stopped, and a pair of footmen opened the door.

"Into the lion's den," Elizabeth said. "Come, Ruxandra."

Ruxandra nodded, gathered up her skirts, and stepped out.

⸻

Lady's Czobor's house was a statement of power, privilege, and excess, made in marble and stone. It stood three stories high. Tall, wide windows ran the length of the walls. Every one was lit up, shining down on the streets below. The women wore gowns even richer than those Ruxandra had seen at the opera. The men wore fur on their collar, and brocade on their coats.

Inside was even more magnificent.

The front hall was done in marble, polished to a shine. A hundred candles flickered in the chandelier above them, lighting the room. A pair of liveried footmen took their cloaks and guided them into a long, wide hall where a hundred people stood in rapturous silence, listening to a woman sing.

It was a sound Ruxandra had never heard. The woman's voice climbed impossibly high, trilling on the words and swooping back down. The woman sang of passion and longing, of desperate need and profound love. Every note, every word, cut to the core of Ruxandra's being.

She was back in Neculai's arms, getting her first kiss from a man. She touched the softness of the skin on his back and chest, such a contrast to his rough, gentle hands. She felt his lips on hers, his body pressed against hers. He looked down at her, his eyes filled with passion, and then she . . .

"Ruxandra!" Elizabeth's harsh whisper interrupted her revelation. "You are crying. Stop at once."

"I'm sorry." Ruxandra pulled a handkerchief from her dress and wiped at her eyes. "The music. It's incredible. It's—"

"It is opera," Lady Czobor said, from behind them. "It's a new form, and one that I think will do quite well."

Elizabeth and Ruxandra both turned and curtsied.

"So very good to see you again . . . Ruxandra, was it not?"

"Yes, my lady."

"I am so glad you like the concert. I do hope you enjoy dancing."

"Yes, my lady." *I am supposed to be a model young lady.* "I am not terribly good at it, but I do enjoy it."

"I have heard this," Lady Czobor said. "In fact, my nephew Ulrik saw you only last night, dancing with a young man in a tavern. Apparently, you were quite enjoying yourself."

Ruxandra looked at her feet. No one had said she should not dance in the taverns, and the young men she had been with had all been gentlemen of the city. Nor had she been the only young woman there. The others had been of equal rank, and had travelled with companions just as she had.

"Elizabeth must certainly trust you"—Lady Czobor didn't even look at Elizabeth as she said it—"to let you wander off alone like that. Does she teach all her students to be so free?"

"I've only been a student for a short time," Ruxandra glanced at Elizabeth. The woman's face was cold, expressionless. On impulse, Ruxandra reached out to feel her emotions. She found a boiling caldron of anger and hate, all directed at Lady Czobor. Ruxandra winced and pulled her mind back. "Also, I was not alone. I brought my servant with me, to ensure there would be no impropriety."

"Ah, yes, your servant. The young girl with a penchant for kissing young men in back rooms."

"It happened once," Ruxandra protested. "And he kissed her."

"They kissed each other, according to my sources." Lady Czobor laughed. "Enough of this silliness. You are young and beautiful and deserve to enjoy your evening. Ulrik!"

She turned away and waved a hand. Three young men detached themselves from a crowd and came forward. They bowed to Lady Czobor. She nodded with a smile.

"Ruxandra, my dear, let me introduce you to my nephew, Ulrik, and his companions Dedrick and Harman."

The three men bowed to her in turn. Ulrik was tall and wide-shouldered, with narrow hips, dark hair, and a pair of brown eyes that smoldered like fire when they looked at her. Dedrick and Harman were blond, shorter than Ulrik, but with the same wide shoulders.

"My dear Ulrik," Lady Czobor said, "Would you and your companions be so kind as to take Ruxandra under your wing this evening? She is a stranger to our court and not well versed in our ways. Would you introduce her to others and show her around?"

"Of course," Ulrik said. "It would be our pleasure."

He bowed and extended a hand to Ruxandra. Ruxandra looked to Elizabeth, unsure what to do.

"Oh, do not be concerned," Lady Czobor said. "The countess and I have much to discuss. When you are ready to leave, you will find her in my company. If you do not mind, of course, Countess."

"Of course." Elizabeth's voice was pure pleasantry. She smiled at Ruxandra. "I have the greatest confidence in Ruxandra, and I cannot doubt that your nephew and his friends will treat her with the utmost respect. Go and enjoy yourself, my dear. I know I shall."

"Then we will see you later in the evening," Lady Czobor said. "Shall we go, Elizabeth?"

With that, Lady Czobor left. Elizabeth nodded once to Ruxandra and followed Lady Czobor. Ruxandra stared after her, uncertain.

"Miss Ruxandra," said Ulrik, his hand still extended. "Will you join us?"

CHAPTER THIRTEEN

Ruxandra looked back at Elizabeth. The woman followed Lady Czobor out the door of the hall. Her back was straight and proud, and she didn't look back.

She trusts me. The thought made her at once proud and afraid. *She believes I will not do anything wrong.*

Ruxandra smiled, put her fingers on Ulrik's, and dropped into a deep, formal curtsy.

"I will happily join you," she said. "I hope you will take care of me this evening."

"We most certainly will," Ulrik said. "The finest care, in fact."

"This is no good," Harman said. "A young woman alone with three men? It is a scandal."

"Not nearly as much as a young woman alone with one young man," Dedrick said.

"True." Harman put his hand to his chin and looked thoughtful. "There is only one solution. We need two more young ladies!"

Ulrik laughed. "One of those wouldn't happen to be Miss Glerisher, would it?"

Harman put on an innocent look. "You know, I had not thought of her, but that is a capital idea. She is over here, I believe."

"You will excuse Harman," Dedrick said. "He thinks of exactly three things: horses, swords, and young ladies. In that order. Since he can't find either of the first two here—"

"Oh look," Herman called. "She is with Miss Widhoezl."

"Then we should go greet them at once," said Dedrick. "Come along, Ulrik. Don't dawdle."

Ulrik laughed. "Would you be so kind, Miss?"

Ruxandra laughed and followed.

The girls curtsied, introduced themselves, and insisted Ruxandra call them Edda and Griffelda. When Ruxandra told them she'd never been to such a grand house before, they insisted on leading her on a tour of the mansion. The young men accompanied them. Dedrick and Harman took the opportunity to link arms with Edda and Griffelda whenever they were out of sight of the older members of the court.

"Do tell us about your home, Castle Csejte," Edda said as they went through the upstairs rooms. "Is it as old-fashioned as they say?"

"I do not know," Ruxandra admitted. "It is very much a fortress, though. It has high walls and towers."

"What a place to have a gymnaesium," Griffelda said. "Where do they hold their classes?"

"In the great hall."

"How strange. What do the other girls think of it?"

They never talk to me. "I only joined the school recently, so I did not have much chance to get to know them before we came here."

"It is strange how she brought you, then," Griffelda said, "if she wants to show off how well her students do. But never mind. Have you been to any galleries in the city yet?"

The conversation turned to the galleries and the concerts the girls had seen recently. Ruxandra mostly listened, though when they discussed the singer, Ruxandra gushed with praise about her voice. She realized it a few moments later and at once felt awkward.

Edda came to her rescue. "The first time I heard it, I felt the same way. Though Griffelda doesn't like it at all, do you?"

"It is too screechy for me," Griffelda declared. "Like a cat being stretched."

The entire group laughed, and Ruxandra laughed with them.

The music for dancing started, and the group half ran back to the ballroom.

The dancing much different from that at Castle Csejte, where the girls moved in emotionless, expressionless steps to the harsh clap of Dorotyas's hands. Here there was laughter and talking and a dozen musicians whose instruments together created music that spun and whirled with the dancers on the floor.

Ulrik took the first dance, which was, fortunately, one that Ruxandra knew. She followed him through the paces, made very few mistakes, and greatly enjoyed herself. The next tune she didn't know at all, and Ulrik gallantly stayed with her while she sat on the sidelines, watching. Dedrick took her for the next dance, then Harman. Then several other gentlemen asked for dances, and Ruxandra obliged.

Hours went by in a whirlwind of candlelight and music and conversation. Ulrik was the best dancer of the group and never missed an opportunity to dance with Ruxandra. His hands were warm and his touch gentle as he led her around the floor. When she didn't know a dance, he stayed with her and brought her mulled wine. Ruxandra drank it greedily; it was so good.

When the musicians took breaks, Dedrick told the girls stories about their training to be knights that put all six of them in stitches. Harman, despite being the quietest of the group, had a sly wit that made the stories even funnier.

A clock chimed midnight.

"Quickly, everyone outside!" Ulrik held out a hand to Ruxandra. "We must see the fireworks."

Ruxandra wasn't sure what those were. Judging from the way the other girls clapped and grabbed their young men's hands and dashed for the door, though, they must have been something exciting.

"Shall we?" Ulrik's hand was still out. Ruxandra took it and let him place her fingers in the crook of his arm. He led them out to the patio.

The gardens beyond were small. Still, it was more than large enough for all the guests who came out to stand on the balconies and patio that stretched the length of the building.

There was a *hiss*, then a *thud* and a *whoosh!*

Ruxandra nearly jumped out of her skin as a rocket shot skyward in a bright streak of light. When the rocket exploded in a starburst of white and a *thump* that shook the air, she let out a screech and covered her head.

The girls all laughed. Ulrik caught her arms and brought them gently back down. He was smiling.

"They're fireworks," he said. "They can't hurt you, and they are very, very pretty."

Now I look like a fool. Ruxandra straightened up and turned her eyes to the sky. Another rocket, then a third, leaped skyward. Ruxandra flinched at both, then again when they exploded in circles of red and blue. *They are beautiful!*

Twenty-five more rockets launched, sometimes singly, others in pairs or threes. They exploded in every color of the rainbow. The audience clapped and cheered, and by the fifth launch, Ruxandra joined in. At the end, a barrage of five rockets flew up at once. Each one of them exploded three times, lighting up the sky as bright as day and leaving the audience amazed.

"That was wonderful!" Ruxandra said as the others began returning inside. "I wish there were more."

"There is nothing as spectacular as that," Ulrik said. "But there is more entertainment. Have you ever seen a man juggle fire?"

Ruxandra shook her head.

"Then come with us!" Ulrik declared. "My lady aunt has arranged for three fire jugglers to light the carriages on their way out. Come this way, and we'll see them first!"

He caught her hand and pulled her down the steps to the lawn. The others followed. He led them around to the side of the house. It was dimly lit here, with not a single window to shine light down upon them. No one slowed down, though. Ulrik dashed forward and turned down an alleyway. The four behind them kept close, practically pushing them forward. Ulrik turned twice more, then stopped.

"Here we are," he declared. "Isn't it magnificent?"

"This?" Ruxandra stared at the dead end in front of them. Windowless brick walls rose up on three sides of them. Two torches hung in brackets on the back wall. A barrel stood to one side. "Where is the—"

A tightly twisted strip of cloth dropped over Ruxandra's head and pulled sharply back into her mouth. She stumbled back against Dedrick. He pulled the cloth tighter. Edda and Griffelda each grabbed one of Ruxandra's hands. Harman pulled a length of cord from his pocket and wrapped it around one of her wrists.

What is happening? What are they doing? Ruxandra tried to say the words, but she could only grunt and mumble against the cloth that bit deep into her mouth.

"Hold the whore tight," Ulrik said. "She is not to make a sound."

Harman yanked her wrist out of Griselda's hand and brought it together with the one Edda held. He wrapped the cord around it.

"Don't worry," Dedrick said. "She'll not get away."

Ruxandra nearly tore her hands free, but remembered Elizabeth's warning. She could not show her power. She struggled and wriggled, her fear and fury growing as she watched Harman tie her wrists together, and felt Dedrick tie the gag behind her head. Then Harman yanked her forward and shoved her face first against the wall.

The Beast growled in response.

No! I'm not supposed to give myself away. I'm supposed to be a normal girl.

The Beast's growl said otherwise. Ruxandra clamped down hard on it.

Ulrik and Harman grabbed her arms and shoved them in the air. They lifted her by them, so her feet left the ground and hooked the cord over a spike driven into the wall. Ruxandra dangled in the air, her feet inches above the ground, her face grinding against the wall.

If I could speak, I could command them to stop.

She tried to tell them to ungag her, tried to ask why they were hurting her, but the words came out as unintelligible moans.

"What should we do to her first?" Edda asked.

"Strip her," Griffelda said. "See if that bitch marked her."

"Excellent idea." Ulrik stepped forward and pressed Ruxandra's face to the wall. Something sharp pushed against her neck. "If you move an inch, I'll cut open your flesh. Do you understand?"

He didn't give her a chance to answer. The sharp point left her neck, and a moment later she heard the fabric of her dress ripping. Cold night air hit her skin, raising goose bumps. The cloth continued ripping until her back was exposed to the air.

"She has not been whipped," Dedrick said. "Check her legs."

Why do they want to know if I have been whipped?

More cloth ripped. Ulrik grabbed the fabric at her hips and yanked it down. Ruxandra squirmed, trying to get her naked flesh away from his touch. He slapped her bare backside hard.

"Stay still, whore," Ulrik snapped. He pulled her stockings off.

"No marks," Edda said. "I told you. I *told* you she wasn't a student."

"Turn her around," Griffelda said, fury filling her voice. "If her front is unmarked, so help me God, I'll do it myself."

Ulrik and Harman grabbed Ruxandra's sides and turned her. The cord around her wrists cut into the skin. Pain blossomed in her flesh.

The Beast growled again, and this time the sound escaped her lips.

"Shut up, bitch!" Edda reached high and slapped Ruxandra's face. "You think you can scare us? That you can fool us?"

Do they know? The thought was terrifying. *If they know what I am, they will kill me.*

"That you could pass for one of Bathory's students?" Edda hit her again, and pain erupted in her other cheek. "My sister wrote to me. She had to use code to keep that bitch from finding out, but she told me what really happens there!"

"Her tit is scarred," said Dedrick. "And her stomach."

Ulrik grabbed Ruxandra's breast hard, his fingernails digging into the flesh as he pulled it one way, then the other. She screeched, but the sound barely made it past the gag. She twisted, but he didn't loosen his grip. The Beast howled and fought inside her. Ruxandra put all her attention to stopping it from breaking free.

"Those scars are years old." Ulrik let go of her breast. "Look how faded they are."

"Since you're not a student," Griffelda said, "you must help Elizabeth torture them."

"Beat the bitch." Edda's voice was hard. "Beat her until she reveals everything."

Ulrik spun and drove a fist into the pit of Ruxandra's stomach. The breath flew out of her. Her legs kicked against the wall. It hurt badly, and there was no way to stop it without showing what she was.

The Beast snarled and threw itself against the cage in her mind.

"Edda's sister hasn't written in a month." Ulrik walked over to the barrel. "Griffelda's sister hasn't written in two."

He reached into the barrel and came up with five long, leather straps.

The Beast screamed in Ruxandra's head.

"We are going to beat you." Ulrik's eyes glittered in the torchlight. "Front and back, as Edda's sister was beaten. Then, and *only* then, will I take the gag off your face, and you'd better tell me exactly what Elizabeth does to the girls in her gymnaesium, or we'll hurt you in ways you can't even imagine."

"Do not think we care if you live, whore," Griffelda said, her voice loud and angry. "We'll *kill* you if you do not talk."

Ruxandra barely heard the words. The Beast screamed and thrashed in her head. It wanted to fight. Ruxandra bent all her thoughts and will into holding it down.

We cannot let them see what we are, she pleaded. *We must not!*

"Me first." Edda stepped forward. "This is for Angela."

The strap whistled through the air and smashed down on Ruxandra's breast. Ruxandra and the Beast together screamed through the gag. Griffelda stepped forward and slashed at the other breast.

No! Don't! Please! You will die!

Dedrick slashed sideways with his strap, right across her belly. He swung it far harder than the girls. Pain tore through Ruxandra's body as the leather cut open the flesh on her stomach. Silver blood welled up.

Edda's eyes went wide. "What *is* that?"

Then the Beast tore through the cord around its wrists as if it were spider web.

No! Stop!

Its feet hit the ground, knees bent to pounce even as its talon-tipped hand tore the gag off its mouth.

Griffelda screamed.

The Beast screamed back, a long, angry wildcat scream that deafened the four in the alley. Edda dropped her strap. Her eyes went wide with horror. Her breath came in a short, stunned grasp. The sharp smell of urine filled the alley as she pissed herself.

Harman, at the back, turned and tried to run from the alley.

The Beast roared and jumped.

It landed on his shoulders, driving him to the ground. He screamed for only a second before the Beast's talons drove into either side of his neck. It twisted its hands, and Harman's head ripped free of its body, bouncing against the wall.

No! Stop!

Ulrik took two steps before the Beast's talons tore through his stomach. His intestines slipped from his body in a glistening pile as he fell to his knees, screaming.

Dedrick leaped forward, a knife in his hand. The Beast's first slash took his hand at the wrist. Its second ripped half his face off. When Dedrick stumbled back, the Beast ripped its talons down, opening up his clothes and his flesh from his chest to his groin.

Griffelda raised her hands to protect herself, but it was too late. The Beast's talon had already slashed open her neck. The muscles shredded, and blood fountained in the air. Her head, still attached to her spine, fell back to dangle upside down a moment before she collapsed.

The Beast advanced on Edda. She trembled and shook but could not move. The stench of her bowels releasing filled the air. Tears ran down her face. Her mouth opened into a silent plea, but no sound came out at all. The Beast sniffed at her hair, at her throat. Edda shut her eyes tight. Desperate, silent sobs shook her body.

Please don't. Please, please, please . . .

The Beast's fangs drove into her throat, and Edda stopped moving forever.

Ruxandra looked at the bloody, broken remains of the two girls and three young men. Horror made her stomach flip. She stumbled back, hand to her mouth.

Ulrik was still screaming, his legs thrashing and his heels drumming against the ground as the last of his life left him. Beyond him and the alley, she heard shouts.

"This way! It's coming from this way!"

Dozens of booted feet slammed against the cobblestones, coming closer and closer.

Ruxandra climbed the wall, her talons digging deep into the mortar between the stones, and fled into the night.

CHAPTER FOURTEEN

SOLDIERS SWARMED THE city like ants.

Ruxandra, hiding on the rooftops, could hear everything, from the cries of "Murder!" to the shouted orders from the soldiers. Her hearing was acute enough to pick up the quiet conversations of the servants, gathered at the front of the house to watch the comings and goings, repeating descriptions that changed and grew more hideous as they were passed on. The names and families of the dead were invoked and prayed for. And beneath all the surface noise, one word was whispered over and over again.

"Monster."

"No man could have done that," a guard captain said as he rode by.

"I heard it scream," one of the party guests said. "It wasn't a sound any person could make."

"There're no wild cats in town," a soldier whispered to another. "What could it have been?"

"It was captive," a servant said. "They had it tied before. Then it broke free and slaughtered them."

The wind picked up, dashing through the streets and making cloaks and dresses dance and flap as it raced through the city. Ruxandra's braids, now soaked in blood, barely moved. She jumped off the roof, landing without a sound. She slipped across the streets and to the Stallburg.

Elizabeth stood in her window, a fur cloak pulled tight around her body. Her beautiful face was twisted with fury. Ruxandra stared up at her, her throat closing in. She wanted to slip into a dark corner of the city and hide.

But she couldn't.

So she let go of the need to be unnoticed and stood, naked and bloody, in the street below Elizabeth's window.

Elizabeth saw her a moment later. She started in surprise and leaned forward. Her eyes went wide at the blood that covered Ruxandra. Then the fury came back, freezing her face. She stepped back from the window. Ruxandra swallowed hard. Then she jumped.

Elizabeth stared at her when Ruxandra landed lightly in the window. She watched her step down, waited as she closed the window behind her. Ruxandra stood in front of her, hands clasped tightly together, her eyes on the floor.

"Ruxandra." The fury from Elizabeth's face poured into the word. "What in God's name did you *do*?"

Ruxandra couldn't look up, couldn't bear to see Elizabeth's face.

"God *damn* you, girl!" Elizabeth's shout echoed in the room. "Do you know what I went through at that party?"

Ruxandra opened her mouth, searching for words, but Elizabeth didn't give her the chance to speak.

"Two hours I spent standing silently behind Lady Czobor while she spoke to everyone except me. Not once did she introduce me, not once did she acknowledge my presence! *Two hours!*" Elizabeth spun away from Ruxandra and stomped across the room. She spun back. The glow of the fire turned her eyes red.

"After that, I got to spend another hour sitting on a hard stool in Lady Czobor's chambers while she relaxed on her settee and interrogated me about my gymnaesium! She asked after the girls there as if she knew them all personally. She demanded details about their care and their discipline. Then she *dared* to show me a letter purporting to be from one of them, detailing abuses, the dog-fucking *whore!*"

Elizabeth grabbed a vase off the table and hurled it against the wall. Ruxandra flinched as it shattered.

Elizabeth turned the full force of her rage on Ruxandra. "*Then*, when I go looking for you, not only do I find you have vanished, but that five of Lady Czobor's favorites, including her *nephew* for God's sake, have been mutilated and killed. As if an animal attacked them. Or maybe a Beast!"

"It wasn't my fault!" Ruxandra cried.

"How could it not be your fault?" Elizabeth demanded. "Did someone else go insane and kill them all? Did someone else leave your clothes in the middle of the alley for investigators to find? Covered in blood, no less? What the hell were you thinking?"

"They hurt me!" Ruxandra shouted back. "They hung me up on a spike, and because *you* said I wasn't allowed to use my strength, I had to let them cut the clothes off my body!"

"You told me you could control people!"

"Not without speaking! And I could not speak because they gagged me in order to beat me without anyone hearing!"

"Then you should have controlled yourself!"

"I *was* controlling myself until the beating started. Then Dedrick hit me hard enough to cut me open, and the Beast got free, and I . . ."

The stench of their blood filled Ruxandra's nose. In her mind, she saw Edda's horrified face as she realized she was dead, heard Ulrik's screaming as his heels drummed on the ground. Her knees gave out, and she fell hard to the floor. When she could speak again, her voice shook.

"Oh God, Elizabeth, I've ruined everything."

"Yes." Elizabeth's cold, hard voice felt like a hammer, hitting her with every word. "You have. I am trying to *save* my family! I'm trying to keep Rudolph from taking everything from the Bathory line and giving it to his cronies! I am trying to save my life and yours!"

"I'm sorry!"

"You stupid girl!" Elizabeth stood over her now. She grabbed Ruxandra's arms in a grip strong enough to hurt and hauled her up to her knees. "Do you know the amount of *grief* you've caused me? The amount of *pain*?" Elizabeth's voice broke. She fell to her knees in front of Ruxandra. "I thought you were *dead,* you stupid girl!"

The change in Elizabeth's tone was so abrupt that Ruxandra could only stare.

"I thought you were dead. When they found your clothes, I thought you'd died. I thought you'd vanished from the earth and I would never see you again. Oh, my Ruxandra!"

Elizabeth wrapped her arms tight around Ruxandra's body. She kissed her hair, then her neck. She grabbed her face and kissed her hard on the lips. Ruxandra felt her body heating in response even as her mind whirled in confusion.

"You're not angry with me?"

Elizabeth leaned in and kissed Ruxandra hard. Her hands ran up her back and tangled in her hair. Ruxandra moaned as Elizabeth's tongue parted her lips. Elizabeth pushed forward until she was pressed hard against Ruxandra's naked, blood-covered skin. Ruxandra pulled back.

"Your dress," Ruxandra gasped. "I'll ruin it."

"I don't care."

Elizabeth pulled Ruxandra to her by her hair. Their lips pressed against one another, and their tongues danced in each other's mouths. Ruxandra fell into the dizzy swoon that was Elizabeth: the taste and smell of her—wild strawberries just pulled from the earth, the animal, metallic savor of her blood—and the maelstrom of power and hunger that defined her soul. Elizabeth let herself fall backward, bringing Ruxandra down on top of her. One hand stayed tight in Ruxandra's hair, the other roamed lower, caressing the skin of her back and cupping her backside.

Elizabeth's touch lit fires in Ruxandra's skin. Her back arched under Elizabeth's trailing fingers, and when the woman's hand rounded her behind, Ruxandra gasped. Her legs began to part. Elizabeth felt it and drove her own leg up, bending the knee so it split Ruxandra's thighs and pressed hard against Ruxandra's sex. The sensation of it rolled through Ruxandra like a wave. Her gasp became a cry only to be smothered by Elizabeth's mouth once more reclaiming hers.

Elizabeth's hips bucked and twisted. She rolled, and Ruxandra was beneath her. She kept a tight grip on Ruxandra's hair as she pulled her mouth away and engulfed Ruxandra's pale nipple. Ruxandra's cry went higher as the wet heat of Elizabeth's mouth enflamed her flesh. Elizabeth's knee pressed harder and began a rhythmic rubbing against Ruxandra that made her squirm and moan.

Ruxandra reached for Elizabeth, tried to caress her, but the pleasure claiming her body was too great for her to do anything but moan.

In the dark larder beneath the abbey kitchen, Ruxandra clutched Adela's hair as the girl pressed her against the wall and ground her thigh hard against Ruxandra's sex.

Elizabeth's mouth came back up and claimed Ruxandra's. Her hand squeezed a breast and then slipped down between Ruxandra's thighs. Ruxandra cried out again.

In the abbey orchard, Valeria clutched her close, their hands beneath each other's dresses, gasping their passion into each other's mouths.

"Oh God," the words came out half-panicked, half-passionate. Ruxandra clutched Elizabeth's dress. *What's happening?*

"It's all right," Adela said, her hands on Ruxandra's breasts. "The sisters are at their prayers."

"It's just the three of us," whispered Valeria in her ear.

Elizabeth released Ruxandra's hair and slid down her body.

"Try to be quiet." Valeria pointed to a picture of a woman kneeling between the thighs of another, her tongue on the other's sex. "Because I'm going to try that *on you."*

Elizabeth pulled Ruxandra's thighs wide and put her face between them.

"Oh God!"

Ruxandra grabbed Elizabeth's hair, held tight as the waves of pleasure shook her.

Neculai kissed her breasts. Adela kissed her mouth hard. Valeria licked the skin on her belly. Elizabeth shifted positions, her fingertips coming up to push against Ruxandra's sex. Neculai moved his hips forward, and she gasped, and then his pulse beat inside her.

The beautiful pale woman with the black wings knelt over her. "Did you know you were to be the sacrifice, girl? Did you come here willingly?"

Adela cried in pain as Sister Sofia dragged her by her hair from Ruxandra's cell. Ruxandra pulled Neculai tight to her, legs wrapped around his waist, gasping in rhythm with his thrusts. She struggled as her father's men spread her arms and legs wide, shackling her to the floor.

"Decide now," the fallen angel said, voice so cold, so inhumanly beautiful. "Do you want to die?"

Elizabeth's finger and tongue moved faster and harder, and Ruxandra's hips thrust up to meet them.

Adela and Valeria knelt in the snow, screaming as the nun's straps ripped into their backs. Her father's head tore free his body in a spray of blood. Her mouth was on Neculai's neck, and she wanted to drink and drink and drink.

The fallen angel's bleeding finger slipped between Ruxandra's lips, and that cold voice uttered her curse. "Soon you will be freer than you have ever dreamed."

Ruxandra screamed, long and loud, and hurled herself away from Elizabeth.

Neculai's corpse chased her through the forest, desperate with hunger.

She snapped his neck and cried and held him close.

His teeth ripped into her throat, and he sucked the silver blood from her.

Her hands moved in a blur of speed as she stabbed his chest again and again. She drove the knife into his eye, sending blood spraying.

"Die!" Ruxandra screamed at him. "Die! Die! Die! Why won't you just die?"

"Ruxandra!" Elizabeth was screaming at her. "Ruxandra! What's wrong? What's happening? *Ruxandra!*"

The visions faded like the life that gushed freely from a savaged throat, then more faintly, then stopped. Ruxandra was curled up in the corner of Elizabeth's room. Her hands pulled against her blood-soaked hair. Small keening cries escaped from between her clenched teeth. Elizabeth knelt five feet away, her face slick and shining and red with juices and blood from Ruxandra's body. Her eyes were wide, and her hands bunched up in her cloak.

"Ruxandra?" Elizabeth's voice was a whisper. "Are you back now?"

"Yes." Ruxandra let go of her own hair and sat up. The wall was cool against the skin of her back.

All of that happened. All of it.

"Are you . . ." Elizabeth licked her lips. "Are you well?"

"Yes." Ruxandra let her head fall back. Tears she didn't know she'd cried slid down her face and fell onto the bloody skin of her legs. "No. I don't know. I am . . ."

Elizabeth crawled forward, worry and confusion on her face. "You're what?"

Ruxandra closed her eyes. A deep, aching weariness filled her mind.

"Ruxandra?"

"Kade said it was the year of out Lord 1609." She didn't open her eyes. *I was born in 1468. I became this in 1476.* "I am a hundred and thirty-three years old."

She opened her eyes. Elizabeth was leaning forward, though she hadn't come closer. Her eyes were wide with expectation and hope and worry. Beyond her, on the other side of the open window, the sky was changing color.

"Ruxandra? Did you remember something?"

"Everything."

Before she could say more, Dorotyas pounded hard on the door.

"My lady!" Dorotyas called. "There are soldiers outside! They demand to see you!"

CHAPTER FIFTEEN

"THEY ARE HERE *now*?" Elizabeth's fist pounded against the floor. "God's blood!"

She rose from the floor, her hands going to her face.

"My lady?" Dorotyas called. "What shall I tell them?"

"Tell them to wait!" Elizabeth's voice cracked like a whip. She undid the ties on her dress. "If they insist on seeing us in the middle of the night, they must wait until we are properly attired."

Ruxandra knew she should get up, knew she should help Elizabeth change clothes and get cleaned up. Only her legs didn't want to work. Her mind filled with a thousand jumbled memories—of the convent, of Adela and Valeria, of her father and her mother.

Memories of what her father had done to her.

Memories of the waterfall beating down on her when she tried to kill herself the second time.

Memories of what she had done to Neculai.

Memories of a fallen angel, asking her to choose.

"Ruxandra! Help me!"

A sharp sting of pain blossomed in Ruxandra's face. Her eyes snapped up from the floor. Her hand went to the cheek where Elizabeth had slapped her.

"*Get up!*" Elizabeth's face was red with fury. She raised her hand again. "There's blood all over the floor. There's blood all over me. I need to get this dress off and clean myself and go out there, and I need your *help*, so get up or I will beat you!"

Elizabeth's hand came down, hard and fast, toward her face again.

Ruxandra shredded the front of Elizabeth's dress and chemise with a single swipe of her talons. The cloth fell back, baring Elizabeth's breasts, belly, and sex. She screamed, short and sharp, and stumbled back.

"I must go," Ruxandra said. "I have to . . ."

"Ruxandra." Panic filled the word. "You can't leave me. Not now. I need you to stay!"

Ruxandra was already out the window and had vanished from notice before she landed. By the time Elizabeth yelled for Dorotyas, Ruxandra was far away, running hard. Even as she ran, her memories threatened to overwhelm her. They sapped her strength and her will, making her legs weak. She stumbled and fell against a wall.

In her mind, she was back in the cave. The fallen angel, with her alabaster white skin and her black wings, cradled Ruxandra in arms so strong that she had felt safe, even in her desperate terror.

"Decide now," the fallen angel had said. "Do you want to die?"

She had said no, then. She was so young, so frightened. Later, when she knew what she was, she had tried to die. Now, with the sky above growing brighter and the full horror of what she had become pounding in her head—feeling a passion she didn't understand for a friend who was not, she knew, the kind of friend she'd had in Adela or Valeria—Ruxandra didn't know how she felt.

I do not know anything anymore. I must find a place to think.

The sun was nearly up when she spotted a servant girl sweeping the stairs in front of a large house. She approached her from behind, still unnoticed.

"Take me someplace safe," she commanded. *"Someplace safe and dark where no one will disturb me."*

"This way, my lady."

The girl led her through the back door of the house, down the stairs to the basement, and then down another set into the wine cellar. Ruxandra collapsed in a corner, wedged behind the wine barrels.

She closed her eyes, and the memories overwhelmed her. She couldn't get hold of them, couldn't slow them down long enough to understand all she had done, all she had become. The memories pulled her under like a whirlpool.

Somewhere, in the midst of it, she passed out.

When she opened her eyes, the day was gone, and despair gripped her tighter than that day, one hundred thirty years ago, when she drove her talons into a tree and waited for the sun to burn the life out of her.

She slipped out into the streets and walked with slow footsteps back to the Stallburg. Around her, the city buzzed with people, even as the darkness filled the streets.

I am an abomination.

She could hear every conversation around her. She knew if she reached out she would be able to sense every emotion as well. She was walking, naked, through crowds of people, yet no one saw her, no one could touch her.

I am a monster.

She had been so happy leaving the convent. She thought she would be married. Instead, she had murdered her father, murdered his soldiers, murdered an old woman, and murdered a boy who she had really, really liked. Then she turned him into a monster and watched him kill a dozen others before she managed to kill him again.

Oh, Neculai. You didn't deserve that.

None of them did.

The prisoners in Elizabeth's dungeon, the old woman and man on the road, the young nobles wanting truth about their missing sisters—all died because she existed.

Now soldiers patrolled the streets looking for her.

"I send you out instead, my child," the fallen angel had said, "to sow chaos and fear, to make humans kneel in terror and to ravage the world where I cannot."

She made me to spit in the face of God.

She remembered the look on Mother Superior's face when she asked if God cared.

I wonder what He thinks of me now?

She found the street leading to the Stallburg. Soldiers with torches and drawn swords guarded it. She slipped past them and around to the side of the palace.

I could run away again. I could go to a place where there are no people.

And become the Beast again . . .

Ruxandra remembered a thousand nights of crying herself to sleep. She remembered days that became weeks and months and seasons and years of seeing no one, speaking to no one. Some days, when she was not hungry or cold, when she had time, nothing but time to think and feel, it hurt so much she had almost gone in search of people. Only the knowledge of what she would do to them kept her away. It was a relief when she began losing herself, when her conscious mind retreated, and the Beast took over.

Then Elizabeth found her and brought her back to herself.

She made me a monster again. A murderer.

But I got to see the city and hear music and look at art, and I got to dance.

Oh, I want to dance.

The window to her room was open wide. A candle sat flickering on the windowsill. Jana stood behind it, the candle's pale light showing the fear and worry on her face. The girl wore only her chemise, and her young, thin body shivered in the cold air.

I have a friend again. A real friend.

I don't want to lose any of it.

Ruxandra jumped and landed on the sill with a puff of air that blew out the candle. Jana stepped forward and froze. She frowned at the window. She clasped her hands in front of her and swallowed hard.

"My lady?" Jana's eyes went wide. "Is it you?"

Ruxandra slipped down from the window ledge and let herself be noticed.

Jana's lower lip trembled, and tears started rolling down her face. She stumbled forward and buried her face against Ruxandra's naked, cold, bloody breasts.

"Oh, my lady." She clung tight to Ruxandra. Tears of relief slid down the girl's face, the warm wetness falling against Ruxandra's skin like blood. "Oh, thank God."

She knows, and still she cares about me. Ruxandra wrapped her arms around Jana, holding the small, warm body tight against her. She began crying, too.

I want to live.

It was afternoon when Ruxandra left her room. She wanted to face Elizabeth during the day, rather than make her wait until nightfall. The sun was still strong outside, though Jana had closed the curtains to keep it out of the bedroom. Jana bathed her and dressed her in a simple gray gown. She'd brushed Ruxandra's hair free of tangles and put it back in a long, simple braid. Ruxandra thanked her and asked her to go out and buy some flowers for the room. Jana opened the door, and Ruxandra, now unnoticed, slipped into the hallway. Two soldiers stood outside Elizabeth's apartment, wearing the livery of King Rudolph. Ruxandra stood outside the door.

"I am sure there must be another solution for this," Elizabeth said as she walked toward them down the hall.

"I have tried," a thickset man with a graying beard said, "but King Rudolph is insistent."

Gyorgy. He met us when we arrived.

"Surely there is something you can do." Elizabeth put a hand on his arm and smiled. "You have always been a good friend, Gyorgy. To me and to my family."

He sighed. "It is unfortunate, Elizabeth, but between that girl's disappearance and the rumors about your school . . . well, people do not think it wise to stand by your side."

"They are nothing but rumors," Elizabeth said in a tone of soft regret. "As for the girl, she was attacked, was she not? Then she escaped."

"Killing five of our young nobility in the process."

"I do not believe it—she was so young and no fighter. How could such a girl commit such savage attacks against five strong young people?"

"I do not understand it myself, but we won't know what happened until she is caught or surrenders. Perhaps she had aid. That matters not. She must come forward." Gyorgy took her hand off his arm and kissed it. "I must leave now, my lady. I will do my best to help you, I swear."

"Thank you, Gyorgy."

Gyorgy bowed and walked past Ruxandra on his way out. Ruxandra followed Elizabeth into the room. Elizabeth stomped over to the bed and threw herself face down on it. She screamed, long and loud, into the mattress. Then she rose, straightened her dress, and began pacing.

Ruxandra appeared and waited. Elizabeth turned and saw her.

"You!" Elizabeth stormed across the room. "Where in the name of God have been? I needed you!"

"I'm sorry," Ruxandra began, but Elizabeth did not wait to listen.

"I spent all day being interrogated by King Rudolph and his men. I have been subjected to every possible slander you can imagine. They practically accused me of arranging to have those fools killed in that alley. Me! Even though I was nowhere near them at the time."

"I'm sor—"

"Guess what they spent the most time discussing? What they continually demanded to know from me?" Elizabeth's face was turning deeper red with every passing moment. "They wanted to know who *you* were, where I found you, and where I was hiding you. They searched the apartments twice. They put guards by my door, and took away my freedom!"

"I'm sorry!" Ruxandra fell to her knees. "I'm sorry I ran away. I had to think. I needed to clear my mind, and I couldn't do it here!"

"I needed you!" Elizabeth turned her back. Her breath heaved in and out, her shoulders rising and falling in angry rhythm. "You said you could command people. You could have commanded them to leave me be. Instead, you ran off—where *were* you anyway?"

"In a wine cellar."

"In a wine cellar." Elizabeth hunched, as if ready to vomit.

"I needed time, Elizabeth. I needed to—"

"I am going to lose everything!" Elizabeth's scream echoed off the walls, driving into Ruxandra's head like a spike. Elizabeth rounded on her. "They are plotting to take my *land* and my *children*, and you run off and hide in a wine cellar!"

"I did not know what else to do!"

"You stay here, and you *trust* me!" Elizabeth's hands curved into claws. "I needed you, Ruxandra! I needed you!"

She dropped to the ground like a broken doll.

"Twenty years ago, even ten, I could have controlled them." The fury in her voice vanished beneath a wave of fear and sorrow. "I could have convinced them to do what I wanted. Even after I lost my husband, I held them in my hand. They saw my beauty, they saw my power, and they saw me as a force to be reckoned with. Now?" A noise like the dying cries of a wounded cat tore out of her throat. "I am old, Ruxandra. I am old and ugly, and I am going to lose everything!"

"No!" Ruxandra crawled forward and caught Elizabeth's arm. "You are not ugly. You are beautiful." She was, even in her fury. Her bright eyes, her rosy mouth, and whatever it was—that ineffable quality . . .

"I am useless! I cannot save anyone." Elizabeth fell silent, her breath coming in ragged gasps. She straightened slowly. Her eyes, bright with tears and hope, came up to meet Ruxandra's. "You could."

"How?"

"Turn me."

Ruxandra fell back, eyes wide, panic welling up in her. "No. I can't. I can't."

"Please!" Elizabeth grabbed at her, trying to pull her close. "Please, Ruxandra! Please help me! For my family, please!"

"I cannot turn anyone. I cannot!"

"Why not?" Elizabeth started crying. "Why not, Ruxandra?"

"Because . . ."

"Don't you love me?" She said the words in a small, plaintive voice. Her hands tightened on Ruxandra's dress. She pulled closer, kissed Ruxandra's cheek, her mouth. "Please, Ruxandra?"

"I don't . . ." Ruxandra began shaking. "I can't."

"Oh, Ruxandra"—Elizabeth's breath blew hot in her ear—"please tell me you love me. Please."

"I . . ." *Is this feeling like it was with Adela and Valeria? Like with Neculai?*

"Please." Elizabeth kissed Ruxandra's neck, sending heat through her body. She pulled at the ties on Ruxandra's shirt so it came loose and kissed her shoulder. "Please."

"I . . ."

Elizabeth pulled at the dress until it slipped down, freeing Ruxandra's beasts. She kissed one of the nipples, making Ruxandra moan.

"Please," Elizabeth said. She squeezed the other breast with her fingers, sucked on the nipple again until Ruxandra panted and cried out. "Please say it."

"I . . . I . . ." Ruxandra tried to say the words, but the pleasure of Elizabeth's touch engulfed her and robbed her of the power of speech.

"Please," Elizabeth whispered. Her hand left the breast, went down Ruxandra's leg, and came back underneath her skirt. "Please, say you love me."

"Oh God!" Ruxandra arched back as Elizabeth's hand found exactly the right place. "Oh God, I love you. I love you, Elizabeth."

"Good," Elizabeth said in her ear. "Because I love you, too."

As the last light of day faded, Elizabeth's ladies-in-waiting entered the room. If they thought or saw anything untoward at the sight of Ruxandra's naked body lying beneath Elizabeth's, they said nothing. They only woke their mistress and helped her to dress. Elizabeth leaned over Ruxandra and kissed her on the mouth.

"I shall be tired this evening." Elizabeth put her mouth to Ruxandra's ear and whispered, "And very, very tender."

Ruxandra smiled. Elizabeth rested her hands on Ruxandra's cheek and then rose again.

"I must go to court," Elizabeth said. "Gyorgy will be waiting for me. We are to meet with several of the king's advisors. Hopefully, I can convince them to support me."

"Of course you will." Ruxandra sat up. "I'm sure of it."

"If my body was still like yours, yes, I would. As it is . . ." Elizabeth shook her head. "Rest here as long as you like. I will see you tonight when I return."

Ruxandra watched Elizabeth leave, felt her heart follow the woman out the door, then fell back onto the covers. She had not felt this way since Adela decided to spend a day giving her pleasure whenever the nuns weren't looking. She had gone to bed tender that time as well.

The memory of it, and the memory of the night she had spent with Elizabeth, made her smile. This night, she decided, had been better. The occasional conflict between them was troubling, but undeniably arousing. She closed her eyes and nestled beneath the blanket. Sleep crept over her and wrapped her in its embrace.

"Here she is," Dorotyas said, startling Ruxandra awake. The woman stood alone in the room, a bulky silhouette in the darkness. "The traitorous little slut."

CHAPTER SIXTEEN

Ruxandra sat up. The daylight had faded, leaving the room dark, save for the light of the fire. "What?"

The blanket fell away, and a sneer spread across Dorotyas's face. Ruxandra pulled it back up. She did not want to be naked in front of Dorotyas. The utter disdain on the woman's face reminded her of Sister Sofia.

"I said you are a traitor and a slut." Dorotyas stepped forward, her bulk and anger making her as menacing as a bear. "You killed five of Lady Czobor's favorites, and then you ran away and left Elizabeth to take the blame. That makes you a traitor."

"That's not—"

"Then, once things were safer, you decided to return and get your cunny filled. That makes you a slut."

Dorotyas grabbed the blanket and yanked on it. Ruxandra tightened her grip, and it didn't go anywhere. Dorotyas pulled again, but Ruxandra didn't let go. Dorotyas dropped it and stepped back, her face going red.

"Oh yes, hide your shame," she said. "Hide the way you hid when Rudolph's guards came looking for you. Slut."

"Why do you keep calling me that?"

"What else do you call someone who fucks to get what they want? Do you prefer whore?"

"That is not what happened!" Ruxandra spotted her shift lying beside the bed. She snatched it up.

"Is that so? Because that's what we all heard!"

"Stop!" She pulled the shift over her head. "Why are you so angry?"

"*Because you are destroying her!*" Dorotyas roared. "Your stupidity, your selfishness, your desires are putting her in a position where they can destroy her!"

"That is not true!"

"How do you know what is true?" Dorotyas's hands balled into fists at her sides. Her body shook with rage. "You know nothing about politics or the happenings at court. My lady is going through hell all because of you!"

She drove a fist into the bedpost, making the bed shake. Ruxandra felt the Beast stir as it had when the five nobles started threatening her.

"Dorotyas," she said. "Don't do this."

"Don't do what?" Dorotyas demanded. "Make you pay attention? Make you responsible for your actions? Make you show you care about my lady?"

"I do care about Elizabeth."

"Do not call her that!" Dorotyas hit the bedpost again. The other hand went to the handle of the strap at her waist. "Do not ever call her that. You have not earned the right!"

"She told me to call her that!"

"I HAVE LOVED HER FOR THIRTY YEARS!" Dorotyas screamed. Her fist slammed into the bedpost again and again, punctuating her words. "I was there for *every* pregnancy, *every* time her husband rode off to war. I was there when he died and my lady spent six months grieving so deeply that she could not even think! I managed her lands and her castles while she recovered, and I helped her find her way back to power when everything was nearly lost. And you *dare* call her Elizabeth?"

"I . . ." Ruxandra's head spun at the words. She never thought of Dorotyas as more than a servant. "I did not know."

"Of course not, you selfish little bitch. You only think of yourself."

Is she right? Is that all I am?

"Do you know where she is right now?" Dorotyas demanded.

"With Gyorgy, talking to Rudolph's courtiers."

"With Gyorgy, being *questioned* by Rudolph's courtiers. They will poke and pry at her for as long as it takes to get her to admit to something—*anything*—that incriminates her. And she will take it because she knows that to fight invites worse criticism and questioning."

Dorotyas stepped closer and pulled the blankets into her fist. "Did you know that fucking another woman is against the law? That your presence in her bed is enough to condemn her if you two are found out?"

Oh God.

"I don't know why she cares for you." Dorotyas threw the end of the blanket at Ruxandra. "I don't know what she sees in a murderous demon like you, but I will not allow you to hurt her again. Do you understand?"

"I never meant to—"

"Meant?" The word came out on a short, sharp bark of a laugh. "You never *mean* anything because you never *think* about anything!"

Ruxandra fell silent. She straightened the shift and got out of the bed.

"Where do you think you are going?"

"I don't know." Ruxandra reached for her dress. "I shouldn't be here."

"Kill Rudolph."

Ruxandra froze. "What?"

"The king. Kill him."

Ruxandra stared at the woman, unable to comprehend what she'd said.

"You can vanish from sight whenever you want, right? So go to the Hofburg and kill Rudolph. Now."

"I can't do that!" Ruxandra snatched the dress up from the ground. "He's the king!"

"You don't even know what being the king means." Dorotyas came closer, her voice dropping. "If Rudolph were out of the way, Elizabeth could leave this place, and we could all go back to the castle."

I do not want to go back to the castle.

The thought shocked her. She'd assumed they would go back together, but now that her memories had returned, she wanted . . .

What? What do I want?

"Elizabeth would be safe at the castle. She would be able to take proper care of her lands and her people and the girls in the school."

The girls.

"She could even take care of you"—a look of disgust flitted across Dorotyas's face—"and not worry about dying for it. Are you even listening?" Dorotyas demanded. "Or do you only pay attention when someone is shoving their fingers inside you?"

"I'm thinking!"

"What is there to think about? Kill Rudolph and solve our problems."

I can kill him. Elizabeth can return to the castle.

But I don't want to return to the castle.

I also don't want to lose Elizabeth.

"If I kill him, everyone will know I did it." The words sounded weak, even to Ruxandra's ears.

"So don't drink his blood," Dorotyas said. "Push him down a flight of stairs. Smother him with a pillow. Put a knife into his spine. I don't care. Kill him so my lady will be free."

Why do I care whether he lives or dies? He is surely not an innocent and it will protect Elizabeth . . .

Why am I hesitating?

"You aren't going to do it, are you?" Dorotyas said. "You're going to let my lady lose everything because you're a coward."

"That's not—"

Dorotyas spat a glob of phlegm and saliva at Ruxandra's face. Ruxandra moved without thinking, and it spattered against the wall instead. Dorotyas watched it slide down the wall. Her face twisted in fury. Her hand squeezed the handle of the whip. Then she turned her back and walked to the door.

"Dorotyas—" Ruxandra began.

"Whore. Coward. Slut." Dorotyas pulled the door open. She turned back, and her anger radiated from her like the sun's heat. "You do not deserve her."

She stepped out and slammed the door.

Ruxandra sank to the floor and put her head in her hands.

She collected her clothes and dressed, as much to cover the shame she felt as to cover her body. Then she opened the window and made herself unnoticed before jumping down into the street.

It was a short run to the Hofburg.

Elizabeth returned to her room well past midnight. Ruxandra heard her slow, tired footsteps far down the hall. She listened as the older woman opened the door to the drawing room and heard the servants there greet her.

"I will need to rise early," Elizabeth said. "Wake me at dawn."

"Yes, my lady."

"I will undress myself."

"Yes, my lady."

Elizabeth opened the bedroom door, stepped in, and closed it behind her. She leaned back against it, her eyes closed. She looked exhausted. For a time she didn't move. Then she sighed again, straightened up, and looked at the bed. She saw it was empty and sighed again, her face falling.

"I'm here," Ruxandra said.

Elizabeth turned. "Ruxandra? Why are you in the corner on the floor? Come here."

Ruxandra touched the wall. "It felt better here."

Elizabeth frowned. "Why?"

"I used to dig dens. In the early years, when I was still me, I used to make each den as perfect as possible. I would beat at the earth until the walls felt as smooth as this one."

"Ruxandra?" Elizabeth knelt in front of her. "What is the matter?"

"I couldn't find Rudolph."

Elizabeth's head titled to the side, and confusion flitted across her face. "Why were you looking for Rudolph?"

"I was . . ." Ruxandra bit her lip. She couldn't meet Elizabeth's eyes. "I went to kill him so we could leave."

Elizabeth sank back to the floor, her eyes wide.

Ruxandra felt miserable. "He wasn't at the Hofburg. I commanded some servants to tell me his whereabouts, but they said he was out of the city."

Elizabeth drew in a long breath. "Oh, my dear."

"I failed." Ruxandra looked at the floor. "I'm so sorry."

"I failed, too," Elizabeth said. "I spent four hours trying to convince Gyorgy's friends of my intentions, and the necessity of letting my lands remain in my hands, but they would not listen. They only discussed Rudolph's desire to strengthen the kingdom, as if taking the lands of one of the largest noble estates in Hungary would do that." She rose. "Could you help me undress, Ruxandra?"

Ruxandra looked up. Elizabeth stretched out her hand. Ruxandra took it and Elizabeth pulled her to her feet.

"Though without the talons this time, please," Elizabeth teased. "I only have so many dresses."

"I am sorry about that," Ruxandra said. "I was . . ."

"In a very difficult place." Elizabeth smiled. "I was not overly fond of that dress to begin with. Now, begin with the strings at the collar."

Elizabeth guided Ruxandra through the steps of undressing her. Ruxandra pulled the pins from her hair and set it free to flow down her back. She undid the ties of her dress and slipped it off her. Then she knelt to unroll Elizabeth's long stockings.

I like being on my knees before her. It feels so right.

"I am glad you did not kill Rudolph," Elizabeth said. She put a hand on Ruxandra's shoulder. "He has no love for me and covets my land, but he keeps the nobles from organizing against me."

"Why do they want to?" Ruxandra pulled the first stocking off and set it aside. She ran her hands up Elizabeth's leg to the top of the other stocking. "Is it because of the girls?"

"The girls?" Wariness crept into Elizabeth's voice. "Why would it be about them?"

"The five nobles I killed . . ." Ruxandra swallowed hard to suppress a shudder. "One of the girls said she had not heard from her sister in two months, that her last letter said she was being tortured."

"Tortured?" Elizabeth sounded appalled. "The girls at my school are Blood Royal, not peasants, and I treat them as such. The discipline is strict, yes, but no one is *tortured*. No one is punished without reason, and those punishments make them stronger and more disciplined."

"I see." Ruxandra remembered the fear and pain on the face of the girls at the school. She remembered also, how Sister Sofia used to beat Adela and Valeria and her. *What do they mean, then, by torture? Is it what Elizabeth does to her peasants?* She rolled down the other stocking. "It is what she said."

"It is nonsense." Elizabeth pulled off her chemise and stood naked in front of Ruxandra. "It is a pretext for action against me. Nothing more."

They looked so scared. The thought came in unbidden, unwanted, and with it the memory of the fear and fierce concentration in the girls' thin, pinched faces.

"They will say anything to destroy me, Ruxandra." Elizabeth let Ruxandra pull off the other stocking and stepped away. "Anything to make me surrender my lands and power."

"I'm sorry."

"I'm tired."

It was a statement, not a complaint, and Elizabeth's tone made Ruxandra look up. In the light of the fire, the lines in Elizabeth's face appeared to deepen. Her back was bent, her shoulders slumped, like a woman twenty years her senior.

"If only I could let it all go," Elizabeth said. "But I cannot. Not as things stand now. If I could secure guarantees from the nobles, I would let my sons inherit and leave this all behind."

The thought of leaving made Ruxandra's heart leap.

"But they won't provide any guarantees." Elizabeth turned away from the fireplace and walked to the bed. "I have no power here anymore, Ruxandra. I have done my best, but I have so little energy left."

"I want to leave, too," Ruxandra said. "I want to go far from here."

Elizabeth held out her hand. "Come to bed, Ruxandra."

Ruxandra wanted to. She yearned to wrap herself in Elizabeth's warmth. "Won't you be in trouble if they find me in your bed?"

Elizabeth dropped her hand. "If they found us fornicating, yes. How did you know that?"

"Dorotyas told me," Ruxandra said. "I should leave, then."

"No." Elizabeth stepped forward. "Please. I don't want to be alone tonight."

"But—"

"Pass me my chemise," Elizabeth said. "You wear yours, and no one shall find fault with it."

Relief spilled through Ruxandra. She gave Elizabeth her chemise and slipped out of her dress. They climbed into the bed together, and Elizabeth pulled Ruxandra's head to her breast.

"There, my dear," Elizabeth said. "This is better. Isn't it?"

"Yes." Ruxandra molded her body to Elizabeth's. "It is."

Elizabeth ran her fingers through Ruxandra's hair. "So red."

Ruxandra smiled. "Sister Sofia used to say it was a sure sign the devil lived in me."

"Sister Sofia?"

"One of the nuns when I lived at the convent. She said that if I didn't change my ways, the devil would take me."

She was right.

Elizabeth chuckled. "I imagine she did."

She let her fingers slip through Ruxandra's hair again. Ruxandra watched the flames dancing in the fireplace.

"I would leave," Elizabeth said, "if I were you."

Ruxandra looked at Elizabeth's face, saw the emotions playing. "Do you want me to?"

"No." Elizabeth's hand went under Ruxandra's chin, cupping her face. "Lord no, Ruxandra. It is only that things are so dangerous here for you now."

"I see." Ruxandra put her head back against Elizabeth's breast. The sound of the woman's breath, of her heartbeat and the blood flowing through her veins, was warm and comforting.

This blood whose scent is so intoxicating but not like food. I don't want to taste it, not even a little. I want . . .

"I don't want to be alone."

"So stay, tonight. Stay with me until morning."

Ruxandra closed her eyes and let Elizabeth's caresses take her to sleep. She woke when Elizabeth slipped out of bed at dawn. Ruxandra sat up, but Elizabeth gently pushed her back.

"Sleep, my dear. Be here when I return."

Ruxandra closed her eyes and let sleep take her again.

Ruxandra's head snapped up off the pillow. She was wide-awake, anxious, and angry and had no idea why.

Then she heard the *crack* of a strap against flesh and heard Jana's muffled scream.

She was out of the bed and out of the room before the scream faded. She raced down the hall, not caring who saw her, not caring of anything except that Jana was in pain. She tore through the Stallburg and smashed the door open with her shoulder, shattering the lock and sending it flying as the strap *cracked* down again.

The curtains had been pulled back, the shutters flung wide, making the room painfully bright with sunlight. Jana was tied to the bedpost, her arms stretched high above her head, only her toes touching the ground. She was naked, save for a thick of cloth jammed between her teeth like a horse's bridle and tied tight on her head. Blood flowed down her back from four wide, fresh cuts. Dorotyas, behind her, raised the strap high for another blow.

CHAPTER SEVENTEEN

"G*ET AWAY FROM her!*" Ruxandra screamed.

Dorotyas's strap came down again, slashing across Jana's backside and opening the flesh. Blood spattered and Jana's back arched as she screamed.

Ruxandra charged.

The Beast screamed its terror of the sunlight. It tried to take control but Ruxandra's fury, even greater than its own, drove it back. She took two steps into the room and leaped.

Her talons cut through the rope holding Jana to the post. Her arm wrapped around the girl and pulled her from the bed. Together, they flew into a shadowed corner of the room.

But not before the sunlight lit Ruxandra's hair on fire and burned her flesh.

She howled in agony, the Beast howling with her, but held Jana tight. She let go the moment she hit the floor and beat at her head with her hands until the flames died. Blisters opened and split over the entire length of her back and legs. The pain was excruciating.

In the midst of it, the tip of Dorotyas's strap came down on the open flesh of her back.

If the sunlight burned like fire, the strap on the raw flesh of her back was like lightning. Ruxandra screamed and spun, her talons shredding the strap as Dorotyas pulled it back. She charged, talons out and fangs bared, ready to kill the woman. Dorotyas backed up, putting more sunlight between them.

The Beast screamed and fought her with every step. If she allowed the sunlight to touch her again, it would gain control. So she stayed in the shadows, screaming like an angry wild cat. "You don't touch her!" Ruxandra brought her talons up. "She is mine, you hear? Mine!"

"Then stop me." Contempt oozed from Dorotyas words. "Or are you too scared?"

"I will kill you!"

"You were supposed to kill Rudolph!" Dorotyas threw the remains of the strap at Ruxandra. "You were supposed to help our lady out of this mess, and instead, you spent the night fucking her!"

"I did not!" Ruxandra's skin began growing back, the pain of it even worse than the burn. It threatened to drive her to the floor, but she refused to fall. She would not show weakness in front of Dorotyas. Not this time.

"This morning, while you were in Elizabeth's bed, Rudolph's men came to tell us they need the rooms. We have until noon to pack, after which we will be escorted, *under guard*, to our new accommodations. *Because of you!*"

"What?"

"Elizabeth says we must obey them. She said nothing about rescuing you!" Dorotyas stomped to the door. "You sit there, bitch, until the sun takes you or Rudolph's men find you. Then, perhaps, I can get my lady safely home!"

She walked out, leaving the door open. Ruxandra fell, her back twisting and arching, as the pain from the healing skin worsened.

"My lady?" Jana's whisper trembled with tears. Ruxandra felt the girl's hand on her shoulder. "My lady, how badly are you hurt?"

The Beast caught her arm.

DRINK!

No!

Ruxandra regained control before the Beast sank her teeth into Jana's throat. She made her body hold the girl at arm's length as she forced the Beast back into its cage. It fought hard, but Ruxandra used her rage at Dorotyas to turn her will into an unstoppable force. She made her hands loosen their grip, and Jana dropped to the floor beside her.

"I'm sorry," Ruxandra whispered through gritted teeth. "I am so sorry. It's all my fault."

"No." Jana shook her head, tears flowing down her face. "It's mine. I was sleeping in the bed when you came in, and Dorotyas saw me. She said I needed to be put in my place."

"She wanted to show me that she could hurt me." Ruxandra's talons retreated into her hands. "That she has power over me."

"Your back, it's . . ." Jana stood slowly, her legs shaking. "You stay there. I'll fetch some clothes."

"You're bleeding," Ruxandra reached for her, but the movement hurt. "You should rest."

"You are hurt worse." Jana went to the trunk at the foot of the bed. "I'll get us clothes, money, and a cloak to cover you. We must leave before Rudolph's men come."

Ruxandra could only watch as the girl limped around the room, finding chemises and dresses and stockings and shoes and cloaks. She piled them up in the corner beside Ruxandra.

"I cannot dress yet," Ruxandra said, imagining how much the touch of those clothes on her open flesh would hurt. "Come here. We'll bandage your back first."

Jana nodded. She brought over the water basin, towel, and pitcher. She filled the basin and dipped the towel in. She held out the towel to Ruxandra.

"What you need to do is—"

"I know." Ruxandra took the towel and knelt beside Jana. "I did this for Adela, after she got caught with one of the farmer's men. Lie down."

"Adela?" Jana frowned as she lay on her stomach. "The girl you talked about—" Jana flinched.

"Sorry. It's going to hurt." Ruxandra dipped the cloth in the water again, leaking red into the clear white basin. "Adela was my friend from the convent."

Jana twisted to look at her. "You remembered?"

"Yes." Ruxandra pushed the girl back down and dabbed again at the ripped flesh. "I remember everything."

"Then you can go back!" Jana sounded excited, despite her pain. "You can go back and see them."

Ruxandra smiled at Jana's excitement but shook her head. "They're all dead now."

"Oh." Jana fell silent, save for the occasional hissed breath as Ruxandra cleaned her back. The water in the basin grew darker red with each dip of the cloth, but the bleeding grew less.

"Want to know what she was caught doing?"

"Was she"—the back of Jana's neck flushed red—"doing *it* with the farmer's man?"

"With her mouth, yes."

"With her . . ." Jana's flush turned bright red. Her hands went over her mouth. "Oh my God!"

"It's not the only thing she was caught for," Ruxandra said. "Once, her fiancé snuck into her room . . ."

The stories did their work, keeping Jana distracted from the worst of the pain as Ruxandra cleaned her back, and keeping Ruxandra distracted from the worst of her own pain as her skin knit together. She healed so fast now.

Because I drink human blood.

The thought stirred her hunger enough that she found herself staring at the bloody wounds on Jana's back. Once or twice the Beast tried to reach for Jana's neck. Each time Ruxandra drove it back into the darkness of her mind.

I will not hurt Jana. I am not like Dorotyas, who would hurt a young girl to show her power.

She remembered the people she'd killed in the dungeon. She had not known why they were imprisoned, had not cared. She'd murdered them and drank them dry.

Because I needed to survive. I didn't hurt them for pleasure like Dorotyas.

Like Elizabeth?

She remembered the haunted faces of the girls in the castle. Remembered what Edda and Griffelda had said about Edda's sister before they beat her and she had killed them.

No! Elizabeth would not do that. She told me. She doesn't torture for fun.

Doesn't she?

As she gently cleaned Jana's wounds, she listened to the chaos in Elizabeth's rooms. The maids scurried back and forth, packing as fast as they could. Dorotyas barked orders and occasionally lashed out with her hand, making the women cry out.

Ruxandra's rage flamed high again.

I will kill her. I will come after her tonight and drain her dry.

Elizabeth would not like it. She did not want to hurt Elizabeth, but she would not let Dorotyas hurt Jana again. She'd kill her first.

Elizabeth needs her.

Ruxandra growled. She didn't know what to do about Dorotyas or what do to about Rudolph.

Jana stopped bleeding, eventually. Ruxandra's skin finished knitting together. It was so red it practically glowed, and still stung when she moved, but it had healed.

Together they helped each other pull chemises and dresses over their injured skin. When they were ready, Jana wrapped the cloak around Ruxandra's shoulders and gave her the money.

"There," Jana said. "Now we can go."

Ruxandra didn't move. *Where do I go?*

I must stay with Elizabeth.

But if Jana stays, Dorotyas will come after her again.

Damn her.

"Everyone out!" a loud male voice called. "Out, now!"

"We're not done yet!" Dorotyas protested. "We were given until noon!"

"The king changed his mind. You're leaving now. All of you. Men!"

Heavy boots tromped and armor clanked as the soldiers came into the apartment.

Anything I carry goes unnoticed when I want it to.

Is it the same when I touch someone?

Ruxandra grabbed Jana's hand. "Listen to me. We're going to walk through the halls. No one will see us, and no one will hear us. All we need do is keep walking and not speak. Understand?"

Jana looked to the door, then back, eyes wide with fear and uncertainty. She swallowed hard but nodded. "Yes, my lady."

Ruxandra willed them unnoticed and led Jana through the halls.

The soldiers, the ladies in waiting, and the servants of the castle all looked away when they walked by. Not one saw them. Ruxandra looked at Jana. The girl was smiling, and her eyes sparkled with amazement. Ruxandra led her through the hallways to the door.

She froze, staring at the sunlight beyond.

Jana looked around before whispering, "There are shadows on the other side of the street."

Ruxandra nodded. Jana stepped outside into the sun. She looked both ways. "There is no one here. So, please, follow!"

She let go of Ruxandra's hand and dashed across the street. Ruxandra gritted her teeth and ran after.

The skin on her back burned as the sunlight hit her cloak. She cried out in pain and put on a burst of speed. She reached the shadows before Jana. She hugged the wall, breathing hard. Even in shadow she felt the heat of the sunlight, digging into her flesh. She had even forgotten to stay unnoticed in her pain. Jana caught up to her and grabbed her hand again.

"I need to get out of here," Ruxandra said. "I need a place in the dark."

"We'll find you something," Jana promised. She took Ruxandra's hand again. "There must be a cellar nearby."

Together they maneuvered through the streets, staying in the shadows wherever possible. The light hurt Ruxandra's eyes so much she could only look at the ground. Jana guided them forward, and Ruxandra concentrated on keeping them unseen.

"Here." Jana pushed open a door. "It's a tavern. They'll have a cellar."

It took two commands and a short flight of stairs before darkness enveloped them. Ruxandra heaved a sigh of relief and took off the cloak.

"Thank you." Ruxandra spread the cloak on the ground and sat on it. She held out her arms for Jana. The girl sat beside her as best she could, her weight on her hip to keep the cut on her backside off the floor.

"We are safe, now," Jana said. "Tonight we can go back to Elizabeth."

Go back . . .

If I don't kill Dorotyas, she will hurt Jana again.

But Elizabeth needs Dorotyas.

"Jana . . ." Ruxandra hesitated. She began again. "If you weren't my servant, what would you be?"

"I *am* your servant."

"Anything," Ruxandra said. "Anything in the world. If you could do it, what would you do?"

"I don't know." Jana turned to lie on her stomach. "I should like to have money. And a family. Mine died. That's how I came to be in Lady Bathory's service. But I am your servant now, so I am happy."

Ruxandra lay back and closed her eyes. "Take some of the money and buy yourself lunch upstairs. I'm going to sleep."

"Yes, my lady."

Jana slipped up the steps. Ruxandra watched her go and then closed her eyes.

Family and money.

I can get the second, easily, I think. But the first?

When night came, Ruxandra led Jana to an inn and got them a room. She tucked Jana into the bed and told her to sleep. Then she headed out into the streets.

It took little time to find the house in whose cellar she had stayed. She slipped inside, found the servant girl in the kitchen, made herself noticeable, and stepped up behind her. The girl started in surprise and opened her mouth to cry out.

"*Hush,*" Ruxandra commanded. "*Tell me about your mistress.*"

Two hours later, Ruxandra shook Jana's shoulder until the girl woke, and told her to dress. She led her through the streets to the house. The servant girl stood waiting at the front door, and escorted them in to the parlor.

A short, plump middle-aged woman in a dark green robe sat waiting for them. She rose when they entered.

"This is the girl?" she asked.

"It is," Ruxandra said. "Jana. My sister."

"Sister?" Jana's eyes went wide. "My—"

"Hush, sister," Ruxandra said. "This is Madame Kovacs. She is willing to take care of you for the next few days."

"What?" Panic rose in Jana's voice. "I cannot leave you! I must stay with you!"

"You must heal," Ruxandra said. "So you will stay here. I insist."

"I want to stay with you," Jana protested.

"You will die, Jana!" The words came out harsher than she meant, and Jana huddled back against the settee. "If Dorotyas doesn't kill you, then Elizabeth . . ." Ruxandra bit her lip. Jana fell silent and looked at the floor.

"Elizabeth," Madame Kovacs repeated. "Lady Bathory?"

"Yes."

"I see." Madame Kovacs sat back in her chair. She pursed her lips and then frowned. "I have heard much unsavory gossip about the countess from the other merchant families. It was not all unfounded, then?"

Ruxandra looked away and didn't answer.

"I see." Madame Kovacs pursed her lips again. "Why did you come to me at this hour of the night?"

"There was no other time, Madame Kovacs," Ruxandra said. "I chose you because your servants say you are a decent woman, whose own daughters are grown and married. They say you are strong and successful and that you run a polite, firm household where servants are not beaten."

"I see." Madame Kovacs looked Jana up and down. "Show me your back, girl."

Jana bit her lip.

"Do it," Ruxandra said. "Please."

Jana turned her back and undid the laces of her dress. She let it slip down, and Madame Kovacs gasped.

"Laryssa," she said to the servant girl. "Take her upstairs at once to the blue bedroom. Wake Mrs. Egger and tell her you need her help, by my orders. I want those wounds cleaned and dressed immediately."

"Yes, ma'am."

"I don't . . ." Jana's eyes filled with tears. "I don't want to go, my lady."

"Go," Ruxandra said. "They will take care of you, and I will be back tomorrow night."

"Earlier in the evening, if you please," Madame Kovacs said. "I am not so young that I can stay up at all hours anymore."

"I will do my best," Ruxandra said. She turned to Jana and held the girl close, feeling her pulse racing. "It will all be right, Jana. Now go with Laryssa, and I will see you again tomorrow. I promise."

Jana cried, but she went. Ruxandra thanked Madame Kovacs and left.

Her hunger was growing, but she couldn't eat yet.

A quick walk back to the Stallburg and a pair of commands got her directions to Elizabeth's new accommodations. It took a bit longer to get across the city, but she found the place easily enough. Lights shone in all the windows, despite the late hour. Men came and went from the front door. In the windows above, Ruxandra saw girls, waving to the men on their way in.

King Rudolph sent Countess Bathory to a brothel.

She will be furious.

Ruxandra sniffed at the air. She sorted through a hundred scents until she found the one she wanted. She followed it around to a stable behind the building. Light from a lantern shone through the open door.

Ruxandra slipped inside and stopped in shock.

Dorotyas hung, naked from a rope around her wrists thrown over the beam above. She swayed gently, and moaned in pain. A dozen oozing cuts crisscrossed her back.

"Oh, thank God." Elizabeth rose from a stool near one of the stables. Dorotyas' strap, dripping blood, hung from her hand. "I thought you'd never come."

"What . . ." Ruxandra stared at Dorotyas. "Why did you . . ."

"Is it enough?" Elizabeth's sounded fragile, as if any harsh word or touch would break her. "I want it to be enough."

"Enough for what?" Ruxandra asked.

"Enough that you won't leave me." Tears filled Elizabeth's eyes. "Please, Ruxandra, don't leave me."

"I won't," Ruxandra stared at Dorotyas, remembered how much Elizabeth depended on the woman. For Elizabeth to beat her like that… "I wouldn't."

"Oh." Elizabeth wavered on her feet. "Good."

Her eyes rolled up in her head, and Ruxandra caught her before she hit the stable floor.

CHAPTER EIGHTEEN

"HELP!" RUXANDRA SHOUTED. "Someone help!"

"No," Elizabeth whispered. "Ruxandra, no."

"Elizabeth!" Ruxandra sank to the ground, cradling Elizabeth in her arms.

"I'm sorry," Elizabeth whispered. "I am . . . so very tired."

"Let me get you inside."

"No." Elizabeth sat up. "You cannot let anyone see you. Not here."

"But—"

"No arguing." Elizabeth looked at Dorotyas. "I found out we were to be moved while I was meeting with Gyorgy. Rudolph's men took me away and escorted me here. When Jana was not here, and you were nowhere to be found, I confronted Dorotyas and . . ." She shook her head. "Help me up. I should prepare for morning. I must keep going. I must protect my lands and my family."

She tried to rise, but her legs shook. She sat back down on the dirt floor of the stable. Ruxandra held her close.

Elizabeth needs to get away from this life. These conflicts, all the danger of the court. She needs to get away from Dorotyas. Then she'll be better.

"You never tire, do you, Ruxandra?" Elizabeth reached up and caressed her face. "But then, you have no responsibilities, do you? You are free to go whenever you like, wherever you like." Tears formed in the corners of Elizabeth's eyes. "Oh, how I wish I was like you."

"If you were"—the words slipped out before Ruxandra could stop herself—"would we travel?"

Elizabeth blinked in surprise. Then she smiled. "It would be wonderful to travel. I have never seen Venice or Rome. I have ruled, and that is all."

She tried to stand again. Ruxandra lifted her and brought her to her feet. Elizabeth wobbled a moment and then found her footing. Her vulnerability slipped away, hidden beneath a layer of polished nobility that returned the moment she straightened her back.

"But I will not travel. Instead, I will go to Gyorgy again, and with his help, make an arrangement so King Rudolph will allow my children to inherit my land. Then perhaps I may be allowed to go home and live out what life I have left at Castle Csejte."

But I do not want to go back there.

Hunger, sharper and more demanding than before, panged in Ruxandra's belly. She looked back at Dorotyas. The smell of the woman's blood caused her mouth to water.

That *would take care of half my problems.*

"No!" Elizabeth said sharply. "Not her. Take one of the girls if you need to, but not Dorotyas. I need her."

Ruxandra's eyes never left Dorotyas's bloody back. "Why is she so important?"

"She is my seneschal, the one who runs Castle Csejte and the lands around it. She helps me run the gymnaesium."

"Does she punish the girls like she punished Jana?"

"Ruxandra, please," Elizabeth put a hand on her arm. "This is a whorehouse. There are thirty women here who no one would ever miss."

Just what Dorotyas would think. Ruxandra shook her head. "No."

"Why ever not?"

Because it is wrong. Ruxandra didn't say it, though. Instead, she looked at the whorehouse. "Why did the king send you here?"

"Pardon?"

"I know it was meant as an insult," Ruxandra said. "A way of showing his disdain for you and to put you in your place, but why here? Why this place?"

Elizabeth's eyebrows rose. "I did not think you would understand such politics."

"The nuns taught us a great deal about them," Ruxandra said. "Mostly as it related to setting a formal table and ensuring we treated all our guests according to their status, but it is the same thing, really."

"It is. And to answer your question, I do not know why he picked this place."

Ruxandra nodded. "I'm going hunting."

"As you wish." Then she asked, "Where is the girl?"

She doesn't even know her name. "Safe. I'll return before dawn."

A man's voice shouted a command, and all around them the streets became alive with noise. Dozens of horses' hooves hit the ground. A hundred boots marched in time. From the front of the whorehouse came shouts of surprise and voices raised in anger.

"Ruxandra!" Elizabeth snapped out the word. "Hide!"

Ruxandra went unnoticed at once.

Elizabeth didn't wait to see it. She went to the front of the house. Ruxandra watched her go and then ran to the back. Behind the stable and on either side of the yard, a line of houses, side by side, blocked any exit.

It's a cul-de-sac. There's no way out.

She ran to the front. Elizabeth was standing before the brothel, facing down a knight astride a tall, black horse.

"I do not know what you are saying," Elizabeth said. "The girl is not here. I haven't seen her since that night."

"She was seen," the knight said, "in your company."

"She is not here," Elizabeth insisted. "You are welcome to search for yourself."

"No."

"Then how should I assure you that—"

"We do not require assurances," the knight said. "We require the girl. You will bring her to us, or you will remain here." The knight took a letter from his belt and threw it on the ground. "Read it."

Ruxandra felt her temper rising. Inside, the Beast sensed her rage.

FIGHT.

No. She slipped up beside the knight. *There are too many of them.*

"*The girl is not here,*" Ruxandra commanded in a whisper. "*Tell Rudolph she has fled. Go now!*"

The knight turned his horse, nearly hitting Ruxandra. She jumped out of the way and let him go by. Elizabeth didn't move until he rode through the ranks of soldiers and headed off into the night. Only then did she reach down, pick up the letter, and walk back inside.

Ruxandra wanted to follow, but the hunger inside her was growing sharper. Instead, she walked away from the brothel toward the city. She went to the areas the gallants had said to avoid, made herself noticeable, and walked through the streets.

She saw the street whores, some waiting on corners, others in the alleys, plying their trade on their knees or against the walls. She ignored them, though the Beast was more than willing to take them. A group of young men, carrying torches and laughing, passed by. She didn't want them, either.

What do I want? The wolves she ran with killed for two reasons—hunger and threat. *Those are the only reasons I kill.*

She remembered the old lady in the woods, how much she hurt, and all her pain and despair.

Wolves cut out the sick and the weak from the herd.

Certainly there wasn't any shortage of dying people around her. While nothing would justify the killing, she could at least make it so she did not take anyone who wasn't dying already. Or anyone who wasn't a threat.

She smelled him before he spoke, sweat and dirt and well-oiled metal.

"What have we here?" the bravo said behind her. "A sweet young thing, all alone in the streets."

Ruxandra turned, but didn't say anything. He was short, but his muscles were wiry and strong. His black hair was slick with grease, his brown eyes narrowed. He reminded her of a ferret. He put one hand on the grip of the sword at his waist.

"Why is a girl like you is in this place at night?" He swaggered forward. "Let me guess: you're running away from your master, or running toward your lover. Either way, you would be in a great deal of trouble, wouldn't you?"

Ruxandra said nothing.

"Imagine what would happen if I dragged you back." He stepped closer. She smelled his arousal now, as well as the beer and onions he'd had for dinner. "You're in for flogging, I expect, or turned out without a position. We wouldn't want that, would we?"

Still Ruxandra said nothing.

"Defiant?" He grabbed her arm and pulled her toward one of the alleys. "Do you know what happens to defiant girls?"

He shoved her into a dead-end alley and pulled out his knife.

"Face that wall," he said, "and raise up that skirt for me, or I'll cut your pretty face up."

Ruxandra retreated farther into the alley. The man grinned at her, showing his puny human teeth.

"You think you can run?" He followed her, the knife weaving back and forth. "I'll fuck you front and back so hard you won't sit for a week." One hand drifted toward his crotch.

Ruxandra smiled back at him. "Try."

His face went red, and the knife came up. "You whore."

She left his corpse in the alley and walked back to the brothel. The place had gone quiet, the last of the customers gone. Ruxandra slipped in, unnoticeable, and sniffed her way through the building until she found Elizabeth's room.

Elizabeth dozed in a hard chair by her window, the letter in her lap. Ruxandra slipped up beside her and picked it up. She read it through, her eyes growing wider and her fury growing more with every word. The Beast, sleeping inside her, roused and growled.

"A whore," Elizabeth said, having awoken, startling Ruxandra. "I am one of his most powerful nobles, and if I do not turn you, and half of my lands, over to him, he will keep me in this wretched place, with no access to my estates, no access to my fortune, no access to my rents. He would rather see me as a whore than a noble."

"I could stop him," Ruxandra said. "I could find him and tell him to—"

"I am weary, Ruxandra." The exhaustion in Elizabeth's voice stopped Ruxandra's words. "So very weary."

"You need sleep." Ruxandra took Elizabeth's hand. "Come, rest."

"I am not tired, Ruxandra. Weary." Elizabeth stood and leaned out the window. "I hide my age well, but I am old. I have been doing this for a very long time. I have spent thirty years ruling my people, fighting wars, and protecting my family. My sons are old enough to reign in my place. If Rudolph lets me turn everything over to them . . ." She laughed, short and bitter. "Of course he will let me. He will be thrilled to deal with men instead of with me. Not that I will be able to travel, anyway. I am an old woman."

"If you were not..." Ruxandra trembled, felt her hands shake. She swallowed hard. "If you were no longer old, would you go with me?"

Elizabeth turned away from the window. Her eyes found Ruxandra's and gazed deep into them. "Yes. If I were not old, I would travel. And if you would have me travel with you, it would be everything I could hope for."

Ruxandra squeezed her hands back. Warmth spread through her entire body. *Travel. Music. Dancing. Love.* There was worry at the edges of her thoughts, a faint doubt, but she ignored it. She leaned in and kissed Elizabeth on the mouth. "I am so glad."

"It is almost morning," Elizabeth whispered. She let go of Ruxandra's hands and closed the window and curtains. "Let us go to bed."

A horn, loud and brassy, pulled Ruxandra and Elizabeth awake. Elizabeth rose first, her naked body pale in the dim light of the room. Ruxandra stayed in the bed, watching the woman put on her chemise and robe.

One of Elizabeth's ladies-in-waiting knocked. "My lady, a messenger from Rudolph has arrived. He demands that you appear at once."

"Demands?" Elizabeth repeated.

"His words, my lady, not mine."

"I will be down presently." Elizabeth turned to Ruxandra. "Be unseen, my love. Can you watch?"

"As long as I am out of the sun, yes." Ruxandra rose and pulled on her chemise and cloak.

"Thank you, my love."

Ruxandra found a shadowy room near a front corner. The bed was large and mussed and smelled of sex and a dozen different men. Three prostitutes lay sleeping in it. None of them heard Ruxandra step in. None saw her open the shutter enough to look out.

In short order, Elizabeth appeared. She wore a rich red velvet cloak over her robe that made her gleam like a rose in the morning light.

"What is it," Elizabeth said, her voice cold and haughty, "that is so urgent that it requires you to forgo all courtesy when asking for my presence?"

The messenger took out a burlap bag dripping with blood from under his cloak. He reached inside, pulled out a human head, and tossed it at Elizabeth's feet.

Elizabeth's expression didn't change. "Is this supposed to impress me?"

"This is the man you sent back to us," the messenger said. "The one who said Ruxandra was not in the building. As several of our spies saw her, he was found guilty of conspiracy against the king and was executed." Ruxandra felt a pang of regret, but stifled it.

It is not my fault the king did not believe his own man.

The messenger, a young man with a lantern jaw and pale eyes, leaned forward on his horse, his mouth tight. "Hand the girl over today, or His Majesty will find it necessary to further restrict your movements."

"I find that rather difficult to believe," Elizabeth said coldly, "as it seems my movements are already as restricted as they could be."

"His Majesty wished me to assure you otherwise."

The messenger turned and rode back through the waiting ranks of soldiers. Elizabeth was on her way inside before the man was gone. Ruxandra went to Elizabeth's room and waited.

When Elizabeth came in, she looked even more tired than before. Ruxandra reached for her, held her, and led her back to the bed. She laid Elizabeth down and pulled the blankets over her.

"Ruxandra," Elizabeth spoke softly. "You should go."

"No." Ruxandra knelt beside the bed. "Let me stay with you."

Elizabeth shook her head. "There are spies watching for you. You must remain unseen and silent. Go down to the cellar. Hide there until night. Once I am rested, I will think of what to do next."

Ruxandra kissed Elizabeth's forehead and pulled the blankets over her.

She slipped unnoticed down the stairs, found the cellar, and found a place to lie down. She lay there, not sleeping, as the hours of the day crawled past.

By noon, she had made up her mind.

At nightfall, Ruxandra left the basement and went to Elizabeth's room.

Elizabeth was sitting in her chair, looking out the window. She didn't get up when Ruxandra came in but smiled at her, a smile of surpassing sweetness. It made Ruxandra's knees weak. *What is it about this woman?*

"Hello, my dear," Elizabeth said. "How are you?"

Ruxandra's mouth went dry. Butterflies danced so hard in her stomach she thought she might start shaking. *She is beautiful, but so are many women. She has helped me, but I know she is not kind...*

"Ruxandra?" Worry filled Elizabeth's voice. "What is the matter?"

"Would you go with me"—the words tumbled out—"if I made it so we could leave tonight?"

"What?" Elizabeth shook her head. "We can't leave tonight."

"If I make it so we can leave," Ruxandra repeated, the words coming out slow and measured, "would you come with me?"

Elizabeth's head went to one side, her mouth falling half-open. She stared at her. "I do not understand."

"You will crave blood," Ruxandra said. "I did. I killed five men—my father and four of his captains. So we'll need blood. I think—"

"Ruxandra?" Understanding crept across Elizabeth's face, like dawn rising through the clouds.

"The soldiers," Ruxandra said. "I will fight them, and you'll drink them. That will get us through."

"Ruxandra . . ."

"Then we'll run and leave the city. I'll teach you how to hunt and how to find shelter. Then we'll travel. We will go anywhere we want."

"Rome," Elizabeth said. "I have always wanted to see Rome."

Joy filled Ruxandra. A smile spread over her face.

"Rome," she said. "That's a wonderful start."

Elizabeth swallowed hard. She looked both eager and terrified. "What should I do?"

"You must drink my blood." Ruxandra held out her wrist. "Bite."

Elizabeth took a step forward. Then another. On the third step, she was close enough and took Ruxandra's arm in her hands. She looked at the pure white skin of the wrist, at the barely visible veins.

"My love," Elizabeth whispered. She kissed Ruxandra's wrist. "My beautiful love."

For a moment, Ruxandra's memory flashed back to the moment the dead thing that had been Neculai sank his fangs into her neck, tearing through the flesh to get at her blood. Then she remembered what had happened to him.

"It will hurt," Ruxandra said.

Elizabeth raised her eyes. "I will try not to hurt you too much."

"Not me," Ruxandra said. "You."

Elizabeth nodded. "I understand."

And she sank her teeth hard into Ruxandra's wrist.

CHAPTER NINETEEN

THE PAIN WAS NOTHING compared to when Neculai had torn into her throat. She felt Elizabeth's lips press hard against the open flesh on her wrist. Then the blood started flowing from her.

Elizabeth suckled hard, nursing on the blood like a starving infant at the breast. Ruxandra had thought it would hurt. Instead, she felt pleasure so intense that it made her knees buckle. Her body shook with it, longer and more intense than any climaxes from her lovers.

Elizabeth fell backward, screaming.

Her back arched so far, it looked ready to snap. Her eyes went wide, the pupils dashing back and forth as if following some horror only Elizabeth could see. Her mouth stretched wider and wider until the skin at either side of her lips tore open. No blood flowed from them. Her hands clenched and unclenched, the nails tearing holes in the palms. Her neck twisted so hard and fast that something cracked.

Elizabeth let out one more long scream filled with pain and despair so great it brought tears to Ruxandra's eyes. Her body convulsed again and then lay still. Ruxandra stared in horror at the twisted, broken remains of Elizabeth Bathory.

She wasn't breathing.

I killed her. She won't turn. She's dead. Oh God, what have I . . .

Elizabeth's skin started to go pale.

It began at her face, the blood draining away from under her flesh like water. It spread over her head, the pale skin shining out between the roots of her dark hair. It spread down her neck and beneath her dress. The blood vanished from her hands next, turning them white as snow.

Her eyes snapped open. The deep brown leached away, leaving them pale blue, like Ruxandra's eyes. Inside her still-open mouth, long fangs tore through the gums. Silver talons pushed out from the tips of her fingers.

For a long moment, she didn't move.

Then she gasped in a breath and snarled.

Elizabeth spun, getting her feet under her and ending in a crouch, moving faster than humanly possible.

But then, she is not human anymore.

Elizabeth snarled again, backing away from Ruxandra, her talons flexing and her head darting back and forth, searching for food.

"This way," Ruxandra said, heading for the window. "You must feed."

A boot crashed hard against the door.

"My lady!" Dorotyas shouted. Her boot hit the door again. "My lady, answer me!" Dorotyas boot smashed against it a third time, and the door sprang open.

Elizabeth let out a snarl and charged at the prostitute who Dorotyas held in front of her with a tight grip.

Elizabeth sprang upward, her talons ripping into the whore's flesh. The woman screamed, short and sharp, her voice cut off when Elizabeth bit through her throat.

Dorotyas ran back down the hallway, moving fast in spite of her bulk. Elizabeth spat the whore's flesh out of her mouth and sucked the blood at her throat.

"Not the women!" Ruxandra shouted. "The soldiers! We must go after the soldiers!"

Elizabeth dropped the girl and raced down the hall. Ruxandra chased after her. Elizabeth dashed down the stairs and to the main floor. She sniffed the air twice, then spun toward the main parlor. Ruxandra tried to grab her and missed. Elizabeth dashed to the parlor, Ruxandra hot on her heels.

Then the slaughter began.

Elizabeth roared and sprang forward. She was in the doorway—the women's faces pale ovals of shock—then she was on top of the closest one, her body swift and agile. She lashed out with her claws and tore through her throat before anyone could even scream. Blood sprayed from the ruptured arteries, hitting the walls and upholstery and Elizabeth's clothes. Elizabeth grabbed the woman and pulled her close, sucking hard at the wound. The other women screamed and scrabbled out of their chairs, dropping teacups and wine glasses. Some ran back against the far wall, looking for escape. Others pressed themselves against the shutters, but they were barred tight from the outside. Three pulled knives, hidden beneath their scant clothing, and lined up together.

Elizabeth dropped the drained woman and grabbed another, a small blonde huddling in a corner. The woman's arm popped out of its socket as Elizabeth yanked her forward. She raised her other hand to claw at Elizabeth's eyes. Elizabeth turned her head and sank her fangs into the woman's wrist. Then she ripped upward, flaying the woman's forearm. More blood spurted, and again Elizabeth drank.

One woman tried running around Elizabeth to the door.

Without looking, Elizabeth slashed out, tearing through the woman's dress and skin and muscle and spilling her intestines to the floor. The woman howled in agony and fell in the slippery, bloody mess. Elizabeth tossed aside the one she had drunk and leaped again.

The slaughter lasted only minutes.

Ruxandra stood in the doorway the entire time, frozen in horror.

Elizabeth didn't stop killing. She didn't drink from all of them, either. She howled with glee as she gutted and ripped off limbs and tore through throats. Blood sheeted the walls and coated the floor. The stench of ruptured bowels and voided bladders mixed in with the heavy copper of the blood, filling the room with a foul stench that made even Ruxandra's eyes water.

In the midst of it, reveling in the slaughter, stood Elizabeth.

The last woman, one of the knife fighters, hung suspended in the air, Elizabeth's talons shoved deep under her ribs, Elizabeth's mouth pressed hard against her throat. She twitched and shook as Elizabeth sucked away the last of her blood.

Elizabeth let the woman slide from the talons to the floor. She looked over the room, her eyes becoming sharp and focused for the first time.

"Oh dear," she said. "Did I do that?"

Then her eyes closed, and her legs gave way, and she fell to the floor. Blood splatted beneath her.

Still, Ruxandra could only stare.

I thought I could lead her outside. I thought we would fight the soldiers and feed her hunger. I did not think she'd do this. She didn't even feed off most of them.

"Is she finished?" Dorotyas asked.

Ruxandra turned. Dorotyas stood at the top of the stairs, looking down.

"Why are you here?" Ruxandra demanded. "Why aren't you hanging in the barn?"

"Elizabeth only had me there to convince you how sorry she was." Dorotyas smiled, looking like a toad about to snare a fly. "She had me cut down the moment she knew you believed her."

She took several steps downward and leaned forward to peek into the parlor. Her eyes went wide, then narrowed.

"What are you doing, letting her lie in the blood like that?" Dorotyas demanded. "Get her out of there. Now!"

Ruxandra turned, her hands tightening into fists. "This is your fault."

Dorotyas laughed. "I'm not the one who turned her into a vampire."

"You're the one who opened the door!"

"Of course I opened the door. Did you think I was going to let her run wild outside?"

Ruxandra's eyes went wide. "You knew?"

"Of course I knew. I've been listening to you two since you arrived here. Why do you think I brought the whore with me? Good thing, too. Otherwise, I'd have been my lady's breakfast."

"I was taking her to the soldiers!"

"So sorry she didn't murder the ones you wanted." Dorotyas came down the stairs. "Too bad, though. It would have been less mess."

She waded through the blood and offal on the floor without flinching. When she reached Elizabeth, she looked back.

"Is she going to bite me?"

"She might leap up at any moment and rip your throat out."

Dorotyas glared at her. "And if she doesn't?"

Ruxandra looked around, heartsick. The women had done nothing to deserve death. She felt suddenly exhausted. Dorotyas was still glaring.

"She'll probably sleep until tomorrow night,"

"Good. That will give us time to get this mess cleaned up." Dorotyas picked up Elizabeth and thrust her at Ruxandra. "Take her to the baths in the back of the building. I'll let the other whores out of the basement and get them to clean up. I'll say the soldiers attacked."

Ruxandra took Elizabeth. She was not light, though for Ruxandra it was an easy burden. "Where are the rest of Elizabeth's party?"

"Upstairs in their rooms, where they are staying until Elizabeth or I tell them to come out."

Dorotyas tromped toward the basement door. Ruxandra took Elizabeth to the baths. As she walked, she heard Dorotyas open the basement door. One of the women there asked what happened. Then came the sound of Dorotyas's strap striking flesh and a wail of pain.

Once Elizabeth is better, I can take her away from that woman. I will explain how Dorotyas ruined my plan and let Elizabeth run amok among innocents.

It took an hour to get Elizabeth clean. Ruxandra wrapped her in sheets and took her upstairs. As they passed the parlor, Ruxandra saw five of the prostitutes on their knees, buckets and rags beside them, trying not to vomit as they cleaned away the mess. Dorotyas stood in the door, strap in her hand, watching.

I don't care if she thinks she needs Dorotyas. The woman is a she-devil.

In Elizabeth's room, Ruxandra closed the curtains tight, then the curtains around Elizabeth's bed. She couldn't bring herself to lie down beside Elizabeth. She was still shaken by the extent of the slaughter in the parlor.

I expected her to feed. I expected it to be bloody, but this . . .

Why did she kill them all?

Why did she enjoy it so much?

I wasn't like that when I turned, was I?

She remembered how she tore her own father's head off, how she chased down and killed his men. She could see every detail of their slaughter, remember every brutal need that drove her to kill them all.

Maybe I was like that.

Even so, those women did nothing to deserve it. It shouldn't have happened.

It's all my fault.

Ruxandra climbed onto the bed and sat in the corner farthest from Elizabeth's sleeping body. She leaned back against the post and looked at the woman.

What will she be when she wakes?

She kept watching until dawn came and exhaustion took her.

"Ruxandra! Wake up!"

Ruxandra blinked twice, shook her head and looked. Elizabeth was standing naked by the window, looking out into the darkness. There was no candle lit, and the fireplace was cold.

"This is beyond belief," Elizabeth said. "I can see so clearly. I can see everything for miles. I can hear everything."

Ruxandra slipped from the bed and came up behind her. She put a hand on Elizabeth's shoulder. The warmth was gone from Elizabeth's flesh. The muscles underneath felt harder. Her scent was different, but not less appealing—instead of reminding Ruxandra of flowers and pastries, she was like stone and ice, like the stars.

Elizabeth looked back over her shoulder. Her face was that of a thirty-year-old.

She smiled. "I am no longer an old woman."

"No," Ruxandra agreed. "You're not."

"You didn't tell me how powerful I would feel." Elizabeth turned back to the window. "You didn't tell me how amazing the world looked through your eyes."

"I'm sorry," Ruxandra whispered. "About all of it. I'm sorry."

"Sorry?" Elizabeth turned. "For what?"

"The women you killed," Ruxandra said. "It should have been the soldiers. The women—"

"Were peasants." Elizabeth's tone brooked no argument. "They were whores, selling their bodies to pleasure their betters. Last night they served me better than they had any man in their lives."

"But . . ." Ruxandra didn't know what to say.

"Peasants," Elizabeth repeated. "We are Blood Royal."

Is this how I seem to others? Cold, monstrous? Yet as soon as the thought came, she put it aside. *We are not monsters. We are lovers.*

Elizabeth turned away from Ruxandra and went to the clothing chest. "Come, help me dress."

"Yes." Ruxandra nodded. "Of course. It's time we left the city."

"No." Elizabeth pulled a dress and chemise from her trunk. "It's time we found Rudolph."

Ruxandra's eyes went wide. "What?"

"First, show me how you command someone. And how you pass unseen."

"I . . ."

"Hurry!"

In the time it took Elizabeth to dress, Ruxandra taught her both skills.

"Excellent," Elizabeth said as she put on her shoes. She went to her door and called, "Dorotyas! Fetch two of the whores."

"Yes, my lady."

Elizabeth preened in front of the mirror. Ruxandra's legs trembled. She sat on the bed. She didn't understand what Elizabeth was doing, didn't know why she wouldn't run away. She tried to find the words to ask her but Dorotyas returned. When Dorotyas knocked and pushed the two women into the room, Elizabeth smiled.

"Excellent." She advanced on the girls. "Now, let's see if it works. *You two stand on one leg.*"

Both girls lifted a leg and stood there.

"Put your leg down, turn in a circle three times."

They did so.

"Perfect," Elizabeth said, her voice low and intense. "Absolutely perfect."

She looked at Ruxandra. "I wonder . . ."

"Wonder what?"

"Ruxandra, stand on your head."

"What?"

"Interesting," Elizabeth said. "It doesn't work on other vampires. And now . . ."

"My lady!" Dorotyas's voice shook. The two prostitutes jumped and looked around. "My lady, where are you?"

"I can see you," Ruxandra said.

"Really?" Curiosity filled Elizabeth's voice. "But they cannot. Dorotyas, can you see me?"

"No, my lady." Dorotyas sounded panicked.

"Interesting." She made herself noticeable again. "Dorotyas, have my ladies pack. We leave before dawn. Ruxandra, go out the window and see where Rudolph's troops are positioned, please. I will meet you at the front door."

Ruxandra frowned but went. The troops had not moved since the night before, although different men now stood at watch. As she looked them over closely, trying to see if any hint of what had happened here had been rumored, the front door swung open, and Elizabeth stepped out. This time, Ruxandra saw a slight blurring around Elizabeth's frame.

Ruxandra went unnoticed as well. Elizabeth smiled and took her hand. She led them both through the lines of troops to a knight at the back. Then she made herself visible.

"You there. Order a carriage at once. I must visit the king."

"Yes, my lady."

The knight wheeled around on his horse and trotted away. Ruxandra stayed unnoticed until the man returned, leading a carriage with four horses attached.

"Very good," Elizabeth said, climbing inside. "Do you know where Rudolph is?"

"No, my lady."

"Then take us to your commander. We don't have all night."

For the next two hours, they crossed the city, going from the night commander, to the lord knight, until they reached Rudolph's chancellor. The man was more than ready to throw them out until Elizabeth commanded him. Ruxandra tried to talk to Elizabeth about where they would travel and how they would live, but Elizabeth kept shushing her, saying she had to concentrate. Ruxandra felt a growing unease, but finally turned her face to the window, enjoying the sparkle of the city at night.

I wonder what other cities are like.

Finally, they arrived at Lady Czobor's house.

Rudolph was asleep until Elizabeth used one of her talons to cut open his cheek. He shouted in pain and sat up.

"Get up," Elizabeth commanded. *"You have work to do for me."*

Rudolph rose from the bed. His nightshirt went only to his knees, showing off a pair of impressively hairy legs.

"Go to your desk and retrieve writing paper."

The door to the bedroom flung open. Lady Czobor and three guards charged into the room.

"What is going on?" Lady Czobor demanded. "You can't barge in and—"

"Sit down and shut up." Elizabeth didn't even turn around. *"Guards, stand watch at the door."*

The guards turned on their heels and left. Lady Czobor sat, her eyes wide with fear.

"Now," Elizabeth said to Rudolph. *"Write as I instruct you."*

It took an hour, including the two copies Elizabeth had him make. At the end of it, she commanded him to write a letter giving freedom of the city to Elizabeth, her knights, and her servants, as well as free passage back to Castle Csejte. In a separate document, he wrote a pledge to forever leave apart the lands owned by the Bathory family. Then, as Elizabeth and Ruxandra watched, he stamped and sealed each document.

"Perfect." Elizabeth pocketed one copy of each document. *"File the others in the morning with the court."*

She turned back to Lady Czobor, smiled at her and asked, "How old is your daughter?"

Lady Czobor pressed her lips tight. Elizabeth's head tilted to the side. Then she slapped Lady Czobor so hard it sent her sprawling onto the floor.

"That," Elizabeth said, "was for treating me like a dog."

"No less than you deserved." Lady Czobor spat the words out with a spray of blood. "You murderous, torturing whore."

"As soon as Rudolph is finished with you, you will send your daughter to the city gates, and have her wait, alone, until I pick her up. From now on, she will attend my gymnaesium."

"Pick her up?" Ruxandra shook her head. "No. We're leaving, remember? We're going to Rome."

"We can't leave yet," Elizabeth said. "Not until my affairs are settled. Now, it is time to go. Rudolph?"

Rudolph glared at her.

"Take Lady Czobor into your bed and fuck her backside until she cannot sit without pain." She turned back to Lady Czobor, whose face was pale with fear and anger. *"You. Let him."*

Rudolph grabbed an unresisting Lady Czobor and dragged her into the bedroom.

"Let us go, my dear," Elizabeth said. She made herself unnoticed and walked out the door. Ruxandra followed.

Once outside, Elizabeth said, "I have several bits of business to settle before morning. I'll meet you back at the whorehouse before dawn."

With that, she got back into the wagon, shouted instructions to the driver, and rolled off into the night.

Ruxandra watched her go, stunned.

I cannot go back there. I don't want to go back there. I want to see the world.

She said we would see the world together.

CHAPTER TWENTY

WHAT DO I do?

Ruxandra walked away from Lady Czobor's house. She stayed unnoticed, the better to avoid the soldiers still patrolling the streets. Her mind was in turmoil.

Elizabeth said she had to sort out her affairs. She has done that now. Rudolph promised to leave her lands alone. Surely that's enough. She can leave her lands to her sons, and we can go away, like she promised.

Surely . . .

A feeling of dread lodged deep in Ruxandra's belly, making it ache. She growled to herself and kept walking. It wouldn't take long to reach the brothel. Then she could wait for Elizabeth to return.

We will talk, and Elizabeth will come away with me, like she promised.

She rounded a corner and saw the sky ahead lit bright yellow with fire.

No. Oh no.

Ruxandra ran. The crackling of flames mixed with the screams of women and the shouts of men and women trying to douse the blaze. As she got closer, the heat of the fire began to permeate the air, and by the time she reached it, it was burning her skin.

The whorehouse was engulfed in flames.

"Elizabeth!" Ruxandra's scream echoed through the square. She tried to get closer, but the flames were too hot. "Elizabeth!"

The screaming stopped, leaving only the sound of the fire and the people battling it.

Ruxandra spotted the knight from the line of soldiers passing buckets. His face was red from the heat. He shouted at his men, encouraging them to keep the pace as they passed bucket after bucket toward the blazing inferno.

Ruxandra ran to him. "Elizabeth! Have you seen Elizabeth?"

"Not now, girl!"

"The Countess Bathory!" Ruxandra shouted the words. "She was living here!"

"She's gone!" He shouted back, even as he kept passing buckets. "The lady came by with her knights with a signed letter from the king granting the entire entourage free passage of the city. They packed up and left while we watched. The place caught fire just after."

She wouldn't.

Would she?

Elizabeth had turned the parlor into an abattoir. Anyone who entered would see it at once. The easiest way to hide it . . .

She must have told Dorotyas to do it.

What about the women inside?

The wind shifted, and the smell of smoke, charred wood, and burned meat filled Ruxandra's nose. She stumbled away, hand over her mouth.

They were just peasants to Elizabeth.

So is Jana.

Ruxandra ran into the night. She reached the door of Madame Kovacs' household and banged on it. It took time before a servant answered, and he nearly refused her admittance. Ruxandra commanded him to take her to the parlor and to wake his mistress. It took the better part of an hour before Madame Kovacs came down. She looked tired and not at all pleased.

Her eyebrows rose when she saw Ruxandra. "You keep strange hours, young lady."

"I do," Ruxandra said. "I am sorry to wake you."

"The girl expected you back last night. She was very disappointed."

"I know. Things . . . happened."

Madame's head tilted, and her eyes narrowed. "Not good things, from your tone."

"No, Madame Kovacs."

"I spoke to Jana today. At length."

Her tone made Ruxandra wary. "Did you?"

"Yes." Her face was stern, her tone disapproving. "I would like to know why you are trying to pass your servant off as your sister."

"She is like a sister to me, and I thought it would be more likely that you wouldn't ask her questions if you thought she was my sister."

"You thought wrong," Madame Kovacs said. "I did not survive the death of my husband and maintain his affairs by not knowing what is happening around me."

Ruxandra could have commanded the woman, but she didn't want to. To force a person to care for someone was almost certainly the way to make things go badly.

She bowed her head. "I am sorry, Madame Kovacs."

"I think you had better explain yourself. Does this girl belong to Lady Bathory?"

"She did," Ruxandra said. "Now she is my servant."

"Who, exactly are you, my dear?" Madame Kovacs asked. "You have not given your name."

Ruxandra smiled, in spite of herself. "My pardon. I am not used to using it."

Madame Kovacs' eyebrows rose, but she said nothing.

Ruxandra stood and did a formal curtsy. "I am Ruxandra Dracula, daughter of the House of Dracula, of Wallachia."

"Dracula? As in Prince Vlad Dracula the Impaler?"

"Pardon?"

"Impaler," Madame Kovacs said. "That is how he was known, was it not?"

Ruxandra had not heard him called that when she was alive, but nodded anyway. "Quite the heritage," Madame Kovacs said. "You are one of the noble girls she educates, then."

Close enough. "Yes."

"My lady?" Jana peeked around the doorframe.

"Jana!" Ruxandra saw worry and fear in the girl's face. "I am so sorry I didn't return last night."

Jana ran to her and threw her arms around Ruxandra's neck. Jana's breath hissed through her teeth as the movement pulled on the scabs on her back. She hugged Ruxandra tight anyway.

"It's all right." Ruxandra held her gently. "You're all right."

"I thought you'd left me." Jana let go with one arm and reached into her shirt. She pulled out the bag of coins. "I still have all your money."

Ruxandra took the purse, lifted Jana off her lap, and sat her down beside her. Madame Kovacs watched them, curiously.

"Jana is my servant, yes," Ruxandra said. "She is also the closest thing I have to a sister now. Unfortunately, if she remains in my company, her life will be in danger."

"My lady, no—"

"Jana is thirteen," Ruxandra continued as if Jana had not spoken at all. "She cannot read. She cannot do basic mathematics. She doesn't know how to run a household. She needs to learn all these things, and she needs a place where she can be safe while she learns."

Ruxandra held out the purse. "This will pay for her upkeep for the next five years while she learns to be a proper young woman. What's left will cover her dowry when she marries."

"My lady, please—"

"Enough, Jana," Ruxandra said.

"She is very attached to you," Madame Kovacs said. "Why do you not stay here with her? With the money you have, you would find a place, I am sure."

"Elizabeth," Ruxandra said. "She will come after me. Also, I'm . . ."

The only one who can stop her.

"The only one who can keep her from coming after Jana," Ruxandra lied. *With Jana safe, I can get Elizabeth to come away with me.*

Madame Kovacs nodded. "Very well. Then consider this your home, Jana. We will start you on lessons tomorrow."

"I don't want to," Jana's whispered. "I want to stay with Ruxandra."

"Shh . . ." Ruxandra kissed her on the top of the head. "It's better for you here."

The farewells with Jana lasted half an hour. Jana cried the entire time. Finally, Ruxandra picked her up and carried her back to her room. She tucked the girl into her bed, kissed her, and left her crying in the dark.

I will never see her again.

The thought left a hole in her heart and brought forth the tears Ruxandra had been holding back. She cried all the way to the city gate.

Four girls waited there, each carrying a bag and wearing clothes fit for the winter. None of them spoke.

Ruxandra kept herself unnoticed and watched, uneasiness growing inside her. As the hours of the night passed, three carriages came by, dropping off three more girls. They also took places against the wall.

All of them looked scared.

Just before dawn, a train of carriages led by knights pulled up to the gate. The lead carriage was embossed with the Bathory coat of arms. Elizabeth leaned out of the window and called, "Ruxandra! It's time to leave!"

Ruxandra made herself noticeable and climbed inside. She heard Dorotyas shouting at the girls to get into one of the carriages. Then the train started moving.

"An excellent night's work." Elizabeth looked pleased. "Seven new girls for the gymnaesium, over a thousand florins in fees to pay for them. Right now Lady Czobor is regretting everything she has ever done to me."

Ruxandra glared out the window at the lightening sky.

"Whatever is the matter, darling?" Elizabeth asked. "Isn't this what we wanted? Freedom?"

"I wanted to leave," Ruxandra said. "I wanted to travel."

"As do I, but one must be patient."

Anger rose up in Ruxandra like a fire. The Beast woke and growled. "Settling your affairs means handing your lands over to your sons, not bringing in seven new girls for the school."

"Is that what this temper is about?"

"And the brothel."

"They were peasants."

"So what?" Ruxandra demanded. "They were people!"

"You feed off people, remember?" Elizabeth's voice was cold. "You drink their blood and leave them dead, so do not pretend you're better than me. I protected us. For now, we must get back to the castle. The girls there have not been disciplined in a long time, and I have much work to do before we can go anywhere."

"What do you mean by disciplined?"

Elizabeth's eyes narrowed. "Exactly what I said. Whether or not I am a vampire, I will not fail those girls by leaving them as an undisciplined rabble." She leaned back in her seat and closed her eyes. "Now please be quiet, Ruxandra. It has been a long and tedious night."

Ruxandra stared at her. She crossed her arms and sank back into the corner.

I should leave.

Leave the castle and go out into the world and . . .

Leave Elizabeth?

I can't. I love her. I made her. I can't leave her.

She argued with herself until nightfall, when the carriages pulled into an inn yard. Dorotyas got the seven new girls out of the carriage and had them line up to await Elizabeth. Elizabeth took her time getting out of the carriage, took longer walking over to the girls, and longer yet looking them over. Ruxandra followed her.

"Come with me," she said. "All of you."

She turned her back on the girls and went to the stables behind the inn. She spoke a word to a small group of her knights and walked ahead with four of them. By the time Elizabeth reached the stables, the knights had the stable hands lined up beside the door.

"Thank you, gentlemen," Elizabeth said. "Ladies, inside."

The seven girls went in. Dorotyas and Elizabeth fell in behind then. Ruxandra stepped in after. Elizabeth made the girls line up in front of her.

"Cristina Czobor, step forward."

Lady Czobor's daughter was blonde, with fair skin and large, blue eyes. She stepped forward but didn't look up.

"Your mother has caused me no end of trouble." Elizabeth grabbed the girl's jaw. Cristina winced but didn't cry out. "Starting today, you will make amends for that trouble. Now take off your clothes and face the wall."

"No." Cristina tried to shake her head but couldn't move in Elizabeth's grip. "I won't."

"Defying me, girl?" Elizabeth said, her tone the same as the man who wanted to rape Ruxandra in the alley. "We'll see about that. *Take off your clothes.*"

"Elizabeth," Ruxandra stepped forward. "What are you doing?"

"Setting an example," Elizabeth said. "The first thing the girls learn is that they must not defy me, and this one is defiant."

"But—"

Elizabeth stepped closer to Ruxandra, her voice dropping low. "Do not show contempt for my authority in front of these girls. If you don't want to watch, you can leave."

Elizabeth released her and watched Cristina undress, the girl's hands trembling so badly it took twice as long as it should have. When she was naked and facing the wall, Elizabeth turned to the other girls.

"All of you watch, none of you move. Dorotyas?"

Dorotyas handed Elizabeth the strap from her belt.

"Elizabeth," Ruxandra whispered. "Please don't."

Elizabeth swung the strap onto Cristina's thighs. The girl screamed and grabbed at the wall. Elizabeth swung it again and again, each time hitting a different spot. Not once did she draw blood, but Cristina wore red welts all across her back, thighs, and backside.

"Dress yourself," Elizabeth said. "Stay here, facing the wall until I come get you."

She looked at the other six girls. All were shaking, their eyes wide with horror.

"Obedience is expected at all times," Elizabeth said. "No failures of respect, discipline, or behavior are allowed. Do you understand?"

The girls nodded.

"You six go inside and have dinner. Now."

The other girls bowed their heads and went. Elizabeth watched them go, handed the strap to Dorotyas, and walked out behind them.

"Ruxandra, dear," she said over her shoulder. "May I speak with you?"

Ruxandra followed, her feet dragging. She felt like she used to when the Mother Superior caught her misbehaving. Elizabeth led her out of the stables, but instead of going to the inn, she took Ruxandra around the back.

"Yes, Elizabeth, what—"

She didn't get any farther. Elizabeth's mouth landed on hers, her tongue ramming between Ruxandra's teeth. She grabbed Ruxandra's breasts and pushed her up against the wall. Ruxandra tried to protest, but Elizabeth wouldn't stop kissing her, wouldn't stop caressing her. One hand slipped from Ruxandra's breasts and began pulling up her skirt. Ruxandra was reminded again of the man in the alley, and her skin curdled with rage. She tried to push Elizabeth away, but the other woman was as strong as she. Elizabeth's mouth lifted off Ruxandra's and went to her ear.

"There is nothing," she whispered as her hand dove underneath the raised edge of Ruxandra's skirt, "so exciting as watching a girl's spirit break."

"Get off me," Ruxandra hissed. "Now."

"No." Elizabeth nipped Ruxandra's earlobe. "I need to touch you."

Her hand drove up between Ruxandra's thighs, her fingers shoving hard inside. Ruxandra yelped and grabbed for her hand. She tried to push it back, but Elizabeth didn't relent.

"I don't want to," Ruxandra whispered. "Please."

"Oh, but I do." Elizabeth began moving her fingers. "You are mine, pretty Ruxandra. Do you understand?"

Elizabeth's fingers shifted and began rubbing her. Against her will, Ruxandra found her breath coming in gasps. She opened her mouth to protest, but a moan came out instead. Elizabeth tore open the front of Ruxandra's dress with her free hand and dropped her face down to engulf one of her nipples. Ruxandra moaned again, the stimulation driving her farther and farther along until she cried out and her knees buckled.

Elizabeth stood up confidently. Ruxandra stayed on her knees, gasping.

She let Ruxandra go and stepped back. "That was excellent, my dear. Now, shall we go off and hunt? Because I, for one, am hungry."

Ruxandra looked down at the ruined gown, at the fading red marks on her bare breast from Elizabeth's lips and teeth.

"I didn't want to," Ruxandra said.

"Yes, you did. You just didn't know it. Now come, let's change into something suitable for hunting."

Ruxandra rose and pulled ragged edges of the torn fabric together. Then she turned and walked away.

"Ruxandra?"

"Ruxandra!" On the second word, Elizabeth's voice cracked like a whip. "Where are you going?"

"Away," Ruxandra said. "I'm going away from you."

CHAPTER TWENTY-ONE

"WHAT DO YOU MEAN going away?" Elizabeth demanded. "You're not going anywhere."

"*You're* not going anywhere, you mean." Ruxandra didn't turn around. "I want to leave. I want to travel. I do not want to be cooped up in the castle again. Not anymore."

"The castle is the one place you're safe, Ruxandra." Elizabeth caught her shoulder. "You know that."

Ruxandra spun, knocking Elizabeth's hand away. "Like Lady Czobor's daughter is safe? Like the girls in your dungeon are safe? There was no reason to do that to her."

"She needed to be put in her place."

““Do I need to be put in my place, too?" Ruxandra closed the distance. "Is that why you did *that* to me?" She felt her fangs come out. She didn't care.

"That?" Elizabeth didn't move. "You liked that. You took it, didn't you?" Elizabeth stepped so close their bodies were touching. Her fangs were showing too. "I felt you spreading for my fingers, and I felt your knees buckle."

Her closeness unnerved Ruxandra. She could smell Elizabeth's desire, as well as the scent of stone and ice and stars that defined the woman as a vampire. It was as appealing as ever, like a tune she would never tire of. Ruxandra tried to turn away again, but Elizabeth caught both her shoulders and held her fast.

"Tell me you didn't like it."

"That's . . ." Ruxandra's hands made fists in her hair. *How can I love someone who thinks like this?* "That has nothing to do with it. I didn't want to!"

"I did."

Tears welled up in Ruxandra's eyes. "What I want doesn't matter?"

"Of course it does."

"Then stop this!" Ruxandra yelled. "Stop this and come away with me!"

Elizabeth's eyes glowed. "We have everything we need at the castle. We will be able to feed, to rule, and to gain more and more power until we are unstoppable."

Ruxandra's lips pressed hard together. When she spoke again, the words came out in harsh, clipped syllables. "I. Don't. Want. To. Rule."

"I *do*. I want you with me. You belong to me, Ruxandra, and I won't let you go."

The Beast growled, long, low, and menacing. The sound slipped passed Ruxandra's lips before she could stop it. Elizabeth stepped back, her self-assurance faltering.

"Control that animal," Elizabeth said, "before you kill everyone here."

"I do not belong to anyone." Ruxandra pushed the Beast back into its cage. "I will not be your pet!" Ruxandra heard the desperation in her own voice and hated it. "Come travel with me. You said we would travel together! Was it all lies?"

Elizabeth said nothing. Her face was perfectly blank but Ruxandra could smell it. Self-satisfaction. *She lied and is so glad it worked.*

Ruxandra turned and walked toward the woods.

"You *will* come back to me," Elizabeth called after her. "You will come *crawling* back to me!"

Ruxandra didn't look back. She kept walking, her back straight, her head high, and tears rolling down her face.

I won't let her see me crying, I won't.

The woods enveloped her like a ragged cloak. The winter had left the trees barren and the grass brown. Ruxandra moved silently through it, disappearing into the woods like a ghost. She listened for pursuit, but none came.

Why did she lie to me?

Her stomach felt like a hollow pit.

I don't need her. I can see the world by myself.

She changed direction, walking parallel to the road to Vienna. With the return of her memories came all her skills at navigating the forest. She kept on direction without trouble.

She would not go back into Vienna, though. It was too risky. She would take the road outside the city. The one heading west.

Maybe Rome. Or Venice. Or maybe I can go to France . . .

The thought excited her in a way she hadn't felt since first seeing Vienna. There were things she could do that she had never done before, places she could see.

I'll need money for that.

Maybe I can find work.

Ruxandra laughed at the idea. She had never worked a day in her life.

I could only work at night, anyway.

No, I'll command people to give me money. Rich people. They won't miss it.

Ruxandra looked down at her exposed breast. *I can't walk around in the cities like this. I'll buy some plain dresses for hunting and for walking about and some fancy dresses so I can be beautiful at concerts and . . .*

She remembered the times Elizabeth had called her beautiful, their laughter and conversation, and the hollow feeling in her stomach grew worse and worse. She started crying again.

No, I won't cry about her. She dashed the tears away with her sleeve. *She doesn't care about me anyway. She wants to rule over people. So I don't have to worry about her at all.*

Even so, the tears kept coming. Her entire body began shaking with grief and loneliness. She leaned against a tree and then fell to the ground, curling her arms around her knees and burying her face between them.

I should go back to her.

The thought came unbidden, unwanted. She shoved it away. With an angry push against the tree she got back on her feet and started walking again.

I won't cry about her. Not anymore. I won't go back to her. Ever.

I won't.

For the first time in months, she spent the night in the forest. She made a small, tight den and crawled inside. The dirt got all over her clothes and skin and into her hair. It was at once comforting and miserable.

When morning came, the hollow in her stomach was worse. She spent an hour crying before she managed to get moving again. She headed for the road, determined to put as much space between her and Elizabeth as possible. It took less than an hour to reach it. She started running, the speed faster than a galloping horse. By the time the night was half gone, Vienna was ahead of her, the torches in the walls glowing in the distance. A quarter hour later, she reached the crossroads and turned west.

A grin lit up her face.

I'll go to Venice. That will show Elizabeth.

Elizabeth.

This time the aching loneliness left her curled up on the side of the road, weeping until dawn. She barely managed to get off the ground as the sky started to lighten, barely managed to find a barn to hide in. She dug a nest in straw—the darkest part of the hayloft and wept there until sleep took her.

She was hungry when night fell.

Elizabeth would feed me. Elizabeth loves me.

The thought made her weep again. She had cried half the night before the call of her hunger became strong enough to drive her from the barn. She opened up her mind. From the farmhouse, she felt only deep contentment of sleep—the farmer, his wife, his children. She let her mind range farther until, at the very edge of her reach, she felt rage and hatred and the desperate desire to kill.

She followed it to a forest glade, where a woman with a red-dripping knife in her hand stood over a naked, bleeding young girl.

"I told you!" The woman hissed. "I told you to stay away from him, you whore."

"I didn't want him to!" Tears streamed down the girl's face. "He came in and did it, and I didn't want him to."

"Lying slut!" The woman raised the knife.

Then the woman screamed.

And gurgled.

And died.

"Who is he?" said Ruxandra as she dropped the woman's corpse, "*Tell me.*"

An hour later, wearing the dead woman's spare dress, Ruxandra knocked on a farmhouse door. The girl stood beside her, weeping. The farmer opened the door and stared blearily at them.

"Her parents are dead." Ruxandra pushed the girl forward. "Take care of her."

She vanished from notice before either of them said anything.

Two hours later, she broke down again.

This time it was more than grief and a hollow feeling in her stomach. This time her stomach erupted in pain, making physical the desperate loss she felt.

Elizabeth. I need to go back to Elizabeth.

NO!

I don't want to go back! I won't go back! I want to see Venice!

She lasted two more days.

Four nights later, Ruxandra arrived at Castle Csejte.

It was only by using all of her strength that she managed to keep on her feet when she reached the gates. She fought a desperate urge to fall to her knees and scream for Elizabeth. She wanted to crawl to the woman's feet and beg her forgiveness.

Instead, she walked to the gate, her back straight and her mouth in a thin, hard line. She commanded the guards to open it and to tell her where to find Elizabeth. They did.

Ruxandra opened the dungeon door and found Elizabeth lounging back in the copper tub, her white skin covered in red. The room was filled with the rich smell of blood. Above the tub hung the bodies of three naked girls, all their orifices plugged, and the last of their blood dripping down their faces and hair. Elizabeth leaned her head back, letting the drops hit her face and hair.

"There you are," purred Elizabeth.

Ruxandra's knees wanted to give way. She wanted to grovel before Elizabeth and beg and plead for the woman to love her. Instead, she gritted her teeth together, locked her knees to keep them straight, and glared.

"What," Ruxandra demanded, "have you done to me?"

"I?" Elizabeth smiled. "I have done nothing."

"Then who did?"

"I don't think you need to know that." Elizabeth lay back in the tub. "Suffice it to say that there are powers other than yours in the world."

Ruxandra's talons came out. She wanted to rend Elizabeth's flesh to pieces.

"Don't be like that, my dear," Elizabeth said. "Hurting me will get you nowhere. It certainly won't make me tell you why you came back."

Ruxandra forced the talons back into her fingers. She stood there, shaking with anger and the fight to stay upright.

"Why are you bathing in blood? You don't need to anymore."

"I like blood, darling. It's so naturally warm, and now it also tastes good." She flicked a tongue out to catch a drop and laughed.

"You are a monster."

"Aren't I? Now, my dear, why don't you visit the baths, then go back to your room. I want you clean, so we can celebrate your return. Oh, and walk through the great hall on your way. We had a little discipline problem, and I want you to see how I've dealt with it."

Ruxandra growled in frustration and left. She stomped back up the dungeon stairs and went to the great hall.

Eighteen girls stood in the middle of the room, naked. Four of the new girls hung naked from chains bolted to the wall, their faces pressed against the stone.

The four on the wall were all bleeding from open welts and cuts on their backs. The others' backsides were bright red from being beaten. Hanja and Agota were bleeding from fresh welts on their legs. Nusi and Sasa both looked ready to collapse. All the ones who had been there when Ruxandra left were so thin she could see their ribs and the sharp edges of their hipbones and cheekbones. The newer ones looked like they hadn't eaten since arriving. They all looked cold and exhausted and terrified.

No one made a sound.

In front of them stood four men with whips in their hands, watching the line of girls. In front of them, Dorotyas strutted back and forth, her own strap swinging in her hand.

She had two holes in her neck.

Elizabeth bit her? Ruxandra listened hard. She could hear Dorotyas's heart beat; hear the blood rushing through her veins. *How is she still alive if Elizabeth bit her?*

"I will ask again," Dorotyas said. "Where is she?"

No one answered.

Dorotyas stepped forward. She stopped in front of a young girl—one of the new ones. Her face was still round with baby fat, her body still plump with youth.

Dorotyas slashed her strap down on the girl's small breast. The girl screamed and fell to her knees, covering her head and chest with her arms.

"We don't know!" she cried. "Please! We don't know! We woke up this morning, and she was gone!"

"There are horsemen patrolling the woods." Dorotyas's voice echoed off the walls. "Soldiers who have orders to teach her what happens to sluts who run away. Do any of you want that to happen to her?"

The girls stayed silent. Dorotyas grabbed the young girl's hair and pulled her up onto her toes.

"Perhaps you all need to see what will happen to her." She threw the girl toward the closest man with a whip. "These four men were arrested for rape. We let them out of the dungeon for this occasion."

"Please," the girl whimpered. "Please no."

"Agoston," Dorotyas said. "Shove three fingers in her."

"Enough!" Ruxandra's roar filled the room. She stomped forward. "Get your hands off that girl!"

"The animal finally appears." Dorotyas sneered. "Do it, Agoston. Now."

The man kicked the weeping girl's legs wide apart and reached down.

Ruxandra's talons went through his wrist, and his hand hit the floor with a spurt of blood. Ruxandra's other hand went through his throat before he could scream.

She caught Dorotyas's strap before it could touch her and shredded it.

One of the men stepped forward, a knife in his hand. She twisted his neck until it snapped.

The girls stood in the middle of the floor, frozen in terror. The other two men threw their whips away and sprinted for the door.

Dorotyas threw a strong, fat fist at Ruxandra's head. Ruxandra caught it and squeezed. Dorotyas face went white, but she didn't make a sound.

"Girls," Ruxandra said. "Go back to your rooms. Now."

"Don't you dare!" Dorotyas screamed, her pain making her voice ragged. "You will stay there until you tell me where she's gone, or I will whip you all within an inch of your lives, do you hear me?"

"Who is gone?" asked Ruxandra

"One of the girls escaped last night," Dorotyas said between clenched teeth. "No one knows how she got out. Elizabeth has her men searching for her."

"They've been standing here since this morning?"

Ruxandra looked again at the shivering girls. They looked ready to collapse. She squeezed Dorotyas's hand tighter.

"Do you think hurting me will make Elizabeth let you go?" Dorotyas gasped.

"What did she do to me?" Ruxandra tightened the grip even more. A bone cracked in Dorotyas's hand. Dorotyas yelped in pain.

"You came crawling back like a dog," Dorotyas gasped. "Didn't you? Like the little cowardly Beast you always were."

"What did she do?"

"I will never tell you. Just know that you were made to come back. You will always come back. Now let go of me!"

Ruxandra looked at the sobbing young girl huddled on the ground, one hand covering her head, the other pressed against the gash in her breast.

She remembered Jana's cries as Dorotyas opened up her flesh with the strap.

She remembered the prostitutes' screams from the brothel, suddenly cut off as the roof collapsed in flames.

Her talons ripped through Dorotyas's throat, and the woman fell to the floor, gasping. Ruxandra left her there and went to the wall. Four more slashes broke the girls free of their shackles.

"Pick them up," Ruxandra commanded the girls. *"Take them back to your rooms and care for them. Now!"*

The girls rushed forward to get the four and ran from the room.

Dorotyas watched them go, her hands clenched tight on her throat, blood spurting between the fingers.

"I will get out of here and I will take them with me," Ruxandra told her. "And you will die knowing you failed to stop me."

She left Dorotyas to bleed out on the floor and went to the baths. The servants who saw her dashed to get out of her way. Ruxandra tore her clothes from her body and plunged into the first tub, not caring if it was warm or cold. The water turned pink with blood. Ruxandra surfaced, scrubbed her body clean, and made herself unnoticed. Naked she walked up the stairs to her tower room, opened the door, and locked herself in.

"I can't see you," Kade said from the chair by the fire. "Is that you, Ruxandra?"

She didn't answer, just threw open the clothes chest. There was a plain dress and chemise there, and a clean strip of cloth to use as a towel. She picked it up and began drying off.

"If that is you, please show yourself," Kade said. "Please. I have knowledge that you need right now."

Ruxandra finished drying. She put on the chemise and slipped the dress over her head. Then she made herself noticeable again and sat on the bed.

"What knowledge?" Ruxandra felt so tired. She wanted to collapse but knew she couldn't. "What could you possibly know that would be of use?"

"I'm the one who made you come back here."

CHAPTER TWENTY-TWO

"YOU . . . WHAT?" The words themselves made sense, but the meaning wouldn't sink into Ruxandra's head. "How could you . . . You weren't even there."

"I am a sorcerer," Kade said. "One of the very few alive today, thanks to the Inquisition."

"What?"

"I came here five years before you arrived." Kade leaned back in his chair. "I had heard rumors that Lady Bathory was in search of immortality. I offered my services to help her. I built the tub in which she bathes. But it wasn't enough.

"Human sorcery has very limited effect on other humans. It can persuade, it can cause accidents, or magnify the properties of some things, like Elizabeth's bath magnifies the rejuvenating properties of the girls' blood." He smiled. "On things that are not natural, human magic is much, much more powerful."

Ruxandra's eyes narrowed. "Things like me?"

"Exactly." Kade leaned forward again, his face glowing with excitement. "I believe magic is God's gift to humanity to ward off evil. Spells that have no effect on people can be devastating on unnatural creatures—like the binding I put upon you. It was even more powerful than I imagined it would be: you were—you are—utterly mesmerized by Elizabeth. Against a person, it does nothing."

Ruxandra felt her hands clenching into fists. Kade didn't seem to notice.

"There were rumors about a wild girl roaming through the forests, going back a hundred years," he said. "I guessed what you might be and set the trap for you. My spells prevented you from seeing the nets or smelling the hunters. Once we had you here, I bound you to Elizabeth. It was so simple. Amazing because, you know, I'd tried it before so many times with people and it hadn't worked. With you, though, you weren't just bound to her. You loved her."

Inside, the Beast began to growl. Ruxandra leaned forward, tension thrumming through her like a bow about to release an arrow. Her fangs and talons descended.

Kade didn't move.

"How do I break it?" Ruxandra snarled the words. "How do I break free of her?"

"There are two ways," Kade said. "The first is to kill me—"

Ruxandra lashed out, her talons reaching for his throat. Then pain—enormous, overpowering agony—erupted from her neck and engulfed her head. It felt as if the noonday sun were burning her skull. She fell to the floor, screaming and slapping at her head to douse flames that weren't there.

Kade rose from his chair and stood over her. He waited until she stopped screaming and flailing before he spoke again.

"Of course, I took precautions to prevent you from attacking me."

Ruxandra reached up for her throat and felt the cool silver of the necklace he had given her.

I forgot I was wearing it. I forgot I even had it.

She yanked on the chain, the links digging into her flesh. Once again pain engulfed her head, leaving her screaming.

"You can't break it, and it won't come off," Kade said. "Not unless I die. Or if you make me a vampire."

Ruxandra stared, stunned, at the man.

"Vampire magic and human magic cannot coexist. Human magic is part of the natural order of things, given by God. Vampires are outside the natural order. If I were made a vampire, the spell you're under would disappear."

"Never." Ruxandra sat up, her head still aching. "I will never make anyone else a vampire."

"Then *you* will never escape," Kade said. "Elizabeth will never let you go."

"Could you release me now?" Ruxandra asked. "On your own?"

"I could," Kade said. "But Elizabeth promised that she would spend a month killing me if I do. And given the number of soldiers she has at her command, she would be more than capable of catching me if I flee. So you see, I do not have a choice in the matter."

"Kade," Ruxandra commanded. *"Take this thing off me!"*

"No," Kade said gently. "Your commands will not work on me, so long as you wear the necklace. If you make me a vampire, I will release you."

Ruxandra slumped back to the floor. "Why would anyone want to be what I am?"

"Immortality is reason enough," Kade said. "The power to live life free from someone else's command."

Ruxandra shuddered. Under *Elizabeth's* command.

"Now I take my leave," Kade said. "Elizabeth will be visiting you soon, and I should hate to stand in the way of your pleasures."

Her pleasures. Not mine.

When he left, Ruxandra got her feet under her. Her legs wobbled as she stood. The agony from the spell had drained her energy. The few steps to the bed seemed a mile. She collapsed on it and began swearing at herself. Adela had taught her a fair number of swear words when the nuns weren't listening. She'd learned more in Vienna. She went through them all twice.

I am such a fool.

Everyone used me for their own ends. None of them care for me. They never did. I just wanted to think so. I was so naïve I didn't even realize my thoughts weren't my own. I didn't question how I could love someone who . . .

I did question it, but I thought . . .

Only Jana was my friend, and she is far away.

Thank God.

She stared at the canopy above, waiting, expecting Elizabeth. Morning came first. Ruxandra closed the shutters and curtains. She crawled into the bed, pulling the bed curtains tight shut, too. Ruxandra half expected Elizabeth to come in, to force herself on her again, even as the sun rose higher. Instead, Ruxandra lay there, staring at the canopy until sleep finally overtook her.

"Get up!"

Elizabeth yanked open the curtains. Ruxandra bolted upright and was met with a slap in the face. Ruxandra's cheekbone broke from the force of it, and her jaw popped out of joint. She fell over, mewling with pain.

"How *dare* you kill Dorotyas!" Elizabeth threw back the covers and grabbed Ruxandra's leg, pulling her half off the bed. "How dare you!"

Ruxandra's jaw popped back into place with a noise that echoed in her head like a shot. She twisted and tried to sit up. Elizabeth lashed out again, hitting hard against the broken cheekbone. Ruxandra yelped and struck back. Her hand smashed into Elizabeth's face, sending the woman to the floor.

Ruxandra rolled off the other side of the bed and came to her feet, talons and fangs out. Elizabeth got to her hands and knees. She shook her head as if trying to clear a fog.

I can hurt her. Ruxandra stayed in her crouch. *I couldn't hurt Kade, but I can hurt her.*

Good.

"That woman served me thirty years"—Elizabeth rose to her feet, her expression as hard as flint—"and you slashed her throat like a pig."

"She was a pig. She was killing the girls."

"She was *disciplining* the girls."

"She was torturing them!"

"Be silent!" Elizabeth raised her right arm, holding up a short, three-tailed scourge. Sharp metal, braided into the leather tails, glinted in the dark room. "Take off your clothes and bend over the bed."

Ruxandra looked over the whip. "I'll kill you first."

Elizabeth lowered the scourge. Her voice became as cold as the water beneath an ice-coated lake. "Right now, my soldiers are strapping the girls. Ten lashes each because of your interference."

Ruxandra dashed for the door. Elizabeth moved faster, blocking her way.

"After, they will stand naked in the courtyard until they tell me how the girl escaped. Because of *you*."

"Do not blame me for—"

"Because of you!" Elizabeth screamed. "If you do *not* do as you are told, if the soldiers see anyone but me approach the girls' apartments, they will cut their throats before you can say a word to them. Do you understand?"

Ruxandra sized up Elizabeth and looked at the door.

"You will not get there in time," Elizabeth said. "If I scream, the girls die. If they see you before me, the girls die. Now, take off your clothes and bend over the bed."

Ruxandra's hands closed tight into fists, driving her own talons into her flesh. She shook with fury.

"When I am done with you," Elizabeth said, "you will never, *ever*, disobey me again, or that is the fate they will suffer. You will not command my soldiers, and you will not attempt to evade me. The girls are being watched at all times now, and God help them if you attempt to interfere or if anything happens to *me*. They will all die screaming. Now *strip*!"

Furious, helpless, Ruxandra pulled the dress from her body and bent over the bed.

The first blow tore Ruxandra's skin and muscles like the claws of the bear she had fought years ago. Silver blood spattered across the room. It hurt nearly as badly as the bear's claws. Elizabeth whipped her from her calves up to her neck and back down, again and again. She made her turn over and tore chunks of flesh from Ruxandra's breasts and belly and thighs. Every time she opened up Ruxandra's flesh, it healed at once. Elizabeth swung harder with each stroke, cutting deeper and deeper.

Ruxandra did not make a sound, could not *allow* herself to make a sound.

The Beast wanted to howl, to grab Elizabeth and rend her to shreds. Only Ruxandra's desperate grip held it back.

I will not let you. We cannot risk hurting the girls.

When the midnight bell rang, Elizabeth stopped.

"Pity you don't scar anymore," she said. "Scars are always the best reminder."

Ruxandra let her legs give way and fell to the floor.

"I am going downstairs," Elizabeth said. "You will stay here until called for. If you behave yourself, I will give you one of the girls to drink tomorrow."

Elizabeth walked out of the room and down the tower stairs, leaving Ruxandra on the floor.

The last of the fresh-ripped flesh pulled back together.

The last of the pain vanished.

The Beast settled.

Ruxandra became unnoticed and headed to the door.

I will not let her keep me here.

I will not be her pet.

I will not let her win.

She didn't bother to dress. Clothes would get in her way. She moved slowly and silently, listening and looking hard, as she made her way down the stairs. Even if Elizabeth could see through Ruxandra being unnoticeable, that didn't mean that Ruxandra would be seen.

She was still a hunter. She knew how to stalk prey.

She slipped through the castle, her nose leading her; her ears open for any sound of approach. She could smell Kade, his scent guiding her through the castle.

She heard the girls, crying in the courtyard.

She heard the men and women sleeping in the bedrooms.

She heard the rats in the walls.

No one heard or saw her.

His scent led her to another tower, away from the main building. The lower room held a large table with bowls and a mortar and pestle. Shelves of strange jars filled with foul-smelling potions and powders lined the walls. Ruxandra slipped through it and up the steps to the bedroom above.

It held only a single shelf of books, a desk and chair, and a narrow bed. Kade was deeply asleep.

Ruxandra took down the first book. It was a treatise on chemicals and their properties, written in Latin. She tried to read it, but Latin had never been her favorite lessons, and the book made little sense to her. The next book was titled *Convocatis Dæmoniorum.* The first page promised spells to summon the most powerful creatures to do one's bidding. Ruxandra closed it and went through the others.

There was nothing about vampires.

She picked up the *Convocatis Dæmoniorum* again, felt the heft of it in her hand. Then she launched it in the air in a neat spinning throw that brought it down on Kade's stomach with a *whap.*

"OOF!" Kade sat up hard and fast. He looked around, his pupils wide as he struggled to see in the dark. "Who is there?"

"Why can I hurt Elizabeth?" Ruxandra asked. "Why her and not you?"

"Ruxandra?"

"Will killing her break the spell on me?"

He pursed his lips but said nothing. She saw his hands bunching beneath the blankets. For a moment hope rose inside her, accompanied by a terrible sadness. Elizabeth had been her friend—*pretended to be my friend.* Even though she had betrayed her beyond all reason, a small part of Ruxandra thought that, somehow, they would be able to reconcile.

Then Kade spoke, and her hope vanished.

"You already killed her," Kade said. "When she drank your blood, she died and became a vampire. She planned for it and made certain the spell would bind you to her in life and death. Even if you destroy her utterly, you will still be bonded to her. You will haunt the place of her death, grieving for her for eternity."

Of course she did. She planned everything and played with me until I fell for it. Ruxandra started shaking with fury. She went unnoticed and slipped out of the tower.

The girls stood in the courtyard, hands on their heads, their skin red with cold. Their bodies shook. Their breath frosted the air in front of them. Tears lay frozen on their faces. Three of them had lost control of their bladders, leaving puddles of urine to turn to ice at their feet.

In her mind Ruxandra saw Valeria and Adela, kneeling in the snow as the nuns' straps slashed down on them, ripping open their backs.

I cannot let them stay like this.

Six soldiers stood guard around them. All looked grim, rather than gleeful, at the sight of the naked girls. Curious, Ruxandra reached out with her mind to feel their emotions. Resentment and anger overwhelmed five of them. They did not want to be there, did not want the girls there. The sixth one was blank, with no emotions emanating from him at all. He had bite marks on his neck.

Just like Dorotyas.

Ruxandra scanned the grounds and the walls, sniffed the air and listened. No sign of Elizabeth.

Ruxandra slipped away from the wall and circled the girls, still unnoticed. She sniffed at the air, breathing in each girl's scent. Halfway through she realized that Cristina Czobor's daughter was not among them.

No wonder Elizabeth is so furious.

Thank God she doesn't know how to hunt. Otherwise, she'd have found the girl by now.

She slipped into their barracks.

It made the convent's dormitory look comforting and warm. The girls slept on mats on the floor, with only one thin blanket for each bed. There were no candles and one fireplace that sat cold and cheerless. Ruxandra dropped to her hands and feet and scurried across the floor, nose to the ground.

That one.

One mattress smelled faintly like Cristina, as if she had only lain there for a moment. Ruxandra breathed in the scent deep. Then she circled the mattress in an ever-widening spiral until she caught the scent on the floor.

It was nearly imperceptible, but it was there. She followed it. It crossed once to the long tables where the girls ate their meals—gruel, from the smell of it—and again to another bed. Ruxandra followed the trail to the latrines.

Ruxandra circled back out. There was no return trail.

No one walks exactly the same path both ways. If she went at night it should lead back to her bed. So what happened to . . . Ruxandra looked back at the latrine. *She didn't.*

A double layer of plain, rough wooden planks with three round holes in them covered the latrine. Ruxandra sniffed again. Her eyes watered from the stench coming from the drains below. She gritted her teeth and leaned closer.

There, on the edge of the planks.

Ruxandra grabbed the planks and pulled up. The entire thing lifted, and the hole below was easily large enough for a terrified girl to descend.

Oh, you foolish creature.

Ruxandra retreated from the barracks. She scanned the courtyard, found no sign of Elizabeth, and slipped out. She walked up the stairs to the top of the wall and jumped down to the uneven, rocky slope below.

She landed wrong and rolled down the hill. She bounced off two boulders, dug her talons into the ground, and skidded to a stop. She lay still, eyes and ears wide.

The guards must have heard me.

There was noise above her. She saw the guards looking over the parapet, but no one raised the alarm. She reached out for their emotions. Like the men in the courtyard, they were angry and resentful.

Is the entire castle like that? Is Elizabeth nearing a rebellion?

Ruxandra sat up, careful not to groan, and followed her nose to the refuse pile.

Even in the frigid cold, it reeked. Steam rose from the rotting garbage and sewage that coated the ground, five feet deep and twenty feet around. She watched it for a moment and circled it for a better look. Then she made herself noticeable and knelt down before it.

"Good job going to ground," Ruxandra said. "No one would think a well-bred girl would stay in a refuse pit, covered in sewage."

There was no sound or movement.

"How long were you planning to stay?" Ruxandra asked. "Until the guards are called off? Because they won't be. Elizabeth will keep searching, and her guards have orders to rape you when they find you."

The pile didn't answer.

"We must get you out of there," Ruxandra said. "We need to get you someplace safe, so I can tell Elizabeth how you escaped, and the other girls can go back inside."

Still, the pile didn't move.

Ruxandra sighed. She turned her head away and took a deep breath. Then she reached in, grabbed the collar of Cristina's dress and hauled her out of the rotting garbage. The girl squawked in surprise.

"Hush!" Ruxandra commanded in a whisper. *"No more sounds until I get you out of here. Understand?"*

Cristina nodded.

"Now get on my back and hang on."

The girl's stench was nearly enough to make Ruxandra leave her, and the slimy feel of her dress made Ruxandra's skin crawl. She pretended it didn't bother her and sent her mind wide, searching for a place to put her. The town below the castle was too close. Elizabeth's men would find her there. She needed to go farther away.

Much farther.

Ruxandra ran hard and fast. In two hours she covered the ground the carriages had traveled in a day and stopped in front of the inn.

Ruxandra hammered on the back door until one of the cooks opened it. Three commands later, Ruxandra and Cristina stood naked in the stables. The women of the inn, led by the innkeeper's wife, scrubbed and rubbed at them with brushes and doused them with buckets of warm water.

"Now don't you worry," she told Ruxandra. "We'll make sure no harm comes to the girl, and that no one finds her before her family arrives. What about you, dearie? You can't wander around like this."

I can't go back now. Ruxandra looked out at the lightening sky. *Those poor girls.*

She spent the day in a darkened room with Cristina.

Ruxandra fretted half the day, worrying about them. She slept fitfully, waking often. Every time she woke, she heard Cristina weeping.

I should comfort her.

I should command her not to say anything about vampires.

She didn't have the heart to do either. *Anyway,* she thought, *it's too late. Her mother knows about vampires now—and so does the king. Maybe half of Vienna as well.*

As soon as the sun sank beneath the horizon, she vanished from notice and ran back to the castle. The road was empty, save for one lone horseman, riding hard through the night, a torch in one hand. She passed him without either he or the horse noticing.

Elizabeth will be furious with me but at least I can tell her how Cristina escaped. Then maybe the girls can go back inside.

Then I must find a way to break the spell.

The last thought occupied her mind until she reached the castle. She stayed unnoticeable, scaling the wall rather than having the guards see her naked. The courtyard was empty.

Where are the girls?

"They're in their rooms," said Dorotyas. "Preparing for their next punishment."

Ruxandra spun, shocked.

Dorotyas's body had changed. The fat and extra flesh had vanished. Her frame was narrow and lean. Her nose was sharp and narrow, her eyes pale blue, and her skin white as snow.

Dorotyas's eyes narrowed, and her face twisted into a rictus of a smile. "You owe me a death, whore."

CHAPTER TWENTY-THREE

DOROTYAS CHARGED FORWARD, fists flying. She caught Ruxandra still flat-footed and staring. The first two punches broke Ruxandra's nose and slammed into her ear hard enough to make her head ring and the world spin. She stumbled back, trying to create distance. Dorotyas grabbed her hair and slammed her fist into Ruxandra's face again and again.

Ruxandra ducked her head and slashed out with her talons, opening up Dorotyas arm from the wrist to the elbow. Her hand fell away, useless. Ruxandra slashed twice more, ripping open Dorotyas's dress and belly before jumping away.

"Slut," Dorotyas hissed. "Slattern. Whore."

Ruxandra growled back. Then she attacked.

Dorotyas moved like the men Ruxandra had seen in the taverns in Vienna, the ones who knew how to fight and were looking to do so. She protected her body and head with her arms and dealt out punishing punches. Her fists bruised Ruxandra's ribs and cracked the bones in her face. In return, Ruxandra lashed out with talons and teeth, tearing and ripping into Dorotyas's flesh.

Both women healed at once.

The men on the walls watched the fight. No one called for reinforcements. No one moved to stop them. They stared at the two women with revulsion and horror.

"Enough!"

Elizabeth's voice rang through the courtyard. Dorotyas froze. Ruxandra dropped to one knee and raked her claws through the woman's knees, ripping out the tendons. Dorotyas fell backward, screaming.

"I said, enough!" Elizabeth dashed out of the great hall and into the courtyard, her flail in her hand. "Ruxandra, stop. Now!"

"Why did you bring her back?" Ruxandra demanded. "How could you do that?"

"Because *she* is loyal," Elizabeth said. "Unlike you."

"She's a vicious, murdering bitch!"

"Unlike you," Dorotyas said. She sat up, her face twisted in pain. "You're nothing but a spoiled brat and an animal."

"*You* were supposed to stay in your room." Elizabeth advanced on Ruxandra, the flail rising.

"*I* went searching for Cristina Czobor," Ruxandra said. "She escaped through the latrines, spent a night in the garbage heap, and ran. I tracked her five miles to the river. I searched up and down the bank for her trail until morning. Then I hid until I could return."

"Liar," Dorotyas said. "You were trying to leave."

"Go sniff the garbage pile if you don't believe me," Ruxandra said, knowing Dorotyas wouldn't. "The girl probably drowned."

"Probably is not good enough," Elizabeth said. "If she is alive, I want her back here. If she's dead, I want her body to send to her mother. After all, why deny the woman her grief? It's a pity I can't see her face when she gets the news."

"I wish I had killed you when I had the chance."

"You never had the chance, dear. You were mine before I ever let you out of the cage." The Beast roared in Ruxandra's mind, and she forced it down.

"What about the girls? What happens to them?"

"They didn't tell me where she went," Elizabeth said. "Their punishment resumes tonight."

"They didn't know where she went," Ruxandra said. "They woke up and found her gone. You're torturing them for nothing."

"I am *punishing* them," Elizabeth said, "for allowing one of their number to leave. When I am done, none of them will *dare* try again." She stepped closer to Ruxandra. "So you know, there will be soldiers with them, with orders to kill the girls if you attempt to rescue them. Since both Dorotyas and I are here to stop you, I assure you that *you* will not be able to stop *them* before it happens."

Ruxandra stood and let her talons retract back into her hands.

"Dorotyas, take Ruxandra to her room," Elizabeth said. "Ruxandra, every time you resist, one of those girls will be flogged. Do you understand?"

Ruxandra glared at her.

"Five lashes for the oldest one," Elizabeth said, her voice implacable. "Do you understand?"

"Yes," Ruxandra ground out. "I understand."

"Good. Dorotyas, you may beat her when you reach her room, but no using her body for your pleasure. It is mine."

While Elizabeth had beaten Ruxandra to punish her, Dorotyas beat her to maim. She broke Ruxandra's arms first. Then she broke her legs. She stomped on her face, and every time the bones started to come together, she stomped it again. She broke Ruxandra's fingers one at a time, every hour, for the entire night.

Ruxandra had not felt so much pain since her fight with the bear. Unlike that time, though, Ruxandra's injuries healed within moments. Knowing it gave Ruxandra the ability to endure and contain the Beast.

The Beast didn't care about the girls, didn't care about anything except destroying whoever was hurting it. If it got free, she would lose everything that mattered. She had to fight with her wits, and that took time. The Beast didn't understand, though, and Ruxandra used every bit of her strength to prevent it from breaking free.

It helped her stay sane, gave her something to focus on while Dorotyas broke her bones over and over again.

Ruxandra waited for the woman to get bored and give up, but Dorotyas reveled in the torture the entire night, muttering the words "whore, slut, animal" under her breath as she did so. Ruxandra held tight to the beast and retreated into her mind. She had not felt such pain since the Dark Angel had first changed her. She almost wished the creature was there, embracing her as she writhed.

It will end with sunrise. I just have to last until then.

As the sky lightened, Ruxandra lay spread out on the ground. Her arms and legs bent at the wrong angles, her head twisted backward on her neck, and the bones of her ribs stuck out through her flesh like jagged-tipped spears.

Dorotyas jumped and landed with both boots on Ruxandra's pelvis. The bone shattered.

"Be thankful Elizabeth wants you for herself," Dorotyas said. "Otherwise I'd fist you front and back until I reached your throat."

She kicked Ruxandra's head once more and walked out, locking the door behind her.

No more of this, Ruxandra thought, as the bones and muscles in her neck twisted back into place. *I need to get the girls out of here, and then I must escape.*

Somehow.

There was a light rap against the door.

"Ruxandra?" Kade called. "Are you all right?"

Ruxandra didn't answer.

"I heard Dorotyas beating you," Kade said through the door. "If you make me a vampire, you will be free of my magic. Then we can flee this castle together."

What about the girls?

"I will come see you later today if Elizabeth lets me," Kade said. "Until then, do think about it."

"Wai—" Ruxandra's jaw hadn't healed yet, and she couldn't speak properly. "Ju wai . . ."

Kade waited. Ruxandra heard his breathing quicken, his heart rate go up. Ruxandra closed her eyes and waited for her jaw to heal. At last, it popped into place. She moved her mouth back and forth a few times. It all seemed to work.

"Kade."

"Yes, Ruxandra?"

"Why did Elizabeth bite her guards?"

There was a long pause. Kade had obviously been hoping for other words. It was enough to make Ruxandra smile.

"Thralls," Kade said at last. "She made them into thralls. A person under the complete control of a vampire. The vampire makes one by draining most of a person's blood. After that, they must do her bidding."

Commanding them does that. Why make them thralls?

"What happens when a thrall becomes a vampire?"

"If the thrall was taken unwillingly, it becomes a vampire and very agitated, I would surmise. If the person agrees to be a thrall, and agrees to become a vampire, it becomes a slave to the vampire who made it. Like Dorotyas."

She inhaled sharply as two of her rib bones retreated inside her body. The pain receded. "Is that in your books?"

"Not mine. Elizabeth's." Kade waited. "Is there nothing else?"

"No. Thank you."

He stood there a bit longer, then turned and went down the stairs. Ruxandra listened to him go. She lay on the ground until her arms and legs straightened out. Then she crawled to the bed and closed the curtains. She didn't sleep. Instead, she stared at the canopy.

I will not turn him into a vampire so I can escape.

I will not turn anyone into a vampire ever again.

But how do I get the girls out?

Two hours after sunrise, a loud, brassy horn broke the air and pulled her from her thoughts. Ruxandra rolled off the bed and went to the window. The horn sounded again. She closed her eyes and listened. The sound came from outside the gate. The horn sounded again. Then came a man's voice, loud enough that it echoed off the castle walls.

"I have here a message for Countess Bathory and words for all who serve her!"

"We'll send for her," said one of the guards. "Will you come inside and wait for her?"

"No." The messenger sounded repulsed by the idea. "Listen to my words and tell your fellows!"

He didn't wait for an answer. Instead, he began reading aloud.

"Let it be known," the messenger shouted, "that Elizabeth Bathory did willfully and with malice use most foul witchcraft upon the persons of His Majesty, King Rudolph, and Lady Czobor! Let it be further known that, having recovered his faculties after this foul attack, His Majesty has deemed all agreements signed and delivered in his name to be null."

Regained his faculties? Ruxandra frowned. *Commands wear off? So that's why vampires make thralls.*

Did Elizabeth know commands wear off? She mustn't have, or she would have made Rudolph a thrall. She imagined Elizabeth's reaction and shuddered.

"Further," the messenger shouted, "let it be known that Countess Elizabeth Bathory is immediately placed under house arrest, where she will remain until such time as the army of King Rudolph arrives, at which time she shall surrender herself to face justice for her actions!"

What?

"Further, that until such time as she is in good custody, her children shall act as security against her actions, and shall, should she fail in her orders, be put to death!"

There wasn't a sound from any of the guards on the castle wall.

"I have here the official letter for the lady," the messenger shouted. "The king has forbidden me to enter the castle or speak to her, so I leave it here for you to deliver."

A moment later, Ruxandra heard the sound of hooves clattering back down the hill at a canter. She leaned against the wall, thinking hard.

As soon as night fell, Elizabeth summoned Ruxandra to her council chambers. Elizabeth's anger from the day before was a pale shadow of her fury at the messenger's news.

"I will *not* be driven from my house!" Elizabeth shouted. "I will not!"

Three large candelabras lit the council chamber. Ruxandra stood in the shadows against the wall. Dorotyas, Kade, and Elizabeth's knight commanders sat at the table. The knight commanders all wore gray beards and scars on their faces. They also all wore fresh teeth marks in their necks.

She's made thralls of them all.

"In that case," said one, "let us send scouts to see the size of Rudolph's army."

"From there we can arrange the appropriate defenses," said the second. "Meanwhile, I will inventory our stores and supplies, should they attempt a siege."

"If they have cannons, the walls will not hold," Kade said. "This place was built before such things were a threat, and cannot defend against them."

"I don't care if they have brought all the armies of the empire together," Elizabeth said. "I am *not* leaving!"

"The girls will serve as hostages," Dorotyas said. "Rudolph will negotiate for their release before they fire upon us. That will give us time to plan a counterattack."

"With what?" Kade asked. "We have no cannons here and not many soldiers."

Elizabeth's eyes narrowed. She looked at Ruxandra.

"Gentlemen, thank you. Please send scouts at once and see to our supplies. Kade, Dorotyas, Ruxandra, stay."

The knights bowed and left. Elizabeth closed the door behind them.

"We do not need cannons," she said. "We have Ruxandra, we have Dorotyas, and we have me."

"Will it be enough?" Kade asked. "Against a hundred men? Or a thousand?"

"It does not matter how many," Elizabeth said. "If it is a large force, we need not destroy it all at once. We wear them down, night after night, until they flee in terror at the very mention of this place."

"That one"—Dorotyas shoved a thumb in Ruxandra's direction—"won't want to do it."

"That one," Elizabeth repeated, fury filling her voice, "is in disgrace for not telling me that Rudolph would return to his senses. She will do *whatever* she is told."

"I did not know!" Ruxandra protested. "I only learned how to command people in Vienna. How could I know it did not last?"

"One more word from you and I give the youngest of the girls to my soldiers for a night."

Ruxandra bit her lip and looked at her feet, fury pulsing through her.

"Get back to your room. Do not come out until I tell you. Dorotyas, lock her in and then return here."

"Yes, my lady."

They walked in silence through the halls of the castle back to Ruxandra's room. Dorotyas's desire to beat her again radiated from the woman. Ruxandra kept her mouth shut, even when Dorotyas shoved her against the wall.

"How does it feel to no longer be the favorite?" Dorotyas whispered. "To learn your true place in the world?"

Ruxandra said nothing. Dorotyas let her go and shoved her toward her tower.

"Walk faster. I'm sick of the sight of you."

Ruxandra did so and as soon as she was back in her room, she threw open the shutters and the curtains. She sat on her bed, opening her ears and her mind.

Fear radiated off everyone in the castle, save Dorotyas and Elizabeth. Even Kade was afraid, though he hid it better than most. Ruxandra caught snippets of whispered conversations from the servants and guards.

"She'll be hung, is my guess."

"Or burned."

"She's brought it upon herself, but now she's bringing it upon all of us!"

"I don't want to be here."

"Will they hurt us, Mummy?"

She stretched her mind as far as it could reach but sensed no one beyond the town.

They must still be far away.

Elizabeth won't go.

Not unless someone makes her. And I cannot make her.

But I won't let her hurt me anymore.

Ruxandra looked up at the bed curtains, then began pulling them down.

Sunrise won't be long now.

CHAPTER TWENTY-FOUR

COLD WINTER SUNLIGHT appeared between the mountains. Light spilled across a landscape of bare trees and wet snow. It crawled up the side of the hill on which Castle Csejte sat and scaled the walls until it peeked into the tower window.

Ruxandra closed her eyes and opened her mind. She sensed every person in the castle, from the guards on the walls to the prisoners in the dungeons. She felt the bright presences of Elizabeth, asleep in her room, and Dorotyas, sleeping in the girl's dormitory.

The light spilled over the walls, over the empty bed and the bare posts where the bed curtains used to hang. It coated the wall with light that bounced and danced through the room, lighting up even the darkest corners.

Then the sun, lagging behind its light, breached the horizon. It climbed the sky, shining down on the town and the castle and the woods around it.

When the sun's light touched the courtyard, Ruxandra leaped out of the tower window.

Long thin strips of bed curtain were wrapped over every inch of her flesh, from her feet to her head. Over the top of them, she wore her heaviest cloak. A thin strip of fabric covered her eyes to keep the sunlight from touching them.

She still felt like she was standing next to a blazing forge.

She dropped twenty feet and hit the ground running.

"Hey!" a soldier shouted from the wall. "What are you—"

"You must leave," Ruxandra commanded. *"Everyone must leave."*

She didn't stop to see if he'd listened. She ran into the gatehouse, startling the soldiers.

"Open the gates," she commanded. *"Open the gates and leave. Now!"*

The soldiers scrambled to raise the portcullis. Ruxandra ran up the steps to the next level. A knight commander sat at the table there. His eyes went wide at the sight of her.

"What are you—"

She punched him in the side of the head, and he flew across the room.

"Everyone," she commanded. *"Out!"*

The other soldiers left without looking at their commander.

Good. Elizabeth only made a few thralls.

Around the walls she went, giving the command over and over. The soldiers on duty dropped their weapons and ran for the gates.

Ruxandra finished her circuit of the walls and went to the kitchen. She commanded the servants and cooks to get their families and go. She raced up the castle floor by floor, telling everyone she met. The only place she didn't go near was Elizabeth's apartments. After, she ran back outside to the stables. She told the stable boys to get out and take the horses with them.

"Ruxandra!" Kade's voice echoed across the courtyard. "What are you doing?"

She ignored him, changed directions and put on a burst of speed. She jumped into the air, twisted, and slammed both feet into the door of the girls' dormitory.

In the moment before she landed, Ruxandra saw the girls. They huddled together, shivering, in the corner farthest from the door where Dorotyas sat, a strap in her hand. She saw the fireplace, the ashes cold. She smelled fresh blood and spotted a dozen new open cuts on the girls.

Then Dorotyas jumped out of her chair and spun. Ruxandra hit the ground, claws out, and leaped again in a low, hard tackle. Her body flew across the ground, and she smashed into Dorotyas's knees, snapping them with the force of the hit.

Dorotyas screamed and swung the strap. It smacked against the layers of fabric on Ruxandra's back but didn't go through. Ruxandra drove her talons into the backs of Dorotyas's knees, and she jumped to her feet. Then she started dragging Dorotyas to the door.

"Get out!" Ruxandra commanded the girls. *"Run to the village and keep running. Rudolph's army is coming to rescue you, so run!"*

Dorotyas twisted and ripped her legs free. Ruxandra grabbed her feet, her talons going through the woman's boots and into the flesh beneath. She ran backward, dragging Dorotyas straight into the sunshine in the courtyard.

Dorotyas hair went up in flames with a *whoosh.* The skin on her face and neck turned bright red, blistered, and split open like a sausage's skin splitting as it burned. Ruxandra let go of her boots, sank her claws through the fabric of the woman's dress and tore it wide open.

Dorotyas's screams echoed through the courtyard and off the hills around them.

Ruxandra leaped back, letting go of Dorotyas and standing in the sunlight between Dorotyas and the running girls. Dorotyas ran the other way, heading for the great hall. Ruxandra let her go . . . Dorotyas slammed through the door and disappeared into the darkness beyond.

"You can't do this!" Kade yelled.

"I already did," Ruxandra turned her back and headed for the dungeon.

"Elizabeth will kill you!"

"No, she won't," Ruxandra said, and inside her the Beast snarled agreement. "Elizabeth has no idea what it takes to kill one of us."

Ruxandra left Kade behind. She ran to the dungeon and, room by room, tore the doors off the cells. Girls, all naked, all terrified, cowered together on the cell floors.

"Get out," Ruxandra commanded. *"Run from here and go to the village."*

She turned and dashed out before they stampeded her.

"Stop!" Kade stood in the courtyard, his eyes wide. "For God's sake, stop for a moment!"

Ruxandra slowed to a walk but kept moving.

"Why?" Kade ran in front of her. "Why this?"

"Because I'm not a pet," Ruxandra said. "I'm not a slave. Without bargaining tools, Elizabeth can't make me do anything."

"You still won't be able to leave!"

"Neither will you." Ruxandra stepped forward and hugged him tight, pressing her body against his. Kade froze.

That's what I thought.

"As long as I'm not hurting you," Ruxandra said, "I can still touch you. And as long as I can touch you, I will bring you back here again and again and again, until you die of old age."

"You think Elizabeth won't stop you?"

"No." Ruxandra's voice was flat. "She won't."

She felt Kade trembling, felt his knees give way. She let him drop to the ground and walked into the great hall.

The smell of burned hair and flesh filled the room. Dorotyas wasn't in sight. Light streamed in from the high windows, creating patches of bright and dark. In the middle of it, in the shadows covering her chair, sat Elizabeth.

"What," she said, her voice clear and strong, "have you done?"

"The girls are gone," Ruxandra said. "So is everyone else except Kade."

"Not everyone," said a man's deep voice from behind them. Ruxandra turned and saw the six knight commanders standing in the doorway, the holes in their necks red and bright against their pale skin. "You called, my lady?"

"I'll kill them all if they attack," Ruxandra said.

"Then what?" Elizabeth rose from her chair. Like Ruxandra, she wore a long hooded cloak. Under it, a long robe covered her body, the sleeves longer than her arms. "You can't leave me. You know that. I will draw you back every time."

"Kade's magic will draw me back," Ruxandra corrected.

"Since you can't hurt him, it's the same thing, isn't it?" Elizabeth said. "It is a pity he didn't extend the same courtesy to me."

"He didn't trust you." Ruxandra began circling the room, moving to a place where she could see the knight commanders and Elizabeth at once.

"How shameful." Elizabeth's scourge uncoiled from her hand. The metal glinted where the sunlight caught it. "I will have words with him."

"Tell him to release me," Ruxandra said. "Please, Elizabeth."

"And if I refuse?" Elizabeth asked. She stepped down from the dais, moving with slow, deliberate steps. "What then?"

"I will kill you."

Elizabeth stopped. Her eyebrows went high on her forehead. Then she started laughing. The sound rang through the great hall. Ruxandra waited.

"You? Kill me?" Elizabeth said at last. "You can't kill me, my dear. I made you what you are."

"I know," Ruxandra stepped into a patch of sunlight. She felt the heat of it at once through the cloth. "You made me a killer again."

"You were always a killer." Elizabeth stepped into another patch of light, ten feet from her. "Just a pitiful one. You don't have the nerve to murder."

"Hunger and threat."

Elizabeth's head cocked to the side. "What?"

"Wolves only kill for two reasons." Ruxandra bent her knees. "Hunger and threat. And when you did that to me, when you said you would kill the girls if I didn't obey you? That made you a threat."

She charged forward, talons out.

Elizabeth was ready for her. The weighted tips of the scourge sliced the air, the metal whistling as it flew. Ruxandra ducked it, going for Elizabeth's knees. Elizabeth spun the scourge once around her hand and sent it down hard. Ruxandra barely managed to roll out of the way.

Elizabeth bore down on her, the scourge singing. Ruxandra scrabbled back and attacked again.

Elizabeth spun out of the way, and Ruxandra felt a line of fire open up on her back. Elizabeth held up her knife, the blade dripping with Ruxandra's blood. Ruxandra's eyes narrowed. She circled Elizabeth, letting the cut heal as she looked for an opening.

"I am a woman, holding land and power in a world full of men," Elizabeth said. "My castles have been attacked by mercenaries, by bandits, and by the Turks. Did you think I would not know how to fight?"

Ruxandra crouched, her hands coming down to touch the ground. Talons came out of her toes, cutting through the strips of cloth. Her legs tensed. Inside her, the Beast howled with glee.

"Ever fight a bear?" Ruxandra asked. "Because I have."

She screamed louder than a dozen angry mountain lions, and leaped forward.

The scourge lashed into Ruxandra's face, ripping it open. The dagger stabbed hard into her belly and tore her flesh as Elizabeth sawed it across.

Then the talons on Ruxandra's hands sank into Elizabeth's shoulders, digging deep into the flesh and hooking underneath her collarbones. Ruxandra's feet slammed into her belly, the talons on her toes tearing through flesh and intestine and coming out of Elizabeth's back.

Elizabeth screamed and fell backward. Ruxandra's feet impaled Elizabeth's body, and she fell on top of her. Ruxandra let out a howl and began digging.

Her hands moved in a blur. Cloth, flesh, muscle, and bone flew as she tore into Elizabeth's chest like a badger tearing into the earth. Elizabeth swung the scourge and stabbed with the dagger, but Ruxandra ignored them both, as she had ignored the claws of the bear ripping her open as she drank its blood. She dug faster, tearing away Elizabeth's breasts in bloody chunks. She ripped open the flesh of her neck and sent silver blood spraying everywhere. Elizabeth's head lolled back, only her spine holding it in place. Her arms lost their strength and fell to the sides. Still, Ruxandra tore at her flesh, eviscerating the woman.

A blur of screaming, sticky, burned flesh slammed into Ruxandra from the side, sending them both flying.

Ruxandra spun in the air, grabbing at Dorotyas with her talons. Dorotyas's own talons descended, and the two tore at each other like animals. They screamed in fury and pain as they ripped flesh from each other's faces. Dorotyas shifted, using her weight to straddle Ruxandra.

In the moment before Dorotyas's fists started raining down, Ruxandra saw Kade sprinting toward Elizabeth's flopping, bleeding body.

Then the world became a blur of fists and pain as Dorotyas pounded her hands down on top of Ruxandra's face. Ruxandra bucked her hips and twisted, sending Dorotyas to the floor beside her. She used her legs to push away and scrambled to her feet.

Kade was sucking the blood from the gaping wound on Elizabeth's belly. Elizabeth moaned in pain and pleasure. Ruxandra retreated, talons still out. She felt the rips in her cloak and the dangling strips of cloth, exposing her bare flesh. Even so, she dashed backward through a ray of sunshine, accepting the agony of the burned flesh in exchange for distance between herself and Dorotyas.

Dorotyas stood between her and Elizabeth, and for the first time, Ruxandra got a good look at her.

The flesh was gone from her face, leaving burned muscle and bone, sticky with silver blood and white pus. Her hair was a short, blackened mess. Even so, she stood between Ruxandra and Elizabeth, eyes narrow and talons out.

Ruxandra glanced behind her. The six knight commanders still blocked the entrance.

I need better coverage if I'm going back out into the sun.

Then Kade started screaming.

The gem on Ruxandra's neck shattered, the chain breaking and falling to the ground. She dashed to the wall, grabbed a tapestry, and ripped it down.

"Where do you think you're going?" Dorotyas demanded. Pain and anger twisted her voice, making it deeper and raspier. "Do you think you'll get by them before I kill you?"

"You can't kill me without dragging me back into the sunlight and burning with me." Ruxandra said. "And I'm not going to get by them. He is."

Dorotyas turned and saw Kade lying on the ground beside Elizabeth. "What did he—"

Kade snarled and leaped to his feet. Ruxandra stepped aside and watched him charge the only sources of human blood in sight. Dorotyas tried to grab him, but Kade bulled through with the power of his hunger. The knight commanders raised their swords.

Kade smashed into them and began to feed.

Ruxandra wrapped her body in the cloak and ran for the door. The knight commanders, fighting for their lives, didn't notice her.

"Ruxandra!" Elizabeth's pain-racked voice filled the hall. "No!"

Ruxandra kept going, into the sunlight, across the courtyard, and out the gates.

She didn't look back.

CHAPTER TWENTY-FIVE

THEY CAUGHT UP TO her two months later, in Budapest. She had a new dress and cloak, and new waterproof boots bought with money from a man who had threatened to sell her into slavery. She was sitting in one of the better taverns, near the window, enjoying the warmth of the fire and their mulled wine. Spring was still far away, and while the cold could not hurt her, there was something comforting about being inside and warm when there was snow on the ground.

She sensed them before she saw them.

Ruxandra put her wine glass down on the table, dropped a few coins beside the glass, and stepped out of the tavern into the cold February air.

The three stood across the street.

Elizabeth wore a long white cloak and dress. Kade had exchanged his gray robes for the long furred cape and heavy blue wool robes of a successful merchant. Dorotyas wore the plain brown clothes of a wealthy woman's servant. All three watched her as she stepped into the street.

Ruxandra stopped in the middle of the street, waiting.

Elizabeth picked up the hems of her skirt and cloak and walked forward. Kade and Dorotyas stayed where they were.

"No closer," Ruxandra said when Elizabeth was ten feet away. "Why are you here?"

"Because I wanted to see you, my dear," Elizabeth said. "Why else?"

"I am not your dear, Elizabeth. Go away."

"We are traveling," Kade said. "We're going to Italy."

Ruxandra looked past Elizabeth to him. "Where in Italy?"

"Rome," Elizabeth said.

"Then I'll be sure not to visit."

"Ruxandra—"

"Leave me alone, Elizabeth. I have no desire to—"

"I am sorry."

The words were enough to make Ruxandra pause.

"I drove you away," Elizabeth said. "I forced you into a place where you had no choice but to fight."

"Yes, you did."

"Forgive me. I was new to this life and blind to the possibilities. I thought only of holding onto what I possessed. I didn't consider what could be mine if I left my old world behind."

"Is that all you care about? What can be yours?"

Elizabeth frowned. "Without power, there is nothing."

"Come with us," Kade said. "Come to Rome and see the eternal city. You don't have to stay if you don't wish, but travel with us, for a while at least."

"Why in the name of God would I do that?" Ruxandra asked.

"Because we are the only ones of our kind," Elizabeth said.

"Because together we can do more, see more, and be more than the world has ever known," Kade said.

Elizabeth took a step forward. "Because I love you."

The laugh that barked out of Ruxandra's mouth was short and sharp. Elizabeth didn't react.

"Ruxandra—" Kade began.

Ruxandra stepped back. "I haven't forgiven you, Kade, for keeping me there. I haven't forgiven any of you for what you did. Not for the way you tortured the girls, not for your cruelty or the beatings or the way you manipulated me."

"Can you forgive me?" asked Elizabeth. "Eventually?"

Ruxandra shook her head. "No."

"Please—" Elizabeth started, but Kade caught her arm.

"We have all the time in the world," he said. "Ruxandra will come around."

"I will not."

Kade smiled at her. "I'll ask you again in a hundred years."

Ruxandra turned and walked away without looking back.

PISA 1730

Ruxandra strutted across the piazza, sword at her side, wide-brimmed hat on her head. The style for men called for tight trousers, and Ruxandra wore them with style.

Here in Pisa, she had become Renaldo, a swaggering young man with money to spare and an easy laugh. She drank her nights away with the bored, wealthy young men of the city and hunted killers and thieves in the alleyways.

An arrogant, selfish rooster of a man named Giaconda had insulted her the night before. He was known for fighting, often over women, none of whom wanted him and most of whom he took anyway. Ruxandra had agreed to meet him for a duel before dawn in two days and then followed him back to his house. Tonight, she planned to lie in wait for him when he came home, and after that, he would not challenge anyone again.

She was nearly at his house when she realized she was being followed.

She didn't see her pursuer, but heard the footsteps matching her pace and direction. She kept walking, changing direction twice to be sure she was being followed. The footsteps stayed with her. She sniffed the air but her pursuer was upwind and she couldn't catch the scent. Ruxandra willed herself unnoticed and stopped, waiting.

Her pursuer stopped, too.

Is he following my footsteps?

Ruxandra frowned. She started walking in the direction of the footsteps. They retreated before her, changing directions and staying out of sight. Ruxandra growled under her breath and picked up her pace. The other one did the same.

You want to play hunter? Fine. Ruxandra leaned against a wall and took off her tall boots. She looked up, picked a building and jumped. She landed on the tile roof, her feet hitting with barely a sound. Her sword hit the tiles with a clatter.

Porca troia. She undid the sword belt, jumped two more roofs until she reached a terrace, and left the boots and sword along with her jacket and cape. Now, wearing only her tight breeches and shirt, she jumped back down to the street.

Now, let's see who is hunting who.

Instead of speeding up again, she slowed down. Her feet made no sound at all on the cobblestones of the streets. She heard the running footsteps slow down to a walk and then stop. She slipped silently through the streets, circling her pursuer until she was downwind of him.

She sniffed the air again and stopped dead, her mouth hanging open.

Here? Now?

She started moving again, hugging the buildings and stalking her pursuer like a deer in the woods. He took a few steps, stopped, changed directions and started again. Ruxandra matched her footsteps to his and stretched out her stride, closing the distance between them. Her pursuer stopped moving. Ruxandra sped up her pace.

She came around the corner and there he was. He wore a short cloak, with tall boots and tight trousers and a brocaded black jacket. He had a sword at his side and a smile on his face.

"I should have known better than to try to follow you," Kade said. "It's good to see you, Ruxandra."

Ruxandra's talons came out. "Where's Elizabeth? And Dorotyas?"

"Spain, last I heard, helping the Inquisition ensure young ladies are on the proper moral path."

"Of course she is." Ruxandra didn't pull in her talons. "Why are you here?"

"Because I have learned a great deal in the last hundred years. And I wanted to share it with you."

"Why?" Ruxandra kept her tone harsh to hide her curiosity.

Kade ignored the question. "There are sorcerers and alchemists in Russia with books and knowledge that the inquisition has purged from Europe."

Ruxandra frowned. "What sort of knowledge?"

"Do you not wonder about the one who created you? Do you now wonder why she did it? Would you not like to ask her?"

"She was a fallen angel," Ruxandra said. "You can't ask her anything unless you plan to go to Hell and talk to her."

Kade's smile grew wide. "Or if we summon her."

"What?"

He held out his hand. "Come to Moscow with me, Ruxandra. Together we will bring the fallen angel into this world and ask her our purpose on this earth."

Thank you for reading Princess Dracula!

Dear Reader,

I hope you enjoyed Not Everything Dies. It was my honor and pleasure to write for you. Of course I was only relaying the information that my Ruxandra was providing, but I hope I did so with clarity and wonder. Thanks for joining me on this fun and wild ride!

Get ready for many more adventures.

Also, if you're so inclined, I'd love a review of Not Everything Dies. Without your support, and feedback my books would be lost under an avalanche of other books. While appreciated, there's only so much praise one can take seriously from family and friends. If you have the time, please visit my author page on both Amazon.com and goodreads.com.

twitter.com/JohnPatKennedy
www.facebook.com/
AuthorJohnPatrickKennedy/
johnpatrickkennedy.net

48358939R10189

Made in the USA
San Bernardino, CA
24 April 2017